PRAISE FOR
RACHAEL HERRON'S
WORK

"A poignant, profound ode to the enduring and redemptive power of love."
– Library Journal

"A celebration of the power of love to heal even the most broken of hearts."
- NYT Bestselling Author Susan Wiggs

"A heart-warming story of family, friendship and love in a town you'll never want to leave."
– Barbara Freethy, USA Today Bestseller

ALSO BY RACHAEL HERRON

FICTION:

STANDALONE NOVELS:

THE ONES WHO MATTER MOST
SPLINTERS OF LIGHT
PACK UP THE MOON

THE DARLING BAY NOVELS
THE DARLING SONGBIRDS
THE SONGBIRD'S CALL
THE SONGBIRD SISTERS

CYPRESS HOLLOW NOVELS 1-5:

HOW TO KNIT A LOVE SONG
HOW TO KNIT A HEART BACK HOME
WISHES & STITCHES
CORA'S HEART
FIONA'S FLAME

MEMOIR:

A LIFE IN STITCHES

The Songbird Sisters

by

RACHAEL HERRON

Publisher's Note: This is a work of fiction. Names, characters, places, and incidents are a product of the author's imagination. Locales and public names are sometimes used for atmospheric purposes. Any resemblance to actual people, living or dead, or to businesses, companies, events, institutions, or locales is completely coincidental.

The Songbird Sisters/ Rachael Herron. -- 1st ed.

HGA Publishing

ISBN-13: 978-1-940785-36-3

CHAPTER ONE

Lana Darling had been home for ten minutes and she already wanted to run away.

Darling Bay, the sparkling little town on the rugged California coast. With every crunch Lana's boot heels made in the gravel and with every chattering chirp her two sisters made as they walked behind her, she wondered if coming home had been the right thing to do.

It was funny – the very light was familiar to her. The sun felt different here, brighter somehow. More cheerful than anywhere else. It smelled like home, too – like pretzels and salt air and sugar from the cotton-candy stand.

It sure as heck had turned into tourist central, hadn't it? It looked like a Hollywood set, with its adorable main street and gazebo. Over by the diner, a man leaned against a tree, playing his guitar, singing sweetly. Townspeople greeted each other with hearty shouts and friendly embraces. Lana had already seen four bear hugs on the street. Her stomach tightened with nerves. She didn't want to be hugged by strangers.

Or worse, people who *weren't* strangers, people she'd have to make small talk with.

Her sisters caught up to her, talking a mile a minute. Lana dragged her suitcase behind her. The rest of her things were in her car, but her suitcase held all her songs and compositions, and she would be damned if those got stolen in a moment's inattention. Of course, Darling Bay didn't have a huge problem with theft, or at least it didn't used to. What did she know, though? It had been years. Almost twelve of them.

"Can I take your suitcase?"

Lana tightened her grip on the handle. She shook her head, opening her mouth to respond, but they weren't letting her talk, of course. Questions tumbled out from their lips like coins spilling from a winning slot machine, but they came so fast and furious that Lana didn't have time to answer one before they moved on to the next.

"Why didn't you tell us you were coming?"

"Where did you come from?"

"Are you okay? Are you hurt?"

"No, look at her. She looks great. Do you have more bags?" Molly, her middle sister, was positively skipping down the sidewalk.

"Are you with anyone? Is it just you?"

"Will you stay? Please, you have to stay." This last was from Adele, of course. Lana's eldest sister always had to know exactly how things would work. She needed to know if she could fix them, make them better. It was and always had been her way.

Adele. Asking her to stay, after all these years of not talking at all.

The incessant questions didn't stop the bubble of joy that rose in the middle of Lana's chest, though. She couldn't prevent the small grin that crept onto her face even if she wanted to.

Molly clutched her elbow. "We won't push you. You don't have to tell us a thing."

Lana raised an eyebrow.

"Except, of course, for everything." Molly grinned.

"Here's my car." Lana pointed at the station wagon. It was small enough to park easily, long enough to sleep in when she had to, and old enough that no one ever tried to break into it. "I've got a couple more things. Not many."

She could almost see Adele making checklists in her mind. "Room one. It's clean, since Molly has been spending more time with Colin than anywhere else. I'm pretty sure she hasn't slept there for a week or two."

Lana looked at Molly, whose cheeks were going pink. "Are you sure? You don't mind?"

Molly shook her head. "Actually – and I hadn't told you this yet, Adele, I'm sorry – I just moved in with Colin."

Adele stopped on the sidewalk and stared. "You did?"

"Yep."

"You didn't tell me?"

Something tightened low in Lana's stomach.

Then Molly laughed. "Nope!"

Lana expected a flash. Adele would yell and stomp off, then Molly would cry, and Lana – Lana had no idea what she'd do.

But Adele only grinned and shook her head. "You crazy kids. Congratulations! That, *and* the engagement, *and* Migration, *and* the café?" Adele looked at Lana. "I'm glad you're here. Maybe she'll take a breather. Relax a little."

Adele the control-freak workaholic was extolling relaxation?

"Huh," was all Lana managed.

"Okay, I've got to get back to the bar. Nate's got a delivery to put away, and someone has to man the beer taps." Adele moved forward quickly, putting her hands on Lana's cheeks. With a big *mwah* sound, she kissed Lana on the forehead. Then she ran to the saloon's porch and disappeared inside.

Lana touched her forehead. "That's what – that's what Dad always did." She wouldn't have been more stunned if Adele had hit her.

Molly smiled. "Yep. Come on. Let's grab some of your boxes and head up to your room."

A few minutes later, with boxes balanced on top of suitcases, Lana followed Molly up the path that ran alongside the saloon.

Lana carefully pulled her load over a crack. "Is Adele okay?"

"She's great!" Molly turned to glance behind her. "Didn't you see the way she greeted you?"

Lana readjusted the top box. "I don't trust it. She was so normal." She followed Molly through the garden and turned left to head toward the room.

"Normal is a bad thing?" Molly heaved the suitcase she was trundling up onto the porch. "What's in here? Rocks?"

Paper. So much paper. Every song Lana had written in the last ten years, plus a couple of old songbooks that helped inspire her when she was stuck. Not that she was going to be writing any songs. She wasn't even really sure why she was lugging them around with her anymore.

"Yeah, yeah. Show me the room, already." The Golden Spike, the property their uncle had left to his three nieces, was divided into three businesses. Her sisters had gotten the dilapidated bar and café up and running, but the hotel was still uninhabitable, all except for room one.

Lana knew both of her sisters had stayed in the room when they were newly back in Darling Bay. Now it was her turn to occupy it.

Her sisters thought it was temporary. A visit.

It might not be. Not that she was ready to talk about it with them yet.

"The door sticks a bit." Molly shoved her shoulder into the door. "Just needs a little weight behind it. Here we go!"

Lana surveyed her new space. It was cute, old-fashioned with its dark wood headboard and ornately curved wooden chairs.

Lana just hadn't remembered how *small* it was. In her memories, the hotel beds were gigantic. She'd remembered the sitting area of this room as big as a house. Instead, the bed was at most a queen, and the grand sitting area she'd remembered was actually just a two-person sofa tucked under a window that faced the green hill. The window was open, and the sea breeze blew in through the screen, smelling of sand and seaweed.

"It's great."

"It is, right?" Molly pushed a suitcase into a corner and dumped two boxes on the couch.

"Careful," Lana couldn't help saying. In one of those boxes was a framed photo of the three of them. It was one of the only sentimental items she'd chosen to carry from place to place. No matter where she'd hung her hat, that picture had sat at the side of her bed. In it, the three girls stood on the beach. Adele and Molly grinned at each other, obviously sharing a nefarious plan, one that probably included running away from Lana as fast as they could run on their then much longer legs. Over Adele's shoulder, Lana could be seen, bent over at the waist, hunting for the perfect shell. Just the side of her frowning face showed, but even at a distance, a viewer could see Lana's frustration.

Yep. Lana loved that picture.

It reminded her of everything she needed to remember.

And it would piss her right off if Molly broke it by throwing the box around.

Sisters.

She was home. Because that's what this was, even though Darling Bay was a place she'd been in for short periods of time in her childhood. Christmas. Summer vacations. Nashville had been their technical home, but this was where their hearts had always been. After their mother had died, when Lana was just thirteen, Dad had moved his girls to Darling Bay and the town had been home full-time.

This was where the band had been formed, when Lana was fourteen. Uncle Hugh had always made them feel like it was their town (and since their great-grandfather Riley Darling had named it, townsfolk had always made them feel the same way). When she was young, Lana had thought they'd stay here, in town, when they were grown-ups. All the Darling girls, home to roost forever.

By the time she was an adult, though, the Darling Songbirds – the band comprised of the three sisters – had broken up. And their sister relationship had shattered into tiny pieces.

Lana had been fine (eventually). She'd travelled. She'd played her songs, and she'd written more of them. She'd kept in touch (minimally) with Molly and had almost no contact with Adele.

Now she was back – there was a place for her to sleep, and there was money in her bank account for the first time ever, and she could stay if she wanted to.

Which she did.

Maybe.

Molly went into the bathroom and opened the small window. "There. Now you'll get the pass-through breeze. We've moved the big dumpster that used to be back there to the side of the parking lot, so you won't even get the oyster-shell stink that guests used to complain about on hot days. Remember?"

Oh, God, she'd forgotten that bit of hilarity. Uncle Hugh, inured to every ocean smell, had always thought the guests were exaggerating.

Something prickled behind Lana's eyes and she realized just how tired she was. "Good. That's good."

Molly frowned and plopped down on the bed. "You okay?"

Lana dropped to her knees next to the suitcase that held her clothing. *I am the kind of woman who can fit all her clothes in one box.* "I'm fine. Why wouldn't I be?"

"Because you're here." Molly's voice was soft. "You haven't been here in a really long time."

"It's not a big deal unless you make a big deal out of it."

"I won't."

"*She* will."

Molly shook her head. "She's changed. You saw how she greeted you."

Lana would *not* ask Molly for clarification. She pulled out her underwear, all eight or nine pairs, and shoved them in the top bureau drawer.

"Okay, I'll tell you what I saw." Molly didn't seem to care that Lana hadn't asked. "I saw a woman who was trying to keep her shit together as her biggest dream started coming true."

Lana narrowed her eyes. "What are you talking about?"

"All she's ever wanted is us all together. Now we're with her. Both of us. I thought the top of her head was going to fly right off."

"You thought she was *happy?*" All Lana had noticed was the speed with which Adele had left to get back to the bar.

"If she didn't cry with joy as soon as her back was turned, I'll eat my cowboy hat, and it's so old that wouldn't be enjoyable, I promise you. You guys will talk, clear the air. It'll be okay."

"You're crazy."

"Crazy about my sisters!" Molly threw herself backward on the bed with a laugh. "I'm thrilled, too! Not to the crying point, but then again, I'm not the pregnant one."

Lana dropped the balled-up socks she was holding. "*What?*"

Molly had already shot back up into a sitting position. Her hand was clapped over her mouth. From behind her fingers, she said, "Adele will kill me. She will literally *kill* me."

"For telling me? I wasn't supposed to know?" Something red and hot pressed itself into the back of Lana's throat. Of course. Adele had always confided in Molly. Never Lana.

"No! That's not it at all. She's just keeping it secret until she starts to show. Doesn't want to jinx it."

By telling the untrustworthy sister. "Sure."

"Don't tell her I told you!"

"Never." It would be an interesting experiment, now that she thought about it. She could see how long it would take Adele to tell her. Would Lana know before the mailman did? Before the regulars at the bar?

Yep, there it was. That rolling ball of discomfort, the one she'd known would lodge itself in her stomach as soon as she hit Darling Bay's city limits. The ball was made of anger and something else ... something that hurt more.

Lana wouldn't call it sadness, because she was just fine.

Totally, completely fine.

She was here on her own terms. Not because she had to be.

"Let's have dinner tonight." Molly glanced at her phone. "The three of us. Like old times."

Old times? Old-time dinners only had two flavors: before the band, when Lana had been young and tiny and utterly unable to keep up with her older sisters when they'd eaten dinner at the kitchen table: good, cheap food that Mama had been great at cooking. And during the years when they'd been a band, when they'd eaten in the tour bus's kitchen. They hadn't eaten out much – they'd always been saving the money. Dad had been good at that, after Mama died. He'd run the band tightly and kept the money close.

Then he'd died too, and everything had gone off the rails.

So Lana wasn't exactly sure she wanted to revisit any of those old times at all. "I'm tired," she began.

"No. I insist." Molly grabbed her hand. "Dinner together."

Lana pulled it back. "Fine. Where?"

"The café, of course."

Well, that *would* be like old times, all right. Lana had forgotten how much time they'd all spent in the Golden

Spike Café as kids. Just thinking about it made her crave a quesadilla and a chocolate malt. "You're still liking being the boss there?"

"Loving. *Loving.* It's better than new. I can't wait to show you everything." Molly's cheeks were prettily pink.

A tight muscle in Lana's chest eased. She pressed her thumb against the tattoo at her wrist. It was still new enough to be tender, and feeling the raised ink lines helped.

Maybe this wouldn't be as hard as she'd thought it would be.

Maybe this would just be coming home. That's what people were supposed to do, right? That's how they found their people, how they built their lives. They came home, to the ones who loved them.

Or who could tolerate them, at least. "Okay, then."

Fear fluttered at the base of her throat.

She'd worry about Adele when she had to. Not a minute before.

CHAPTER TWO

Taft Hill groaned. He took off his cowboy hat. He set it on his manager's glass desk so he could lean all the way back in Sully's uncomfortable modern chair and groan harder. "I can't do it."

"You have to do it." Sully looked cheerful.

"Why do you look so all-fired pleased about that?"

"I'm not the one who has to write a song, so it's easy for me. I just get to tell you to do it."

"I could fire you."

"But you wouldn't." Sully interlaced his fingers over his small, round paunch. "Because you couldn't have gotten this far without me. You need me."

"Those words would sound like a threat from anyone else, you know that?" Taft lifted his head to glare at Sully and then let it fall backward again.

"Yeah, it's just the truth. Do you even know the password for your email?"

Taft thought for a moment. "Is it Taft-Hill-Is-A-Superstar?"

"Five years ago it was."

"Dang," said Taft. "Why'd you change it?"

"Because you actually became one, just like I said you would, and I didn't think it was the best choice of unbreakable passwords. Now it's twenty-two letters and numbers long."

"So I'll never read my own emails again?"

"Are you telling me you want to?"

"Hell, no, I don't." Taft could barely keep up with the texts on his phone. "Speaking of that, we may need to change my number again."

"You gave it to another reporter at a bar," Sully guessed, giving Taft a knowing look.

"She just looked like a regular gal." He shrugged, remembering. A cute one, with sparkly green eyes and freckles on her nose.

"Who'd she work for?"

"*Daily Star.*" Those freckles had been bait.

"I'll get your number changed today."

"Thanks."

"In return, write a damn song. Only three to go, and you're done with this album."

"I can't." Taft considered groaning again, but Sully was getting that sharp tone to his voice. More moaning wouldn't be tolerated. "Every time I try, all I get is crap."

"Then give me a crap song. You think the label will know the difference?"

"Yes."

"We'll tell them it's a first draft."

"You have to have some words on a page to call it a draft, and I ain't got nothing but the words flipping around in here–" he tapped his forehead, "–like goldfish trying to get away from a cat."

Sully's eyebrows drew together. "You've never had trouble with writing like this before."

"Yeah, well. Now I am. How's Ellen doing?"

Sully scowled. "Don't change the subject."

"Honestly, I'm not. I've been thinking about her. I got a wooden spoon from Thailand from a friend who just came back from there. I'll bring it to her this weekend."

Sully's eyes softened. "That woman and her spoon collection. You know some online magazine called her to talk about it? She grinned like a kid for a week."

"She deserves some happiness." Taft loved Sully's wife, a woman with a sweet voice and even sweeter eyes. The cancer had thinned her, leaving her bald and too skinny, but she still had every drop of sweetness she'd ever possessed.

"She's got me!"

"Who could ask for more?" His tone was teasing, but Taft was serious. He had rarely seen a man more devoted to anything or anyone than Sully was to Ellen. "Give her my love."

"Will do." Sully popped a mint into his mouth and sucked. He spoke around it, the mint clacking on his teeth. "Back to your writing. What's wrong with you?"

Wrong? Taft was a fraud.

He was an imposter.

And that was a secret he'd never share with Sully, a man he loved almost as much as he'd loved his father. Taft would take the secret to his grave. Which, at this point, was probably only a few years away since he'd obviously never write another song and he'd never have another hit. He'd lose all his money and he'd die of exposure from living under a bridge somewhere. "Nothing's wrong," he replied. "I just can't find my mojo." And that was the truth. Despite his recent lack of self-belief, he had always been able to write, but lately his willpower had decided to abandon him.

In his no-bullshit voice, Sully barked, "Where'd you leave it?"

"If I knew that, I wouldn't have this problem." If only Taft could buy the mojo from someplace. Go into a store and hand over enough money to purchase it back. At this point, he'd give almost anything to find it.

Trouble was, it had been taken from him, and it damned sure wasn't coming back.

"Is it because you bought 'Blame Me?'"

Taft shut his eyes and shook his head. "I don't even like to think about that song."

"That's unfortunate."

"I know." It was at the top of two charts, number one in country *and* in pop.

"You're going to have to sing it on stage until the day you die, so you might as well get right with it."

"But it's not my song."

Sully made a loud, impatient noise – it reminded Taft of the sound a horse gave when it was being directed the way it didn't want to go. "It's yours. You paid for it. That's what everyone does."

"Yeah, well. *I've* never done it before."

"You never had to. But if the well dries up, you don't go without water, do you? You drive to town and you fill up your – your, um, cistern, or something."

"Your metaphor's a little ragged."

Sully cracked his mint with a snap of his teeth. "Is it the money? The royalties going to her?"

"Of course not." Taft was nowhere near bridge-living just yet. There were still so many dollars in his bank accounts that it didn't quite make sense sometimes to him, and "Blame Me" was just pouring more money in, download after download.

"Well, are you embarrassed? That you co-wrote a song with someone? Just because you'd never done it before doesn't make it a shameful thing."

"I didn't co-write it." Lana Darling had written it. He'd changed the point of view and a few pronouns, that was all.

"Get over it, boy. Every country star co-writes or buys songs. How many of them lie about it, straight up?"

Taft groaned again. "A few."

Sully jabbed a finger in Taft's direction. "A few? Most of 'em. You don't know the things I know, and because of non-disclosure agreements, you're never going to. But I can tell you this, *most* singers – and I'm talking about singers you respect – buy songs outright and never tell anyone."

Taft shifted in the uncomfortable chair. "What about the royalties? They have to send them to the songwriter."

Sully raised his arms above his head. "This never occurred to you? That some people don't play that way? You were *raised* in the scene. How does the son of Palmer Hill,–" Sully crossed himself, "–may he rest in peace, not know how Nashville works?"

"You can't keep that kind of thing secret," Taft said. "Songwriters would talk eventually."

"Not if they were paid extra – *a hell of a lot* extra – to keep their mouths shut about it."

"You mean, buy them out?" Taft was genuinely shocked.

"You never even considered that was a thing?"

No, Taft had never thought about the idea. Why would he have? His whole life, he'd watched his father write his own songs. Taft had learned at Palmer's knee how ideas took shape into words. First just a few, the rumbling of an idea. Then a phrase, caught in writing if you were lucky, if you always carried your lucky pencil in your pocket like Palmer had.

Taft had followed in those hallowed footsteps. He even carried the same damn mechanical pencil, given to him by his father. The pencil was a 1924 Wahl Eversharp in engraved sterling silver with a chevron pattern, and with it, Taft had written all his own songs. He'd made them hits, just like his father had before him.

Then, suddenly, Taft had stopped being able to write. "Why didn't you get me to buy out that girl, then?" he asked.

"By that girl, you mean Lana Darling?"

Taft had no real yen to say her name out loud. "Yeah."

"I asked if you wanted me to explore that option with her."

"You did?"

Sully raised an eyebrow. "You don't remember."

Of course Taft didn't.

Lana Darling was the worst sex he'd ever had.

One-night stands were supposed to be fun. They were supposed to be exciting and awesome and dangerous and hot. They were *not* supposed to make a man feel like a failure, like he didn't know the female body (he *did* know it), like he didn't even really know how to kiss a girl (he knew that, too).

She'd been a bad idea, followed by an even worse one – to buy her song and make himself accountable to paying her royalties for the rest of their natural-born lives, and then some, since royalties kept right on being paid even after death.

If Sully had mentioned it, Taft sure as hell hadn't heard him when he'd said it. After all, he'd been trying so hard not to think of the way Lana's mouth had tasted – of sweet berries and the wine they'd had and something richer, darker. He'd been trying to forget what had happened after he'd kissed her – the way the heat had leaped between them, a fire that neither of them had had to work to stoke. It had blazed.

Taft would pay good money to have someone remove the memories of what had happened next. The way nothing had gone right, even though everything had felt like it should. Their limbs had tangled awkwardly. From their mouths fusing like they'd been made to kiss each other, they'd gone to two separate bodies who'd been obviously never meant to fit together in the same bed.

It had been an embarrassment. Taft had a pretty good idea that he'd been the most embarrassing part of the equation.

Sully smacked his hands on the enormous desktop, snapping Taft out of his reverie. "I've got an idea. Go write some more songs with her."

Like Taft hadn't thought about it every day since that night. Like it had never occurred to him. "Nope."

"No, it's great. Where's she at? Is she in town?"

She had been. He'd seen her singing at the Bluebird eight moths ago. No one had been listening except him. The bar had been packed with tourists who'd given Lana a cursory glance, seen that they didn't recognize her and commenced to trying to outdrink each other. Only Taft had watched, only he had listened to the whole set. So he was the only one who'd been blown away by the sheer, raw power of "Blame Me." He had only himself to thank for that.

"Nope."

"How do you know? You're in touch?" Sully's eyes lit up. "You'll call her. Write a couple or three more like the one you did together."

"*She* wrote that last one. Not us."

"So when you do write together, it'll be an automatic smash. Who's her agent again? I can't remember." Sully turned to his computer and started tapping.

"I'm serious, Sully. I'm not going to do that."

Sully peered more closely at the screen. "Well, holy hell."

"What?"

"She was with Myers and Wright, but the latest *MusicRow* says they split. Amicably." Sully shook his head. "Only teams who don't part amicably say they do."

"Oh yeah, she said they fired her."

"Now it looks like ..." A few more taps at the keyboard. "Nope. She was singing in Ontario, but that was a few weeks ago and there's been no news about her since."

Taft fought down a strange mixture of relief and disappointment. "Good. There you go."

"What about her sisters?"

"You want me to write with her sisters?" Taft's eyebrows shot up.

Sully ignored him. "They did that fundraiser recently – some women's hotline thing the two women started, called, what was it – here it is. Migration. Adele and Molly, working together again. Two-thirds of the Darling Songbirds, back together. Stands to reason she'll be joining them, right?"

"They've been broken up a long time. Maybe for a reason." Not that Taft would know. He and Lana hadn't really *talked* that much. He'd asked if he could buy the song. She'd said yes. He'd asked her back to his place. Then there had been a lot of not talking and even more awkwardness. If he could erase one night from his life, it might be that one. That day – before he met her – had been one of the worst of his life, and it had just gotten worse.

"Hang on. Let me shoot off this email. I know a couple of people at Myers and Wright."

"There's no reason to do that." Taft straightened in his chair.

"There. It's sent," Sully said, shocking Taft for the second time that day. "We'll find her. Then you can meet up with her and you'll both write some songs that will make everyone cry. We'll all be rich." Sully looked down at his mahogany desk. "Even richer. I can't wait for you to do this."

"Jesus, Sully, I said no!"

"No means no with women, dogs, kids and horses. In business it's a soft yes."

Taft slid lower in his chair. If Sully did find Lana, it might be worth talking to her.

Just talking.

"Blame Me" was bigger than any other hit he'd ever had. Her words tapped a deeper vein than his own, even when he'd been writing well, had ever gone. If she could do that again, if he could – ah, shit.

The truth was he wouldn't mind seeing her again. Taft bridled at the thought that he hadn't made a good impression in bed. He was proud of always satisfying his lovers. It was part of his brand, as it were. He wasn't the kind of guy who picked up a girl in every town, just to be next to someone at night. That would be easy, obviously. In his line of business, women were always around, always plentiful and always ready to please.

Honestly, they were usually pretty boring.

Lana had been grumpy and taciturn. She'd been reluctant to talk to him at all. When she'd finally laughed at something he'd said, he'd felt like the sun had come out after a week of rain. When she'd agreed to sell him the song, he'd thought he could fly.

When they'd failed so spectacularly at being naked together, he'd been so frustrated he'd wanted to grind glass with his teeth.

More computer clicks. "Ha! He's always been fast at returning emails," Sully was saying. "Lana Darling's in California. Here's the address. I can have you on a flight by morning."

"That's crazy, Sully."

"Just do it. For me."

Taft thought about it. What if he did go find her?

If Sully really thought it would be good for his career, who was Taft to say anything? After all, Sully was great at his job.

California probably had some damned nice wooden spoons. He could bring a couple back for Ellen.

Lana Darling.

"Okay," he said finally. "For you."

He knew it was for himself, and he bet Sully knew it, too.

"Good kid."

"Love you, Sul." Taft didn't say it often, but he should. God knew he hadn't told his father enough, and Sully was a second dad to him.

Sully's round cheeks went pink with pleasure. "Ah. Cut it out. Go write me a song."

CHAPTER THREE

Lana was so tired from travelling that she wanted to use the hour before meeting her sisters at the café to have a gigantic, drooling nap.

But when she lay on the squeaky bed, her eyes snapped open. She traced the crack in the ceiling with her gaze until she could see a panda in the design. Or was it a horse? No, what it actually looked like was a baby pacifier.

A baby.

Adele was having one of those.

She could have told me. It's not like I ignore every single one of her texts.

Just most of them.

Sudden nerves kicked in her stomach. Lana swung off the bed. A nap was not in the cards for her right now.

Exploring it was, then.

Molly had warned her the place was bad. *There's mold. And dry rot. And there was the fire, of course. Small, but it did a lot of smoke damage.* Lana had an active imagination. She was pretty sure the place couldn't be more run-down than she'd thought it was. She picked up the master key Molly had left with her and looked in the mirror.

She sighed. That fateful night she'd spent with Taft Hill – she almost wished it had never happened. Sure, months later, she was glad for the money flying into her bank account as if someone had aimed a fire hose of cash into it. Mechanical, performance and synchronization royalties – that's where the money was, when it came to a hit, and without an agent, she was getting all of it. It was enough money to truly retire. Her best friend, Jilly, had been so incredulous. *You? You're retiring from music?* It had felt great, so phenomenal in fact, that Lana had gone and dyed her hair.

She'd always kept it blonde, bleaching it so light it looked white in photos. A country girl's hair. Even though she'd been the Songbird voted least likely to know how to put on false eyelashes (seriously, in *Country Music News*), she knew how to blow-dry her hair so that it kicked out at the ends. Long, soft waves, that's what country-singing women had. Taft had said it was gorgeous. He'd held up a strand, running it through his fingers. *This is what I wanted to do while you were singing.*

Yeah, he'd heard her song and liked it enough to buy it, but what he'd really been drawn to was her country-girl hair.

She'd dyed it dark brown – almost black – a week ago. It was her natural color, after all. Too bad it didn't really suit her complexion. She didn't care.

She'd cut it shorter then, too.

Now it swung unevenly, just hitting her shoulders. It looked like a botched home job – which it was – and she'd told herself she didn't care.

Lana had come very close to believing it.

She sighed and jammed the master key into her jeans pocket.

The room next to the one she was staying in wasn't as bad as she'd imagined. It had a foot-wide hole in the ceiling, but the hole was covered with blue plastic, and the rest of the room didn't seem to be too bad. The carpet was filthy, and the furniture needed deep cleaning, but it didn't look awful.

The next room, though. Upon opening the door, she could smell the mildew, a rank, green smell that seemed to climb so far into her nasal passages that she would probably never get it out. A wooden bed frame stood in the middle of the room, off kilter, as if it had started creeping toward the door, trying to escape. Both back windows had been broken inward, and the glass shards on the floor were so dirty from the open roof that they didn't even shine.

The next room had been the one most affected by the electrical fire. The roof was open to the sky above, and while the corner of a blue tarp flapped in the breeze, it wasn't big enough to even cover a quarter of the ceiling. The far wall was charred, and Lana realized she was looking inside it – the beams were blackened inside the roasted drywall.

Lana covered her nose and swallowed hard. She hadn't expected this.

She was an idiot for *not* expecting it. Both Adele and Molly were forces of nature. If they said it was bad, she should have known they were under-reporting it, if anything.

This was her big idea? Come back to Darling Bay and take over the motel? Lana had known the electrical needed work, but she'd thought that would be the big part. She'd imagined a few weeks of scrubbing walls and maybe some light redecorating.

This restoration would be a full-time job, even if she hired a crew to help her.

Inside her chest, the initial dismay gave way to something she didn't recognize at first.

Relief.

That's what it was. She wouldn't have to think about music, about lyrics or chords or hooks or riffs or gigs or fans.

This would take *forever*. Thank God.

Lana took a quick peek into the other rooms (most of them horrifying in their dirty condition and falling-down chaos). Then she shut the last door, carefully locking it even though most of the eleven rooms hadn't been. Why bother? Squatters wouldn't even be interested in rooms like these.

In the falling twilight, she made her way through the garden toward the café. This patch of land between the hotel rooms and the saloon, at least, was still gorgeous. More beautiful than ever, actually. The roses Mama had planted so long ago were in full bloom, sending their heady scent into the purple sky. The jasmine vines were loaded with small white explosions of sweet fragrance and someone – Adele probably – had painted the rocks in the walkway white.

Adele had always loved painting over things. Covering them up. Refusing to see problems, even when they were right in front of her.

God, Lana was nervous. Being back in town was like a massive case of stage fright, nerves and jangled thoughts and all.

As she pushed open the door of the Golden Spike Café, a hunger pang rumbled through her belly. How long had it been since she'd eaten? She'd driven for hours today, surprising her sisters in the Migration office. Molly had told her all about the shelter hotline on the phone a month or two ago. It was Molly's idea, and with Adele's help they'd made it happen.

Just another case of her sisters being awesome.

It was possible Lana hadn't eaten since the peanuts she'd chowed on at the rest stop early this morning.

She'd driven the remainder of the day, speeding up the closer she got to Darling Bay, like a horse smelling the barn.

She'd rushed here. Now, a large part of her wanted to rush away. It was the part she was going to silence. Lana was going to give this a chance. A real one.

Straightening her shoulders, she pulled open the café front door.

CHAPTER FOUR

She took a quick, surprised breath.

It was wonderful. Lana shouldn't have been surprised, but she was – was this going to be her default in Darling Bay?

The place smelled much like it had when Uncle Hugh had run it – of cheese and fresh bread and clam chowder – but there was more in the air, too. She could smell herbs: basil and rosemary. She reached out and touched a plastic-coated menu that rested in the menu holder. Her finger came away clean, not sticky like the old days.

"Well, hi there! Just one?" A pretty blonde grinned at her.

Lana nodded automatically, and then caught herself. "No, sorry. For three. If you have it. The other two should be right behind me."

The blonde looked around. "You bet. That booth just opened. Let me wipe it down and it's all yours."

The café was packed, another surprising thing. All the booths except the one she was waiting for were filled. Long, wide tables ran down the middle, full of people chatting and laughing over burgers and bottles of wine. The walls were covered in the crap Uncle Hugh had loved – ocean floats, old wooden oars, rusted license plates and fruit-stand signs. Lana remembered the wall decorations being covered with a thin layer of grime and the occasional spider web. Now they were as clean as the rest of the place seemed to be.

Molly's influence was strong here. Adele, of course, had always been the fixer-upper, the one who insisted on setting things to right. But Molly was the warmest of the three – the caretaker. This room felt like a place everyone would want to be.

And they obviously did.

A short woman with grey hair touched her elbow. "You. It's you."

Lana jumped. "Just waiting for a table."

The woman wore a blue muumuu-like dress and her eyes were as wide as the fat-bottomed candles on each table. "Lana! You're home!"

Only in this town would she be recognized. "Hello, there." She stuck out her hand politely. "It's nice to meet you."

The woman brushed aside her hand and drew her into a full-bodied hug. Her breasts were pillowy and she smelled vaguely of gin. "Oh, my heart, my heart. I drew the Four of Wands and I *thought* that's what I was reading, but then again, I thought they were telling me to learn how to walk on stilts that one time, and boy, were they wrong. I broke my leg *and* took out three boxes of tomatoes at the farmers' market."

"Mmm?" Lana pulled back as best she could, but the woman kept leaning forward, following her, until Lana ran into the back wall with a thud. "Oh, my God. Stop. Please stop." Lana scooted sideways.

"Sorry! I forget hugs make some people uncomfortable. I always mean to ask permission. I mean, that's what you do, right? In today's society? I was told that, by someone. I should say *Are you a hugger or a non-hugger?* But by the time I get in there, it's too late. I've already forgotten. Oh! I'm Norma, did I say that? Do you remember me?" She didn't wait for an answer. "Nikki! Girl! Look who I have here!"

The blonde hostess turned with a smile, a blue rag in her hands. "Your booth's ready." Then she gaped. "Oh, my *God*."

"Right?" Norma bellowed. "It's her!"

Fantastic. Lana held out her hand to the hostess. "I'm —"

"*Lana Darling.*" Nikki dropped the rag on the floor, clapped twice, and then reached out to shake her hand. "I can't *believe* it."

Lana felt, rather than saw, heads turning all over the restaurant. Even if they'd missed Norma's bear hug at the door, there was no way to miss this top-volume exchange. She slid into the booth and prayed to disappear.

Nikki clapped again, then stamped her feet. She gave a small scream while turning in a circle. "I can't believe it's you. I'm just going to pass out right here."

It had been years since Lana had had a fan girl freak out on her. "Please don't. It's very nice to meet you. My sisters will be here soon to have dinner with me ..."

"Of course. Of course. Good. Oh, wow, did Molly know you were coming?" Nikki picked up the rag and stuck it in her apron strap.

"Nope."

"A surprise!" Nikki laughed. "How wonderful! Can I get you a drink? On the house, of course. Wine? We have an amazing local chardonnay. Or beer? We have six on draft, which isn't that many, but they have a lot more at the saloon – oh, you know that. A mixed drink? We don't do them here, but I'm *totally* happy to run next door to get you whatever you want."

"Just water, thank you."

Nikki gazed at her in reverence. "Water. Of course. You got it. Ice? No ice?"

Lana was a no-ice kind of person, but this woman would obviously be happier if she could help. "Ice, please. That would be amazing."

Nikki clapped again. "Yes! Yes! I'll be right back!"

Lana exhaled deeply, pressing herself into the booth. The loud woman named Norma chugged away, muttering something about her tarot cards. The people who had spun around to see what the excitement was had turned back to their food. It was quieter in the restaurant now that Norma wasn't filling her ear. It seemed as if everyone had piped down. It felt as if they were all trying not to stare. Lana heard snippets of phrases: *Youngest one, right? Did she move to Canada? I heard Cuba. Drugs? Nah. Maybe? This one song* ...

Lana used to have a way of dealing with this. Back in the day, when they'd been in Darling Bay, Lana had possessed a method of tilting her head, looking up and to the left, as if trying to remember something, and then setting her chin on her fist while she stared at a piece of paper.

Paper. She rummaged in her bag and pulled out her journal. If she stared at the page hard enough, she'd look so busy that no one but the waitress would interrupt her —

"There you are."

Her big sister, Adele, had never had a problem interrupting her. Years ago, it had seemed to be Adele's full-time job.

"Hey."

"Oh, man." Adele slid into the booth opposite her. "Just looking at you does my heart good."

Lana blinked. Where was the side-slung insult?

It would come in a minute. Adele would wonder why her hair was cut crooked, why she'd dyed it so dark. Or she'd comment on Lana being too thin. Something. Lana was ready for it – ready for the criticism. "You, too," she managed.

"I'm not going to ask you anything. I know you hate it when I want to know everything too fast."

Adele was right. Lana *had* always hated that.

If Adele didn't push her that way, though, where did their relationship stand? What in the world would they talk about? Lana sure as hell wasn't ready to talk about the elephant in the room – the real reason she'd run away and stayed away. "Where's Molly?"

"She was right behind me, but she said she had to do something in the kitchen first. She's probably in there now."

"Doing what?"

"Who knows?" Adele shrugged. "She's always back there. This place has turned into her baby. The other day she burned two loaves of sourdough to a crisp, and I thought she was going to cry."

Alarm jolted through her. "That doesn't sound like her. Is she okay?" Asking Adele about Molly. She swore she'd never fall back into this habit.

"She's in love. She cries at the drop of a hat, but she laughs all day long. Her emotions are just pretty close to the surface."

Lana took a breath. She could handle making small (big) talk with Adele. She was an adult, after all. *Come on, Molly, hurry up.*

If Adele wasn't going to ask why Lana had cut her off so long ago, Lana wasn't going to bring it up. Not yet, at least.

She would swallow the lump that felt like a block of tears and keep pretending she was okay.

As if reading her mind, Adele said, "I'm sorry ... I'm sorry we didn't talk for so long."

"What? I texted." *Stupid.* What a stupid thing to say. They hadn't talked because Lana hadn't wanted to talk to her eldest sister.

Adele had barely even tried to figure out why she hadn't.

"I should have reached out to you more." Adele's eyes were sad.

Lana hadn't predicted how much that would get to her. All these years of wondering what Adele would say when they were finally face to face, but she hadn't thought about what her expression would be. "Yeah," she managed.

"I'm sorry."

"What are you sorry for?" Did Adele even know?

Adele looked at the table. She touched it with her fingertips. "Do you want to do this now? Here?"

Something inside Lana's chest released. "Not really." She sighed. She could pretend a while longer. She could give Adele this. "So you know this sheriff of Molly's?"

Adele nodded in what looked like relief. "Colin McMurtry. He's a good man."

"Are you sure?"

"You know how some guys become cops because they really want to be criminals but don't quite have the balls?"

"Yeah."

"He's the opposite. He won't even hire those guys."

A knot loosened in Lana's neck. She hadn't even known she'd been worried about Molly and Colin. "Good."

"They're engaged, did you know that?"

Lana sat taller. "Yeah." She was the first person Molly had told. Or at least, that's what Molly had said on the phone.

"She ..." Adele reached for a paper napkin from the wicker basket on the table. "She told you about me?"

Caution crept back into her blood. "What do you mean?"

"Me and Nate?"

"The bartender. At the saloon." Adele had claimed the Golden Spike's bar as the third of the business she'd wanted, and Molly (of course) had been fine with it. Lana hadn't cared enough from a distance to fight about it. It was fine, really – Lana had spent all the time in country dive bars she'd ever wanted. She wasn't interested in the place.

"Yeah."

"She told me." What did you say to someone who was in love? Congratulations didn't seem quite right ... but holy crap. She'd almost forgotten about her sister's pregnancy. "And she told me you're knocked up."

Adele started. "She *what?*"

"She didn't mean to."

"She *told* you?"

"I think she's excited, that's all." Great, now Adele would be mad at both of them. Par for the coming-home course, she supposed. Lana wondered if the café did room service. It probably didn't, since the hotel was mostly uninhabitable. Of course, the overeager hostess probably wouldn't mind running a grilled cheese up to her, and Lana would tip her well for it.

"Oh, well." Instead of looking angry, Adele grinned. "I wish I'd seen your face, but now's as good a time as any, right? What do you think?"

"Huh?" Her sister couldn't possibly need reassurance, could she? From Lana?

"About *this.*" Adele patted her very slightly rounded stomach. "The fact that you're going to be an aunt."

"Holy shit." They were barely sisters anymore. What kind of aunt would that make her?

"Right?"

It literally hadn't occurred to Lana that's she'd be *related* to Adele's fetus.

Uncle Hugh had been so important to all three of them growing up. The girls had loved their parents, but their uncle had been something special. He'd had more sparkle, somehow. Uncle Hugh had meant sun and sand and ice-cream cones dripping on the rough wooden pier. He'd been lazy mornings and late nights, crayfish in the creek and trout from the lake. He'd been *fun.*

What kind of relationship would Lana have with Adele's child?

A kid. A baby.

"Wow." Lana's voice was soft. Again, she felt that weird pressure behind her eyes, but she was *not* going to cry, not in Darling Bay. "I'm happy for you."

She was.

"Thank you. You have to meet Nate. He's amazing."

Well, of course Adele thought that. People thought that about their significant others, and very often it wasn't borne out.

Molly said he was a good guy, though. Adele said Molly's dude was great, too.

Handy, that's what it was.

And, honestly, sweet.

She slipped out of her seat and moved around the table to slide in next to Adele.

Adele leaned left.

Lana leaned right.

Their shoulders held each other up, and then the sides of their heads pressed against each other. The words warred within Lana, but finally she said them because they were true. "I'm happy for you."

"Thank you."

An audible sigh came from the booth behind them. Lana turned to look. The tarot-card woman, Norma, was staring at them unabashedly, wiping a tear. "That's beautiful, girls. Just beautiful. Adele! I can't believe you didn't tell us until now!"

Lana frowned. "Oh, no.–" This was her fault. She'd spilled the beans.

Adele shook her head in Lana's direction. "It's okay. We were going to tell the whole town, as soon as you knew. I just wanted you and Molly to know first." Adele folded her hands as if in prayer. "I got my wish."

Norma lit up as if she'd been plugged in. "Now you can tell everyone!" She clutched the back of the booth and twisted further in their direction. "Can I tell them?"

"No!" Lana didn't know this woman, but she was pretty sure that was the right answer.

"Yes." Adele put a warm hand on Lana's arm. "Sure, Norma, go ahead. The more good wishes the better, right?"

Norma cackled in glee. She scooted and thumped her way out of the seat and then stood. "*You guys! Everyone! I've got something to say! Adele Darling is gonna have a baby!* And it's Nate's!" Norma turned her head. "Oh, damn, I didn't actually confirm that. Is it Nate's?"

Adele gaped. "Of course it is!"

Norma bellowed into her cupped hands, "It's Nate's, for sure!"

CHAPTER FIVE

A round of applause followed Norma's shouted words. Six women diners rushed the table, and Lana slid out of the booth, back to her side so Adele could collect the congratulatory hugs.

Molly burst through the swinging door that led to the kitchen. She rubbed her hands on a red apron at her waist. "Seriously? I missed you telling Lana?"

"Oh, really? *I* didn't tell her."

Lana watched Molly squirm. There was some satisfaction in this, at least.

"Oh, yeah. Whoops." Molly squinted as if trying to focus on something in the distance. "Sorry about that."

"It's okay. It's fine. I wouldn't have been able to keep it secret, either." Adele's cheeks went pink. "My sisters are here. Both of you are here to share this with me. I'm so *happy.*"

Molly sat next to Adele. Lana faced her sisters. There was still an older woman with dyed pink hair busily congratulating Adele and offering her nursery-school advice (too early, surely?), so Lana had a moment to stare.

The two of them. Right there. She could reach across the table and touch each of them. She could press her fingers against the skin of their arms, see how strong their muscles were, feel the bones inside. She *wanted* to.

But she didn't.

Molly said, "I ordered us bacon cheeseburgers with the fixings. And fries. Sound okay?"

Adele nodded while keeping a polite gaze on the woman who was now telling her how many bibs she would need.

"Sure," said Lana. She kept staring.

Adele, still so pretty and fair, with her honey-blonde hair and blue eyes. Molly, looking brighter than Lana could remember, her hair glossy and dark, her brown eyes shining. The girls shared the same-shaped eyes, but the color of Lana's had always been muddy, neither bright like Adele's nor dark like Molly's. Hers were light brown. Boring.

Neither of her sisters looked boring. They were both startlingly pretty.

The last time she'd seen both of them at the same time, Adele and Molly had been on television. As the last congratulator left the table, Lana said, "I saw you on the *Jack and Ginger* show last month."

Adele leaned forward. "You saw that?"

"You both looked great. You sounded amazing, too." It was the least she could say. They really had. Their song "Fly Up" had tugged at the back of her throat, always the sign of good writing.

It was a mistake, though, bringing it up. Adele had that look on her face, the look she got before she asked them to do something entirely too sisterly. It had been a long time, but Lana still recognized it. But instead of asking them to sing something together, Adele just said, "Thanks. We were proud of it."

That *we*.

Adele and Molly were a we.

Would Lana ever be that with them again?

Did she want to be?

Lightly, she said, "It was pretty. You wrote it together?"

"Yeah."

"No way," said Molly. "I had the idea, but Adele is the one who rewrote it and made it good."

Lana nodded, her heart aching. Once, she'd thought she'd become the best songwriter in the family, but she hadn't even managed that. A one-hit wonder was nothing to brag about. "Still writing for Nashville?"

Adele nodded, ducking her head as if a little embarrassed. "Sometimes."

Molly bounced in her seat. "Have you heard 'Easy' by Toby Keith? Adele wrote the whole thing, but I came up with the last line, so I make her give me free beer at the bar sometimes."

Lana had heard it. A lot. The song had rocketed up the chart in what seemed like just a day or two. She'd been jealous she hadn't thought of the chorus. *I'm not easy like Sunday morning, I'm easy like Saturday night.* "Good for you."

"What about you?" Adele's voice was so soft, as if she were being careful with Lana.

"Me?"

"Have you been writing? There's some good stuff out there right now." Adele was acting like talking about Nashville was the most important thing in the world.

Lana was grateful for it. It was something to hang their conversation on, and she could avoid the question. "Have you heard George Strait's new one? You know Shirt Turner wrote that, right?"

Molly and Adele both gasped. They leaned forward. Molly said, "But didn't he ... we heard he killed himself."

Lana coughed. "Rumors of his demise are greatly exaggerated. He lit his hair on fire when he fell asleep with a cigarette in his hand."

"But ..."

"Yeah, he only had that combover. Now he has a scar and even less hair. But he's fine. Drunk most of the time nowadays, but fine."

Adele's gaze was eager, her eyes bright. "More gossip. Tell me. I've been sending songs to where they need to go, but I haven't heard good dish in forever. What about Gavin?"

"Broke."

"Stacey?"

"Broker."

"Jones?"

"Oh, he *married* Stacey, which is why she's broke."

Her sisters laughed, and something warm ran laps in Lana's empty stomach. This was getting *too* good. She needed a nap. A break of some kind. So much happiness would probably curdle her. Lana was used to struggling. This felt way too easy. "I'm starving. And I'm suddenly exhausted. Any chance we could get room service around here?"

"Ooh!" Molly nodded. "Great idea. I'll put together some plates and we'll eat in your room?"

Oh, no, that wasn't what she'd meant.

Adele wasn't paying attention – she seemed to still be stuck on Nashville news. "What about Taft Hill? Who's writing for him? Have you heard that new song? "Blame Me," I think it's called. I can't decide what I think about it."

Lana, stunned, could only say, "Sorry?"

Molly said, "Oh, man, if you haven't heard it, you have to. It's really good. I'm dying to know who wrote it for him."

"It's different," said Adele.

What did "different" mean? Lana wished to hell she didn't care, but she did. She should derail this particular train. "Doesn't Taft Hill write his own stuff?"

Adele inclined her head. "Well, sure, that's what he says. We know how it really goes. *This* song was written by someone else, I know it."

Lana tried to give a scoffing laugh, but it came out more like a choked wheeze. "Maybe he's just gotten a lot better with time."

"Oh, I didn't say it was better. I said it was different."

Molly turned to stare. "You don't like it, Adele? You listened to it like four times in a row the other afternoon."

"I'm not sure if I like it."

Lana's heart beat faster. "Why not?"

"I don't trust it, somehow. You really haven't heard it?"

Should she lie? Instead, she deflected again. "Why don't you trust it?"

Adele waved her hand in front of her face, as if pushing away the thought. "I don't know. I need to let it go. It's just such a strong song, subject-wise, but something's lost in the way he sings it."

"What's it about?" *Now* she was straight-up lying by omission. But she had to hear more.

"An abused woman. Typical fare, you know. Boring. Of course, there's the normal alcohol references to make it feel more inevitable."

It was like Adele had slapped her. She managed to say, "Yeah?"

Molly jumped in. "Now that's not fair. I think Taft is saying something pretty big in it. It's not about a woman getting abused, it's about her not being allowed to choose the hand she's dealt. I think it's pretty deep, and it says a lot that he's the one listening in the song. The abused woman is telling her story *through* him, I think."

Adele shook her head again. "Maybe it's deep and I'm not getting it. There's something I really like about the song, even though on the surface level I actually kind of hate it. Maybe the songwriter is just really young? Really naive?"

"No." Oh, great. Lana should stab herself with a fork. That would distract them.

"What?"

"I mean, if Taft Hill bought it, it has to be someone established, right? He's too big to work with someone renting a White Bluff apartment and eating Top Ramen."

"It's just weird. That's all. What about you? Hey, you didn't answer earlier. Have you been writing?"

A leaden lump settled in Lana's chest and she didn't feel hungry anymore. The diners around them were loud again, happily tucking away their dinners, indifferent to sibling drama. "Nope. Not a word." What a lie. Even when she wasn't actually physically writing songs in her notebook, Lana was writing them in her head, singing each line over and over in her brain until it was stuck there, impossible to dislodge.

It was something she loved about herself – the inability to move more than a few yards on a walk without coming up with a new hook that begged for a song to fit it in.

It was one of the things she hated most about herself, too. That her talent was second-hand, passed down from Adele, the real songwriter in the family.

Lana folded her knife and fork back into the paper napkin she'd taken them from. She'd eat a protein bar in the room, and she'd call that good. "You know what I always hated?"

Molly was distracted, waving at a red-faced baby at a nearby table, but Adele was listening. She looked startled. "What?"

Don't start. Quit it. Don't do it. Lana spoke anyway, hating herself as she did. "The jeans."

CHAPTER SIX

Adele tilted her head. "Jeans?"

"Yours, in particular. You always got them new."

Molly turned to join in. "True! Adele, you were the only one with new jeans when we were growing up."

"So?"

"By the time they got to me, they were worn out." It was so *stupid* to bring up that old hurt feeling.

Adele smiled. "You got the patches, though! Mama made those jeans so cute, you know she did."

Lana started to scoot out of the booth. "They were worn. You got them when they were cute and new, and I got them covered with patched butterflies and elephants."

"So cute!" Adele insisted.

"Not when I was in junior high."

"Oh, come on." Adele looked like she was going to laugh. "You're not seriously still upset about that."

It stung. It always had. When Adele decided what she thought about another person, she didn't give up on that, though. If she thought Lana had loved wearing jeans with animal patches stitched into the crotch, she'd believe she was right till the breath left her body.

"Come on, Lana." Molly was the peacemaker. She always had been. "It's not a big deal, right? It was so long ago." Molly's smile was wide. Pleading.

Lana would swim across a lake of fire for Molly. "I'm just saying."

Adele nodded. "Besides, look at you now. You're the real star of the family. Still out there working, singing. Still making money with your music. I sell songs, yeah, but I don't sing them."

"What about that album you two did?"

A short, sharp look flew between Molly and Adele.

"We thought you didn't mind," said Molly weakly.

Lana didn't.

Well, she had thought she didn't. The album was to raise money for Migration. Lana had been nowhere nearby. It was great that her sisters had done it. They were making a difference in the world.

Lana had given herself a crooked haircut and a bad dye job.

Their lives weren't parallel – they were perpendicular.

"I don't mind." No matter what, she had to make that be true. "I really don't."

Adele smiled warmly, so warmly Lana almost believed she was as special as the smile said she was. "Will you stay?"

Next to her, Molly rolled her eyes and groaned. "No pressure, though. I'm sure that's not what she wants to talk about right now."

But Lana nodded. "Yes."

It was as if she'd pulled out a paper bag full of kittens and dumped them all over the café table. Her sisters both screamed and squealed in the same breath. They got up to hug her, but the embrace was less like a hug and more like a homecoming. Lana blinked hard and rubbed her nose with a napkin, mumbling something about allergies in Darling Bay. Restaurant patrons looked on with renewed interest. Why had she told them now, here? In front of everyone.

On the other hand, maybe she'd done it on purpose. Now she could make her escape, plead exhaustion, which was true, and go to bed.

The words were tumbling out of her sisters, and it took effort to parse their meaning. "You mean it? You'll stay? Like, forever?"

"Will you run the hotel? Oh, God." Adele's eyes were huge. "You have to run it. Molly and I can't figure out one damn thing to do. We have no idea where to start. You would be perfect for it. You *have* to stay."

What an Adele move.

Lana had just said she was staying, and now Adele was trying to make her do so. As if it were her idea.

Molly put her soft hand on Lana's forearm. "What about singing? Touring? Will you still do that if you stay? Go out on the road?"

"Nope." The word was nothing but bravado. The only thing Lana knew was the road. She hadn't lived in a town for more than a month since she was a little girl, since the last time they left Darling Bay. "I'm done with music."

Somehow, she'd expected they would congratulate her. It had been something she'd thought about for so long, after all, the idea wasn't surprising to her anymore. It still felt sad and deep, like a cold dark well of black water, but it was water she was used to. Water she was willing to drink.

Adele gave a short laugh. "Oh, my God, I thought you were serious for a minute."

Molly scanned Lana's face. "I think she is."

The food arrived then, mercifully. For a few minutes, they focused on moving plates, grabbing extra mayo, salting the fries.

They carefully didn't look at each other until Nikki had refilled their waters and walked away.

"Okay," said Molly. "More, please. You can't be serious."

Adele nodded but kept quiet, thankfully.

Lana held a too-hot fry in her hand. "I'm as serious as sin. I'm out. No more dingy bars, no more drunks grabbing my ass, no more songs being sung by people who don't understand the emotion behind the words."

No more late nights searching for hours for the right word, the word that would make this song lift off and soar. No more joy as the right chord found the next one, each line making the song better, stronger. No more meeting with other songwriters, no more collaboration, no more incredible surprises, no more breath.

No more hope.

Just regular life. With regular people.

Lana was going to be someone with an interesting history and a boring future.

Honestly, after so many years of trying to be fascinating enough to captivate strangers with nothing more than a well-turned phrase, a boring future sounded kind of okay.

Adele broke the short silence that had fallen with a clap. "Okay, we have to celebrate. You're *staying*. Our last Songbird. Home. I'll go grab a bottle of wine so we can really celebrate. And by "we" I mean you two, since I'm not drinking."

"I'm good with water." Lana threw a smile at Molly. "And this delicious burger."

Adele kept up her chirping. "Okay. What about money? It's not going to be cheap to upgrade the hotel rooms, and I know it might be hard to ask, but —"

Even though most customers had by now made their way out into the night, there were still enough people in the big room that this was the wrong place to make this revelation. But Lana couldn't help herself. "I have enough money."

Molly grinned. "I knew it."

Adele looked sharply at her. "Knew what?"

"That she had an ace up her sleeve."

Molly would, of course, be the one who guessed. "I like an ace, that's true."

"You're rich."

"Well ..." Lana wasn't ridiculously wealthy. She couldn't run off and buy a castle or anything. She'd never have a private plane. The money to upgrade an old hotel and make the rooms rentable again, though? To make them clean and pretty and old-fashioned and home-like? Yeah, she had that money, with more of it pouring into her bank account every day. "I have enough."

Molly pumped her fist. "You always said you'd never come back until you'd made it. Now you have. I'm so proud of you. And happy for *us*." She grinned. Lana was the lucky one with a sister like Molly.

Adele, however, was suspiciously quiet. She examined a pickle slice carefully and then ate it.

Lana jammed two fries into her mouth. She spoke around them. "What?"

"Nothing."

Molly held up a hand. "We don't have to get all the particulars right n–"

"How did you make the money?"

Funny, Lana would've happily told Molly. She'd planned to. But when Adele asked like that, it made her want to lie, the same way she had every time Adele had blamed her for finishing off the animal crackers when they were little. Lana lowered her voice. "I ran a whorehouse for a little while. Good money in it, you know."

Adele's eyes widened. "No."

"Um, seriously?"

Adele shook her head. "I knew you were kidding."

Pain sliced inside Lana's chest. "Dude. For a minute you actually thought I could make money selling women's bodies – that was easier to believe than maybe I just did well in Nashville?"

Adele rubbed her cheeks. "Of course not. That's not right. It's just ... but how?"

"I sold a couple of body organs. Expensive ones. Heart and both lungs."

Molly said, "You guys ..."

"I'm happy," said Adele. "I'm fucking *thrilled* you're home. This has been my dream for just about forever."

"*You've* been here less than a year," Lana accused.

"It's always been my dream."

"To have us all back in the same broken-down town?"

Adele shook her head. "To have us all back together. I didn't give a shit where." Her eyes were glossy, as if she were about to start crying, and honestly, that was going to do nothing but piss Lana off.

"Don't cry, for God's sake."

Adele glared. "I'm *not*."

Lana stabbed a fry in her direction. "Good. Because that would be dumb."

"How did you get the money?" Adele demanded.

"Does it actually matter?"

Molly groaned. "I give up on you two. Give me more fries."

"Here." Lana shoved them in her direction.

"Tell me they're the best."

"They are." They really were. But as delicious as the fries were, the topic wasn't going to throw off Adele.

"Did you do a tour we don't know about?"

"No." Lana knew Adele still worked with the biggest names in the business. She'd have heard if Lana suddenly had gone on tour with Jason Aldean or Reba McEntire.

"Has to be songwriting, then."

"There's nothing else in the industry? That's pretty reductive, isn't it?"

Adele frowned. "True. You're right. Okay, tell me."

"No." Lana took a huge mouthful of the cheeseburger so she wouldn't be tempted to say more.

Only, as she chewed, she wondered what the hell her problem was. Why couldn't she tell her sisters? She'd done nothing wrong. She'd written a song that had rocketed to the top of the charts since months ago and showed real staying power. It had been optioned by four different movies and one major national ad campaign. That, plus the others she'd sold in the past, would keep royalty cheese flowing into her account for the next twenty years at least, checks that meant she never had to go on the road again.

Was it possible *that* was her problem?

That she'd lost the only adult life she'd ever known?

Why the hell was she trying to hide it from her sisters, the ones who loved her more than anyone? It was just stubborn misplaced pride and embarrassment.

She'd wanted to be a star.

Instead, she just wrote songs, exactly like her big sister, who'd done it for longer and who'd been better at it.

She had to face it and quit pushing them away. "I –"

"What is that tattoo?" Adele reached forward and pulled at Lana's wrist. Lana instinctively pulled back, but it was too late.

Adele's eyes were wide. "That's the piece, the one I sent you in the mail. The *Sorry!* game piece you bit off when you were a kid."

As a child, Lana had pretty much chewed her way through most of their toys. She shrugged. "Yeah."

Molly said, "It looks like a blue volcano."

"Could be that, too." But it wasn't. It was the *Sorry!* piece, with its round blue base, its conical stem, and the ragged edge where Lana as a child had gnawed off the round head. Adele had mailed it to her. It had made Lana cry. The tattoo had made her feel close to her sisters. Silly, really. She pressed her thumb into it. "Look, I made enough money to quit the business. That's all."

Adele crossed her arms. She had a smudge of ketchup just to the right of her lip, and she'd hate finding it there later. Lana sure wasn't going to tell her. "And you're stubborn enough to not want to tell us how."

"Yep." Lana's heart thumped hollowly inside her chest.

"Fine." Adele nodded. "It's really fine. I'm just so glad you're home."

That was it? That was all she was going to get? Something like disappointment slid down the back of Lana's throat. She managed to say, "Me, too." She wasn't sure it was the truth, but she also didn't know it to be a lie, so somewhere in there the truth probably existed.

CHAPTER SEVEN

Taft Hill had never seen a town like Darling Bay that wasn't on the big screen. It was like something out of a romantic comedy made just for women.

The main street was called, of course, Main. There only appeared to be one stoplight. There was a line outside the ice-cream shop and a balloon guy – who just looked like a college kid making some money, not the creepy clowns Taft remembered from carnivals – was laughing while a baby tried to grab a balloon in the shape of a puppy. A police officer held up traffic as – Taft wouldn't have believed it if he hadn't seen it with his own eyes – a mama duck and her babies crossed from one side to the other. An older woman honked her horn at Taft from inside the Library Mobile, but it was only to wave his car in front of hers.

Jesus.

Even though Taft had never been comfortable around perfection, and even though the sweetness of this town should make his teeth hurt, it felt good to be driving carefully down a main street, the top of the rental open to the sun, watching a town function in a way that could make them proud as a nation. All races seemed represented. All ages were present. No one was shouting. In fact, everywhere he looked, people were laughing in the morning sun. The whole town seemed to be scented with fresh coffee, rising dough and a whiff of ocean spray.

Too perfect. *Way* too perfect. Had to be a cult or something.

In a minute, someone would recognize him, and then the world would shift back into place – greedy people would kowtow to him and self-serving ones would make a big deal that he was there. Taft would go back to the life he knew, the life he hadn't enjoyed in a long time.

You never knew what people really thought when they never told the full truth.

Taft hated that.

He parked in front of the Golden Spike Café. According to Sully's research, the Darling girls owned the property now. Was Lana planning on starting a recording studio here or something? Alan Jackson did it, after all, with that studio he had in Miami, and another singer he'd worked with last year had up and moved to Iceland, of all places. She said, "I can do everything I need to do online, except for tour, and I can start a tour from anyplace in the world."

He pulled on a black SXSW ball cap. It wouldn't keep him from being recognized for long, but it might take longer than if he wore his cowboy hat.

The diner was as busy as Nashville's Loveless Café. A blonde woman waved at him and gave him the sign to sit anywhere.

Instead, he stood at the hostess podium. Even with as good as the place smelled – like blueberry muffins and maple syrup – he wasn't here to eat. Later, he could fill his belly with old-fashioned diner fare. Right now, he needed one thing – another song.

"Sorry, I thought you saw me, anywhere's fine." The woman had a pretty face and a perfect-ten body, curves in all the right places.

Taft thought briefly of Lana's slim frame. "I don't mind waiting for you to finish."

"Nah, just choose a seat. Your waitress will be right with you. I have a DEFCON level-five clean-up over there, and if I don't get back to it, the milk will seep through the floor and into the groundwater, and I'll be in trouble for something that I don't want to be in trouble for." She made a move to step away.

"I'm not here to eat. I'm looking for Lana Darling."

"Oh!" The woman's eyebrows flew upward. "Well, she's probably around."

"Would you mind telling me where I could find her?" It was a small town, it couldn't take too long to find a gorgeous hellcat who wrote songs like a goddess, could it?

"Hmmm." The blonde leaned on the podium. She looked him up and down. Then she shook her head. "No."

"Sorry?" Did the woman not like his music?

"You look like my ex, Todd. Therefore, I don't trust you at all. If you don't know how to find Lana, there's probably a reason."

"Well, that's remarkably direct."

"Refreshing, isn't it?"

"I lost her phone number." It wasn't true. Lana had refused to give it to him, and they'd done all the contract negotiation through his agent.

"Okay, then." The woman reached under a side counter and pulled up a coffee pot. "Like I said, I have to clean up the milk, and do another coffee round. If you don't want anything else ..."

"She owns this property with her sisters, right? So she'll be around at some point. You really want me to just stick around, like a stalker?" He heard how it sounded only as it came out of his mouth.

"Well, now that you put it like that, seems like a *very* bad thing for you to do. I'd suggest leaving before I call the cops. And since my boyfriend – also named Todd, but he's Good Todd – is the cop on my speed dial, I suggest you move it on out." The woman's voice was pure sugar, her face showing nothing except a friendly smile. Anyone looking at them would think they were chatting about the weather.

Taft shifted his weight. He was doing this all wrong. "Look, I promise I'm not a stalker. I barely know Lana Darling."

"That makes me feel even better about not telling you where she is."

He took off his ball cap. He gave her his biggest smile, the same smile that more than one magazine had called heart-stopping. He upped the wattage by giving her a wink. "What's your name, darlin'?"

The blonde cocked her head. "No, thanks. Good luck to you."

It was worth one last try. "You listen to country music?"

She shook her head as she walked away and spoke over her shoulder. "I do. The Darling Songbirds is my favorite group."

Taft wondered if the whole town would rally around Lana in the same way.

Somehow he got the feeling they might. That must be something.

A short, round woman sidled up to him. She had so many beads draped around her neck that she clacked like tumbling rocks every time her head moved. "Lana said she was headed to the hardware store."

Taft slapped the cap back on his head. "Hot damn. Thank you, ma'am. Will you point me the right direction?"

"Down the street, on the left."

"Thank you!"

"Don't thank me. The cards told me to tell you."

He touched the brim of his cap. "Ma'am."

"Lord, have mercy. Do I look like a ma'am?" The older woman looked down at her shoes, which were just big leather strips. Her toenails were painted blue. "Maybe I do. Anyway. Go easy on her."

"Sorry?"

"I assume the cards told me about you because you're going to be important for some reason."

The hairs rose on the back of Taft's neck. "What's the reason?"

"Humph. If I knew that, I'd have just asked for the lottery numbers. Do I look stupid to you?"

For the second time in two minutes, a woman stormed away from him without a goodbye. Taft hadn't been this unpopular since he'd had glasses and braces in seventh grade. Even then kids were mostly nice to him because he was Palmer Hill's son.

He had to admit, it was refreshing. Bracing, like jumping into an icy stream on a hot day. He wasn't being recognized. He was just a normal guy. Looking for a girl.

No eyes followed him as he turned.

No one raced after him for an autograph.

No customers whispered their suspicions. He'd gotten used to the way a room sounded when he was trying to go unnoticed and not succeeding – there were murmurs, all shushed sibilants. There were small exclamations, tiny explosions around the room. *Is that him? It's totally him. You go ask. No, you go. Oh! You think?*

Now he heard none of these. Spoons clattered in coffee mugs, and a table full of women laughed over something that sounded like a dirty joke. The coffee machine gurgled and spat. A low rumble came from behind him, out on the street, and when Taft turned, he saw a tractor making its slow way down the main street. Cars were lined up behind it, moving at a crawl.

No one honked. Not even once.

This sure as hell wasn't Nashville.

CHAPTER EIGHT

O ne of Lana's favorite places in Darling Bay always had been Floyd's Hardware. The door still creaked the same way when she pulled it open, and inside, it sounded just the same as it always had. A key being cut shrieked, and nails clinked metallically as they were tossed into a bin. It smelled like citronella and fresh-cut wood and something else clean and sharp, redolent of Pine-Sol.

At the hotel, she'd tried pulling down some drywall. She'd found to her astonishment that not much at all stood between her and the studs of a building. She needed some tools, and some guidance of some sort. She'd always been good with her hands, with building, and she'd spent long hours on every tour under the stages, building with the set crew. Back then she'd had her own coveralls and her own tool belt. She'd been just a kid, though, good with a hammer but not versed in actual repair. Back then, she'd just followed directions. While her sisters had tested mics up above, Lana had crawled below, running cables from one end of the set to the other.

It was all so long ago now.

"Hey! Is that you, girl?"

Floyd Huppert had owned the hardware store since the end of the Spanish–American war, or so he'd always claimed. He'd been old when Lana was a girl rifling through the nail bins, and though he should have looked ancient by now, incredibly, he didn't seem much different. He still had a full head of white hair, and he wore the same old blue shirt with his name embroidered above the pocket.

"Floyd!" Lana leaned over the counter to give him a peck on his cheek. She rubbed her lips. "You're scratchy."

"What?" Floyd scraped at his chin. "I shave twice a week, whether I need it or not."

"Ida lets you get away with that?" As the words left her mouth, Lana felt a pang. She had been away so long – what were the odds that both Floyd and Ida were still alive and healthy?

But Floyd beamed. "She lets me get away with just about anything, as long as it doesn't involve licorice or other women."

"Licorice?"

"She hates the smell. She'd throw me out of the house if I ever came home with it on my breath. Think I could come home reeking of ladies' perfume first."

"You ever tested that theory?" she teased.

"Lord have mercy, no, I haven't. There's a reason I've been happily married so long. You in town to sing with your sisters?"

Two other old men rattled and coughed in their direction. The siren call of the hardware store – it was always like this, in every town she'd been in over the years. In every single store, three or four old men held up the walls with their shoulders. Lana would bet the two – no, make that four now – men headed her way spent most of their waking hours telling old war stories with Floyd. No matter where she was, Lana usually made an excuse to go to the local hardware. Sometimes she needed a better plug for the hotel bathtub drain. When she was staying on friends' couches, she'd offer to paint something, anything. Any excuse to wander the aisles and look at all the things she didn't quite know how to use, all the things she wanted to learn about.

Now was her chance.

"Look." Lana put her hands flat on the counter. Men like Floyd were expert in small-town gossip. They were worse than women when it came to chatter and conjecture, Uncle Hugh had always said. *Best to be straight with a man, right up front. Otherwise they'll imagine too much.* "You're going to see me in here a lot. I'm going to spend a huge amount of money. I'm fixing up the old hotel. I know you mean well, but I'd very much appreciate it if you don't get on my case about music, in any form. I'm out of the business, and I need one part of my life where it's not going to come up. Can this shop be that place?"

Floyd's eyes widened. "Why, yes. I believe it can. I appreciate the business."

"Thank you."

"It's a big job, girl."

"Yes."

"Where're you gonna start?"

"Room twelve."

"No, I mean, what are you going to do first? Roof? Inner walls?"

"I figured I'd go room by room."

From behind her, Lana heard the store regulars grumble. *Can't do it that way. That won't work. That's a girl for you.*

A man who wore his big nose like it was something to be proud of said, "You know how to roof, girl?"

Another said, "What about electrical?"

"Repairing sheetrock?"

"Have you thought about the HVAC?"

Lana opened her mouth to say something snappy, something smart, something that would shut them down. *Of course I know about heating and ventilation! I'm strong enough. I don't spend all my time in hardware stores dreaming of bygone days. I can probably do more push-ups than all of you combined.*

"I'm fine." It was all she could get out. She chewed quickly on the side of her thumb, then stuck her hand into her pocket.

"You ain't got a man around to help you?"

She smiled as sweetly as she could, but she'd never had a good poker face. It felt more like a grimace. "I don't do well with help, gender aside."

A white-haired man who hadn't spoken until now said, "You better *get* good with help. You cain't do that job alone."

Of course she could. She had money and she had time. Lots and lots of time, which was good, since it would take a while to learn everything, to buy everything, to figure out how to use the tools, to redo whatever she screwed up ... Her resolve flagged for a second, but she bucked herself up again.

Lana didn't ask for assistance, not even when she couldn't find something in Target. If you were patient enough, you could do anything that needed doing.

Too bad she couldn't buy extra patience, though. "Yeah, well, I'm a fast learner."

Then Floyd jumped in. "Don't try the electrical by yourself. I knew a guy who did that once."

Lana rolled her eyes. "Burned the house down? Yeah, I'll be careful. Not much more damage I can do."

Floyd frowned. "He got fried. He left a widow and three kids behind. Never seen a woman angrier than his wife, I tell you what. He'd been supposed to wait for his friend to help him, a friend who knew what he was doing, but he was impatient."

Chastened, Lana took a breath. "That's terrible."

"Yeah."

"I promise, I'll try not to be impatient. And you promise me something."

"What?" Floyd's face was open even as the other men puffed out their chests, obviously at the ready to spout instructions.

"Promise you'll stop thinking about me as just some girl. A woman can do just as good a job as a man."

Floyd nodded. "I promise. I truly agree with you. Now, take this." He slid a white card across the counter.

She took it. "Ballard Brothers Building and Realty?"

"They're good."

Lana wanted to rip it up into little pieces, but she controlled herself. "Thanks. If I need help –"

"When," interjected Nose Man.

"*If* I need help, I can find my own workers."

"They employ women, that's all I'm saying."

Lana blinked. "They do?"

"Got a woman electrician on their crew, and maybe a plumber, too. Right, Howard? The Fellows girl working with them?"

Lana decided she'd just ignore the use of the word "girl." "Fine. Thank you for the card."

"Great. You'll do great. Now, what are you looking for today?"

"A book."

Floyd stared again. "Sorry?"

"Don't you have a book about construction?"

"Well, yeah. But no one's bought a book in at least five years." He cocked his head and looked at her like she'd lost her mind. "Don't you have the YouTube?"

Lana sighed. "I'm old-fashioned."

"Well! That's refreshing! Follow me. I've got a whole shelf of books. Even ordered new ones last year, in case anyone wanted one. Which, I have to say, no one has. You know, there are three of those Ballard boys, just like there are three of you girls. Too bad y'all didn't get here earlier. Liam and Aidan are already spoken for, I hear. Your sisters, too. Everyone your age shacking up, I guess." Floyd smiled warmly. "Let me show you those books now."

As she trailed behind him, the wind left Lana's sails. *Shacking up.* That was a good enough phrase for it.

Love.

Honestly. Who had time?

"Hey!" An old man wearing a red T-shirt with "I Heart Bingo" printed on the front said, "Isn't that ...?"

"Lord almighty! I think it is!"

Lana's cheeks heated. Floyd had remembered her, but she and Uncle Hugh had spent so much time in here when she was young that she hadn't been surprised. And he hadn't said her name out loud. If those other old men recognized her, then it meant Molly was right – that this town still remembered them. Maybe if she pretended she couldn't hear them, maybe if she just kept following Floyd down the aisle, they'd get over their surprise.

"I have to get an autograph."

"Me first!"

"I'm going to get him to sign my cane!"

Lana frowned. Him?

"He's not his father."

"He's still good."

"Palmer Hill was a real musician. I'm not sure about this boy of his."

Um, no.

She must have heard that wrong. She slowed and looked over her shoulder.

"Is he coming in here?" The old man in the red T-shirt poked the one wearing blue.

"I think he is. Oooh, I'm going to ask him if he really dated Taylor Swift."

"You're as bad as a woman. Play his father's music at my funeral, but not that kid's."

Sparks ran up Lana's spine, adrenaline shooting electricity to her wrists. It couldn't be Taft Hill.

Not in Darling Bay.

Impossible.

She couldn't see outside – whoever had walked in front of the window who resembled Taft Hill had already passed by.

The bell over the door jangled as it opened.

Floyd was halfway down aisle three, ignoring the other men. "Down here. I've got just the book for you."

Lana ducked past the end of the aisle and peered around a stack of air filters.

There he was.

Shock colored her vision black and white.

Taft looked good that way, too.

Large as life, and about six times as handsome. The man was too good-looking – it wasn't healthy to be so pretty.

"Taft Hill! I told you, Benny, didn't I tell you?" One man nudged another in the ribs so hard he wheezed.

"Hi, fellas."

"What are you doing here?"

Thank God someone was asking it.

"Strangely enough, I'm looking for a woman. Someone said she might be here. Lana Darling – have you seen her?"

Something like heartburn rose in Lana's chest. She sucked in a breath and stumbled backward. She spun around, barreling down the aisle, away from the front. "Floyd," she hissed. "Floyd!"

He turned. "Yeah? Heck, I think I moved 'em. Like I said, no one buys books. Maybe over on eight. Let's go check."

"Can I use your bathroom?"

Floyd pointed. "Down there, just turn at the fertilizer."

Lana ran, not caring that Floyd looked surprised. She turned at the stack of bagged soil and pulled open the first door she saw. She slammed it closed, locked it, and fumbled for the light switch.

She wasn't in a bathroom. She was in a storage closet.

CHAPTER NINE

Old men still listened to country music, and these old men knew who Taft was. He'd have to tell his Taylor Swift story, he could feel it.

He *really* didn't want to tell it again.

"Hey there, nice to meet you." He shook a man's hand, then another's. "So, Lana? Did you see her?"

They almost tripped over themselves to tell him. "She went back there!"

"Looking for a book!"

"She doesn't use the YouTube!"

"Floyd!" The old man's voice was a hoarse excited screech. "You got yourself Taft Hill in your store!"

Taft headed down the direction they pointed him in. Three aisles over and around a corner, he found another old man standing stock-still in front of a wall lined with paint cans.

The man looked at him in surprise and stuck out his hand. "Floyd Huppert. At your service."

"Taft –"

"I know who you are. Big fan of your father's."

There was a certain breed of man who would never get on board with new country. They loved everyone up to and including Merle Haggard and no one newer. Taft always liked these men more than anyone else – it was good to have honesty directed at him. No false praise for a shoddy job.

"Thanks. Me, too."

Floyd scratched the top of his head. "This day sure keeps getting weirder. I've got two country stars in my store now."

"Lana Darling? Yeah, I'm looking for her. Someone said she might be here."

Floyd looked at the closed door he'd been staring at. "Yeah, well. She seems to have locked herself in the closet."

A squeak came from the other side of the door.

"Really?"

"Said she was going to the bathroom, but I hope she's not, 'cause there's nothing in there but some old buckets. Well, I suppose *that* would be all right, except –"

"I'm not using a bucket!"

The door banged open. There she was, in all her glory. Lana Darling looked as fierce as she sounded – her hair was shorter now than it had been, and it was dark, almost black. She looked *mad*, looked like a sexy ass-kicker, as if she were about to punch a vampire. She wore a black T-shirt halfway stuck into black jeans and big black combat boots. She wore a wide black leather bracelet, and she had not a lick of make-up on her skin. Her lips were pink and her eyes shot sparks at him.

She couldn't have been sexier.

"Lana."

"What the hell are you *doing* here?"

"What do you think? Looking for you."

He hadn't known a woman in combat boots could sweep past regally, but somehow she pulled it off. "Well, let's pretend you haven't found me."

"What were you doing in the closet?"

"I was trying to get away from you, and it was the first door I opened."

He laughed. She was so *honest*. He'd liked that about her immediately – she didn't seem to have the social-nicety filter most people came with.

Lana didn't slow down. Over her shoulder she called, "Floyd, I'll be back for the book later."

"You sure? I've almost found it, I'm sure I have!"

She was already outside, though, on the sidewalk, moving fast.

Taft walked behind her. She was obviously hurrying, but when it came down to it, she had shorter legs, and he didn't have to lengthen his stride too much to keep up. The morning sun shone on the crown of her head. "I'd love to buy you a cup of coffee."

"Had one."

"One's never enough." Taft almost tripped over an uneven section of sidewalk.

"It is for me." She shot a pointed look back at him.

They'd had once. That once had kind of sucked.

"Come on. What about a drink?"

"It's not even eleven o'clock in the morning."

"Good point. Lunch?"

Lana spun and put her hands on her hips. "What. Do. You. Want?" Her anger was real, and it threw him.

"Hey, now." Taft raised his palms. "I didn't know if you'd be pleased to see me, but I sure didn't know you'd be mad."

"I'm not mad."

She was. She was radiating fury.

"Okay, then. So you'll consider letting me buy you lunch?"

Without saying another word, she turned her back and walked away again.

Taft followed her. The eyes of the men at the hardware store burned into his chambray shirt, and embarrassment crawled down his spine. He'd done something wrong, and since he didn't think it had anything to do with the money that was most likely flooding her bank account, it had to be about the night they'd spent together.

"Lana, can you stop for a minute? Talk to me?"

"No, thanks." They were at the Golden Spike, and she plowed through the parking lot.

"I feel like a stalker here."

"Then stop following me."

It would be easy to ignore her. To assume she was just playing hard to get (but why was she? He wanted music, not her body – they'd already established it didn't work out real well that way between them) and just follow her up to the hotel area he could see from the parking lot.

But Taft had been raised to respect a woman's wishes. Always.

So he stopped.

He needed her help, but he'd have to figure out what he'd done wrong. Then, whatever it turned out to be, he'd apologize for it. He watched her go. Her back was straight, her head so rigidly affixed atop her body that he wondered if it hurt her neck.

Damn, though, he couldn't help admiring the sway of the back of her jeans as she went.

CHAPTER TEN

L ana went into room twelve because she knew off the top of her head that she'd left it unlocked earlier. She wouldn't have to fumble for a key, even for a moment. His footsteps had stopped, but she wouldn't let herself relax until she knew for sure he was gone.

Once in the safety of the room, she slid down the door so she was sitting on the floor, facing into the trashed area. The ceiling was open to the sky, allowing the sunlight to stream through. A pool of light fell on the toes of her boots, and her feet felt warm, which was nice since the rest of her was so cold.

They'd had one bad night. That was all. She'd told him too much. She regretted it. But she'd assumed that he was out of her life for good, except for the very welcome money she got from "Blame Me."

She'd been fired by her agent group (though in the tabloids, they called it a "mutual split", which was what they always said), and while she'd hoped that they'd put together one last small tour for her, all they'd gotten her was the Bluebird gig at the very last minute.

It was a Monday night, always the worst night of the week. Rumor had it she'd only gotten the slot because a bluegrass band from Boise had broken up on the revelation the fiddler was sleeping with the bass player's wife.

The only people in the audience were tourists. It was always easy to tell who was from Nashville and who was just visiting. The tourists watched the stage for a while, eagerly waiting to be impressed. They held up their iPads and phones, hoping for a real country star sighting. When it was just her, when they realized that no one more famous than a girl who used to be in a female band that wasn't the Dixie Chicks was on stage, they turned around and started showing each other pictures on their phones. Tourists always spoke in normal voices, as if they were at a bar anywhere, as if whoever was on stage was just background noise, like the cover bands at their watering hole at home.

Locals, on the other hand, stayed quiet. They waited in the dark to listen. Locals were ready to be impressed, but even when they weren't, even when the act let them down, they stayed respectful. The space's heritage demanded that. John Prine, Clint Black and Townes Van Zandt had played right in the spot where Lana sat by herself with her guitar. Locals were reverent to the space itself if not always to the singer.

While she'd played that night, Lana just sang over the tourists' heads. They didn't notice, of course, too busy looking at their phones. Instead, she sang into the back, where it was dark. She let herself imagine there was an indie label scout back there somewhere – a man or woman just looking for their next big break, and that it was her. They'd see her singing and rush the stage afterwards.

Somehow she'd missed Taft Hill when he came in. It wasn't easy to miss a man like that, all shoulders and swagger and goodwill. He was like a friendly missionary, kindly smiling, then he got that glint in his eye, the one that made a girl feel like a woman. That's what he managed to do on stage, on screen, on a television, looking out into the audience. It was nothing compared to what he could make a woman feel like up close.

And damn, he was getting close.

Lana watched him walk toward the stage. She pretended to be tuning her guitar, but under her lashes, she saw every move he made. *Why* was he coming her way? There were no free tables at the front – there never were, even though those were the people least likely to listen. Tourists who thought they liked country but really only liked Garth Brooks, and nineties Garth Brooks, at that. Was he coming up to try to play with her?

Lana tightened her grip on the neck of her guitar. Her finger slipped on the E-string and fed a sour note into the mic.

He pulled out a chair and said something low to the couple who'd been looking at their phones the whole time they'd been sitting down.

That was just weird.

So she sang. She tried to keep her eyes from drifting to him, but it took physical effort. Her gaze wanted to rest on him, to travel from that shock of thick sandy hair down to those darker eyebrows, to trace his square jaw, and wander down the muscled cords in his neck. He wore a western shirt (naturally), but it was subtle, a dark blue with the pattern at yoke in a darker purple.

Up close, well, damn.

He was hot.

Even sitting still – and he was sitting *so* still, like a piece of chiseled rock – he was magnetic. People in the audience had stopped taking desultory, obligatory pictures of her (*Who is she? Is she someone? Part of a girl group, I think? The Honeys?*) and had turned their cell phones on him and those impressive broad shoulders of his.

That was fine.

All Lana had to do was sing. Luckily, that's what she knew how to do.

The last song on her set list was "Blame Me." For a second, the intensity of his eyes on hers made her think about playing something else.

Should she play it tonight?

A staff person in the back dropped a tray of something glass. The resulting crash made everyone in the place jump, including Lana.

Taft didn't jump, though. He kept his gaze on her, his hands open in his lap. He leaned back in his chair as if he were sitting in his living room, and suddenly Lana wanted to play the song.

So she did.

And even though the room was still bustling, even though people were still chatting and laughing, even though the really drunk woman in the back was finally getting politely escorted to the door, Lana felt every word move through her like she'd just written the song.

Blame me, the way I do.
Blame me, for not saying yes.

Taft nodded at the end. He nodded right at her, and Lana felt something in the pit of her stomach overheat. Taft Hill.

Huh. She'd heard his music, and she liked it, but then again, she'd heard a lot of country music over the years. Maybe all of it. His was as good as anyone else's – not as good as his father's but better than most.

The way he looked at her, though – yeah, that made her think again.

CHAPTER ELEVEN

I
t wasn't like he'd gone to the Bluebird to find anything.

It was more like he'd been trying to escape everything else.

He'd found something out that day. Something that was impossible to face just yet, so he figured he wouldn't.

So yeah, Taft had been running away. It was funny, when he thought about it, that he'd run straight into the one place so many of his friends had gotten their start. Not him, of course. Palmer Hill's son didn't need the Bluebird to kick off his career – Taft had been born into the country-singing world, and he'd die in its rhinestone-decorated arms someday.

It was still a good place to get a drink, it turned out. Tourists crowded the front tables (they had reservations now, something that they'd never had in the old days), but the back of the bar was still dim and the alcohol still full proof. Watering down a drink like they did in big cities was a hanging offence in this part of the state.

Taft didn't plan on talking to anyone except the bartender to order drinks. For the first hour, it worked. A man and woman crooned pretty harmonies on stage, but there was nothing in their vapid lyrics that required attention. Taft sipped his bourbon on the rocks and let his mind drift, thinking about everything and nothing, as long as he didn't think about what had happened, what he'd learned. The thing that would change everything.

You're the best thing that ever happened to me.

It was what his father had always said to him, over and over again.

Yep, not thinking was definitely in order. Taft ordered another drink.

Then she came on stage.

She didn't look like everyone else in Nashville. Her hair was long, of course, and blonde, done in those long country curls. Her eyes were light brown, almost tan, and wide set. She had high, flat cheekbones. Her mouth was pink, but not from lipstick – it looked as if she'd been biting her lips.

She had not one lick of nervousness.

She sat on the single stool, making sure her guitar was amped right. She checked the cables herself, which meant she was a real musician, not just someone with a pretty voice.

Because her voice was pretty, that was for darn sure.

"Who is this?" he asked the bartender.

"A Darling girl, I think. The little one."

The Darling Songbirds. Lord, it had been a while since he'd heard that name. They'd been broken up for ten years now, maybe more. The eldest, Adele Darling, was still writing – they'd almost collaborated once, but then she started writing with Kenny Chesney. Taft and she had never worked on a song together. What were the other sisters' names? Molly, that was it, she was the rounder one, so that left Lana.

Lana Darling.

He watched her sing.

Charisma.

The real deal, she had it by the truckload. When she was singing, she transformed into something different, something electric. She'd been cute when she walked out, eccentric and kind of adorable in her plain black shirt and black jeans. But when she sang, she was beautiful. Her eyes went darker brown, smokier. Her voice seemed to hold up her spine, and her whole body sang to the crowd.

The *ungrateful* crowd full of sons of bitches who didn't have the courtesy to even watch her. They were too busy texting and taking selfies. They were in a historic room, with someone in front of them making damn history itself, and they couldn't see it.

As Lana Darling's first song ended, Taft stood. He walked to the front table, where a man and woman were involved in a heated discussion about the jalapeño poppers they'd ordered that afternoon.

"I'm telling you, they used light cream cheese."

The woman shook her head. "It was probably full fat. You're not allergic, anyway. Just shut up."

Taft rapped the tabletop with his knuckles so hard he made their Long Island iced teas jump. "Hi. Why aren't you clapping?"

Startled, the couple clapped.

Taft could feel Lana's stare on the back of his neck.

The man's mouth dropped open. "You're ... wait, are you –?"

"That I am. You mind if I sit down here with y'all?"

The woman stuttered. "Taft Hill, my God. Of course, sit with us."

Taft pulled out the chair, straddling it backward. "Great."

Both scrambled for their phones, but Taft raised a hand, palm down. "Put 'em away. Enjoy the show."

"Can you just – one picture with me?"

"After." Taft raised a finger to his lips. "You're in the presence of a legend."

"Sorry," the woman said. "Sorry. Of course. You are a legend, I know."

Taft blew out a sharp breath. "Not me. *Her.*"

Lana, only six feet away, snorted. It wasn't a giggle, and it wasn't a chuckle. It wasn't ladylike. It was a snort of derision. It was loud and held no apology. She fiddled with her C-string and started the next song.

Taft fell a little bit in love.

The couple left four songs later, and they missed the best part.

Lana sang "Blame Me."

Blame me, for not saying no.
Blame me, for wearing that dress.
Blame me, the way I do.
Blame me, for not saying yes.

He wanted it.

The song, that was.

Taft wasn't ready to admit he wanted anything else. That song, though – it was perfect. Even the people who'd rolled in drunk and got drunker listened to it. Lana's last line rolled over the tops of the audience's heads, and the room felt blessed. She'd anointed them with the truth. This was church in Nashville, and she was a conduit to a country god.

"Thank you." It was the first (and last) thing she'd said to the audience. She didn't have patter or snappy dialogue. She'd just sung.

Now she was done and stepping off stage.

Taft waited until she came out of the green room to accost her. "Lana Darling. I'm Taft Hill."

She shook his hand and nodded. She didn't pretend not to know him, which was a relief.

"Can I buy you a drink?"

She shook her head, and the long white-blonde tips of her hair hit the tops of her breasts. "Thanks, but I've had a pretty shitty day."

"Me, too. Can I buy that song? The last one?"

Lana stared at him. "Seriously?"

Taft crossed his heart, something he hadn't done since he was in second grade. "It's the best song I've heard in years. Do you sell your writing?"

"Hell, yes."

"Has anyone else offered on it?"

She shook her head. "My agent fired me today. This was my last gig in town. I haven't sold a song in a year, and I'm pretty sure my career is over, so yeah, if you want it, you can have it. You'll have to change it quite a bit, though. It couldn't be more in a woman's point of view if it tried."

Sheer happiness, that's what the feeling was. And for the shit day he'd had, the relief of it was even sweeter. "Help me revise it."

The surprise on her face was exquisite. "You're really into this."

"I can't even tell you. Please let me buy you a drink."

Lana narrowed her eyes, and Taft felt a thrill run right down his body, through his boots and into the floor. "Hmm."

"Tequila was made for bad days and new partnerships."

"I can't argue with that."

Taft ignored the people snapping pictures of them. They'd hit *The Tennessean* tomorrow, but that was fine. He didn't care. On second thought, he found he actually liked the idea that the tabloids would pair them up. Huh. "Well, right up until I heard you sing, today was the worst day of my life."

She looked up at him. If she stepped forward, the top of her head would fit right under his chin, and for a second, he wished she would. Just so he could see if he was right.

Finally she spoke. "Tequila sounds good, but I'm tired of this place."

"You want to go somewhere else?"

"Not to a bar."

Her meaning didn't hit him for a moment. When it did, the lust that gut-punched him almost brought him to his knees. "My place isn't far."

"Give me the address."

Fifteen minutes later, he handed her a shot of Cazadores. Nerves, sudden and unwelcome, jumped through him.

Lana didn't look tense, though. She looked as cool as she had on stage. She stood at the floor-to-ceiling glass window that looked over Centennial Park. "Great view. A little high up, though. Does it make you dizzy, looking out?"

The only thing making him dizzy was her. "Nope. Where's your place?"

She gave a half-smile, that pixie mouth of hers twisting sideways. "Over in the Gulch."

"Great location."

"Yeah, well. It's not mine. I'm couch surfing, staying with my friend Jilly, before I head west."

West. That wasn't what he wanted to hear. "Why are you ...?"

"Let's do some revision, huh?" She tossed back her tequila and held her glass out for another shot. "And let's get drunk."

CHAPTER TWELVE

I t wasn't a surprise to Lana when Taft Hill had asked
her to get a drink with him.

It *was* a surprise when he'd asked to buy the
song. Her first impulse had been to say no. It was *her*
song, a hard song, a song that told the truth but still
covered up the most important thing, a thing she still
couldn't get close enough to name. Her second impulse
– the one she sensibly acted on – was hell, yes. She
could use the money.

It took until they were in his apartment – his glorious
penthouse of a place, a far cry from the futon she was
borrowing at Jilly's place – that she fully understood they
were going to rewrite it. Together.

She took the tequila he offered her and sat on the
floor in front of his coffee table. It was irregularly
shaped, made of shiny black stone, and it had probably

cost more than a month's rent. When she touched its top, it felt like icy velvet. On second thought, it probably cost more than her car.

Carelessly, he set down two glasses of ice-water. No coasters. "One glass of water for every drink, that's what I always say."

"That's not exactly the cowboy way, is it?" Lana leaned back against the buttery leather couch she couldn't even begin to financially appraise.

"Yeah, this cowboy has had his share of hangovers. I might be too old for them now."

"How old are you?"

He appeared to think. "Thirty-five. No, thirty-six. I just had a birthday."

"Happy birthday."

Taft shrugged. "It wasn't, not until the end."

"What happened at the end?"

"You came over."

That was how he'd spent his birthday? Alone in a tourist trap? "Okay, then. Happy birthday." Lana lifted her glass, and they clinked again.

"Thanks."

The air grew thick. Lana felt a fine trickle of sweat between her breasts. It wasn't hot in here. *He* was the heat. "Okay. Let's do this."

He raised his eyebrows.

"Revise the song, I mean," she clarified.

"Oh, that."

"*Then* we'll fuck."

Taft, sipping his drink, coughed violently. "Wow."

Lana pulled a pencil out of her bag. "Let's get to it."

He caught his breath, and they started at the top, working their way down.

"So. The male point of view." Taft tapped on the words.

"Yeah, well, if you're singing it, the whole thing has to be, right?"

"Can we fit two more syllables in somewhere? If we can fit in 'she said' then we can change less. It turns into a story I'm telling about someone I care about." Taft moved sideways and angled the page so she could see it better.

Their thighs touched. Neither drew away.

Lana wondered if it was possible for jeans to spontaneously combust. "Yeah," she said. She wanted to kiss him. No, she wanted to *bite* him. To chew on him, to see what he tasted like. Instead, she stuck the side of her finger in her mouth and gnawed on the skin. "What about if we take out 'today.' Then it would be ... no, wait." She drifted off, feeling the heat of his leg against hers.

Song, song, back to the damn song. Getting the songwriting royalties on a song with Taft Hill would do wonders for her bank account, and if it actually charted, she'd be rich. "This is hard."

Then she thought about what else was hard in the room, and she lost the ability to focus on the black marks on the page.

"Here, let me." As he reached out to take the paper, his arm brushed across her breast.

He knew it. He made eye contact with her as he drew back his arm.

Holy fuck, she wanted this guy.

Taft scratched some notes on her paper. "Okay. This might be it."

Lana looked over his shoulder. She scratched out his words. She wrote over them. "Better now."

"Yeah, you're right."

Lana couldn't take much more. She took the pencil out of his hand and laid it on the table. She lifted his wrist, bringing it to her mouth.

His eyes widened, and she saw the intake of breath he sucked into his lungs.

Then she bit him.

Hard.

"Ow!" Taft jerked back his hand and rubbed his wrist. "I didn't expect that."

He had tasted like she thought he would, a little soapy and a little salty. "Did you mind, though?"

"Hell, no." He offered his hand back. "You want more?"

She laughed. Taft's dark-blue eyes were easy to read. He was as turned on as she was. He was delighting in putting off the next move, too. It felt delicious, like being thirsty all day and just looking at the glass of ice-water, delaying the pleasure of drinking it.

Four more lines tweaked, and they were done.

He sang it under his breath and she joined him on the chorus. She inserted a harmony she'd always heard in her mind, but since she'd sung it by herself hadn't been able to try.

It was good.

It might be really good.

Taft leaned his head back on the couch, looking up at the ceiling. "I'll get my agent to contact yours."

"I don't have one," she reminded him.

"To contact you, then. Standard royalty split."

"Yes."

"This is going to be big."

She couldn't help the smile of disbelief that crossed her face. "If I had a nickel ..."

"I feel it. It's my superpower, to know a hit when I hear it."

"That's a damn fine superpower." And she believed it. She looked around the room, the tall windows, the heavy drapes, the gilt-painted Fender Telecaster propped on a steel stand in the corner. "And that's obvious."

He laughed. "I wish. This is what you get when you're Palmer Hill's son. The hits are just extra."

"Must be nice."

"Yeah," Taft said slowly. "I thought so."

"Anyway." It was time to have sex, before she burst into flames. Then she could get out of here and recover from this unexpected man.

"Anyway," he echoed. "Is this song about you?"

It was a punch to the throat. "No."

"You sure?"

Lana turned to face him, putting six inches of extra space between them as she did so. "You new to songwriting? It's not usually autobiographical, no matter what people say."

"I'd say it's not *always* autobiographical. Sometimes it is. I'm just checking. This song is about a girl who got attacked, and I just want to make sure that girl isn't you."

"Yeah, well. No, it's not." Anger seeped from her blood into her bones. What if everyone really did think that? What if it got big, and her sisters found out she was the songwriter?

He narrowed his eyes. "So it *is* about you."

"I said it's not and I meant it." Lana slid up from the floor to sit on the couch. She was above him now, which felt better. "But I don't want people thinking it is. I have a business account from when I was thinking about starting my own label – you can pay that instead of me."

Taft shrugged. "It's your song. Whatever you want. I just think you're protesting too much, that's all."

"If I'm upset that some people might try to track it back to my life? Of course I am. Are we agreed? You'll buy it from my business name?"

"What about a pen name?"

"Not a bad idea."

"Can I pick it?"

Her default answer, the word that sprung to her lips, was *no*.

Taft held up a hand. "Before you say no, just think about it. My other superpower is naming things."

God, his eyes sparkled. Could a person get plastic surgery of the eyes to make them do that? Because the way they caught the light was practically unnatural. "Really."

"Really. So can I?"

Lana crossed her arms. "Try."

"Candy Floss."

"Excuse me?"

"Flossy Petal."

She snorted. "No."

"Petal Whispers."

"That's a porn name."

He nodded hard. "*Oh*, yeah. All right, what about Whisper Frankfurter?"

"You're terrible at this. I don't need a pen name." No one would notice who'd written the song with him. It didn't matter.

"Birdie Sweetiepie."

"Oh." It was adorable. It sounded like a name her mother would have called her in teasing. "That's ..."

"That's your new name. I'm going to start calling you it immediately. Hey, there, Birdie."

"Come on."

Taft grinned. "You love it."

She kind of did love it.

And that made her stomach clench.

She was selling this song to him? *This* song? She'd already verbally agreed. In Nashville, a handshake agreement was as enforceable as a signed contract.

This song was about her.

To prove it wasn't, she was going to sell it to one of the biggest stars in the industry.

She was a freaking idiot. Anger started, low in her chest. What kind of moron was she?

"Birdie." He chuckled.

She should have kept the song. She should never have sung it to begin with. This was all her fault.

It was always her fault.

Lana tugged on a bracelet. "Okay, so whatever. We're done with the song?"

"We are if you say we are." He was still looking at her questioningly, as if she were a puzzle he wanted to solve.

There was only one way to derail a man who had that particular curious look on his face. "Take me to bed."

Taft stood.

He pulled her to her feet from the couch.

Then he threw her over his shoulder, and Lana went into a full-blown panic attack.

CHAPTER THIRTEEN

L ana was hot as hell, and Taft wasn't sure how he'd gotten so lucky. He had, though, and he wasn't going to throw away his shot.

"Take me to bed," she said.

That's where Taft made his mistake, or at least that's what he guessed later. He stood, tugging her to her feet. In a move he thought would be funny and sweet, he picked up Lana and threw her over his shoulder. "I drag you to my bedroom," he roared. "Like a caveman!" She was so light he felt like he could carry her for hours. He tossed her onto his bed with a laugh.

Then Lana went sideways.

She launched at him like a wildcat. Yeah, she was into it – that didn't seem to be the problem. She ripped at his belt buckle and tore his shirt in her haste to get his clothes off. She hit his hands away when he tried to help her with her own shirt and jeans. In a blurred few seconds, they were both naked.

Her skin was clammy, as if she was covered in sweat. "Hurry up," she panted.

Was she actually okay? "Hey, slow down a sec."

Lana bit at his mouth and Taft realized he hadn't even kissed her yet. Not properly. He took her face in his hands and tried, but she pulled away with a brittle laugh.

"I don't like slow," she said.

"We have time." He wanted to study her body, to run his hands down the planes of her ribs, to cup her ass, to see if she was sensitive at the back of her knee. He wanted to lose himself in exploring her.

"I don't care." She pushed him backward, hard, and then flung herself to straddle him. She had a condom in her hand – where had it even come from? – and she rolled it onto his cock, which was traitorously eager for her touch. He should slow this down – this didn't feel right – but then she was on him, above him, taking him into her and moving fast. She was tight and wet, and God help him if he could stop her. Her breasts were high and small, her nipples dark.

But her eyes were closed, her chin turned so that even if they were open, she'd be looking out the window. Not at him.

And while she felt like sex on a stick, while he wanted to come so bad he literally hurt, it wasn't right. He held her waist and slowed her. "Hey."

She slapped at his hands. "Stop it. Let me."

"Lana." Using more force than he thought he would have to, he physically lifted her off him with a grunt. Then he scooted backward, panting, so his back was against the headboard, and she was straddling his knees. "This doesn't feel right."

"What?" Her mouth was a sneer. "Too much for you?"

"Hell, yeah!"

A surprised look crossed her face. "What?"

"If we're going to do this, I want you here for it."

She blew out a breath, pointing to her breasts with both hands. "I'm here. Naked. Did you not notice?"

She was so *angry*, Taft realized. At him, for some reason. "Did I scare you?"

Lana jerked at the sheet below them, pulling it up around her. "Scare *me*? No way."

He wouldn't rise to the bait. "What's wrong? Tell me."

Lana tossed her head. "Apart from the fact that now I have blue balls? Nothing."

They were big words, meant to shock him, Taft knew, but then Lana rubbed her nose roughly and Taft saw through the move to what it was – she was trying not to cry.

"Birdie." The word came easily to his lips, and he opened his arms. "Come here." He'd hold her for a while, and listen to her heartbeat slow. Then maybe they could try again. Or maybe they'd wait and she'd sleep, and then he'd make her coffee and pancakes in the morning when the sun flooded yellow through his dining-room windows.

She flopped onto her back instead, throwing off the sheet. "I'm just going to get myself off, that okay with you?"

She wasn't really checking in with him, that was clear.

Taft lost his breath as she reached down between her legs. Her fingers – the ones he'd watched play her guitar so adroitly and emotionally on stage – did the same with her clit. She played her own body well, her back arching, her cheeks reddening. She turned her head to look at him, her eyes dark with lust. "You do it, too. You touch yourself. I want to watch."

But Taft'd had just about enough of being ordered around in his own bed by a total stranger. "Nope."

"Come on."

He laughed. Her voice was imperious. This was a woman who took care of herself, who was used to getting her way. He loved it. "You're so fucking hot, woman, but I'm just going to watch and there's nothing you can do about that." He slid down the bed so her body was flush against his. He could smell her: lightly floral with a slight musk of desire. His cock pressed against her hip, and with incredible effort, he restrained himself from pushing against her. He palmed her belly and felt the muscles contracting there as she continued to touch herself.

"Fine," she growled. "Whatever." She arched again and kept her eyes closed, her fingers thrumming faster.

Well, hell. She was already pissed off at him.

So he kissed her.

She gasped, but she didn't draw away. Her mouth was soft – so much softer than he'd expected, and smaller, too. She tasted like tequila and something lightly minty. Taft had the feeling that he could kiss her for a year or seven without getting tired of the feeling. She breathed into his mouth and then kissed him back. Taft felt the bed lurch below him.

Her mouth was hot, so much hotter now. Her tongue met his and the kiss went deeper, harder. She challenged him and he responded. Her teeth clacked softly against his, and she gave a moan low in her throat that made him almost blind with desire. He'd never felt so hard in his whole life, and it didn't matter – the only thing that mattered was that she made herself happy.

Her hand was moving faster now, and he could hear how wet she was. He kissed her harder – she gave a small cry.

In a surprise move, she grabbed his hand from her stomach, moving it to her pussy. "In?" she said against his mouth. This time it wasn't an order. It was a question.

He slipped one finger inside her. "More," she demanded, but he was in charge now.

"Maybe." He drew his head back so he could look down at her. Her whole body felt flushed and hot, and her skin was pink at her chest. She arched again, pushing herself against his hand as she kept working.

"*More!*"

"Who am I to argue with a lady?" He gave her lip a quick nip, and then pushed three fingers inside her. He curved his hand so he could stroke her G-spot, and she gave a scream. He felt her start to come, the muscles inside her clenching so hard it almost hurt. Good thing he was used to strumming. He caressed her velvety, wet skin, pressing, pushing. Lana held his wrist, holding his hand inside her as she bucked against him, and her other hand continued to play her clit. He kissed her then, claiming her mouth as his, and she gave it to him as if it was what she wanted more than anything, and her eyes flew open and she looked right at him, right *into* him, and then she came around his hand with a roar.

Lana shattered.

It felt like a gift.

He got ten seconds – maybe fifteen – of her lying quietly next to him, her chest heaving. Then she rolled away from him and was off the bed in an instant.

"Hey."

She ignored him as she put on her clothes. She didn't meet his eye.

"Wait." Lana was back to pushing him away, back to being angry, and he had no idea why.

Lana gave him a scathing glance. "Hey, pal, you don't need me. If I have to get myself off, then you do, too."

"I couldn't give a *shit* about that."

She looked surprised at his vehemence, but not enough to slow her stride. Still stark naked, Taft followed her. "Tell me what the hell just happened back there."

She pulled open the door and was gone before he could even repeat the words.

He sat on the couch, the leather cool on his heated skin. He took a deep breath.

What the actual *fuck*?

CHAPTER FOURTEEN

L ana waited in room twelve, her back against the
door, until enough time had passed that she
knew he must be gone.

Taft Hill, here in Darling Bay.

The man she'd given her song to.

Okay, she'd sold it. Fair and square. She was rich because of it.

But she was still so angry with herself for selling the song.

And with him for taking it.

It wasn't his fault, she was smart enough to know that. None of it was. Her reaction to him certainly hadn't been on him, not at all.

That had been all her.

As soon as he'd thrown her over his shoulder in his apartment, Lana had been covered in sweat. She'd lost every bit of oxygen she'd ever had in her blood. Her head had pounded, and she could feel her hands start to shake. Everything had gone dark, even though she could tell he'd turned on the lights in his bedroom.

Taft had deposited her on his bed, and there'd been nothing in the man but desire and fun and lust. She'd hurled herself at him anyway. She'd been a hellcat, and she'd confused him immediately, she'd known it, but she hadn't cared.

He hadn't felt safe.

So she'd taken control.

She'd put the condom on him.

She'd taken him inside her.

When he'd pushed her off (who *did* that? Jesus Christ!) she'd given herself pleasure, as a kind of *fuck you*. She would show him, throwing her around like a slab of butchered beef.

But as she'd bolted from of his apartment building that night, pulling her sweatshirt around her like it could possibly warm her, she'd realized she hadn't shown him a thing.

He'd shown her kindness.

Taft had lain next to her, and he'd touched her perfectly. Expertly. He'd slid his fingers inside her and *he'd* been the one to make her come. She'd stroked herself, getting her to the almost-top. But the way he'd touched her inside had been what had made her explode.

He'd been so *nice* to her.

Screw that guy.

Lana Darling didn't need nice. She'd needed money, and now she had it. She'd needed out of the business, and now she had a hotel to rebuild.

But now Taft Hill was here.

In *her* town.

I'm the kind of woman who hides from men in a hotel room with no roof.

No. No. *No.*

Lana pulled open the door carefully. She looked out into the garden.

No one.

She skittered to her room, cursing herself as she went.

Lana sat and thought. Hard.

Then she called Ballard Brothers Building. She left a message. She didn't *need* them. No. But it might be useful to have extra hands. It would make the work go faster.

Her cell rang, and it was a number she recognized, thank God.

"Hey." Jilly, her best friend in Nashville, sounded as chirpy as the damn birds outside. "What are you doing?"

"Hiding."

"From what?"

"The world," said Lana.

Jilly laughed, the sound of it easing the tension right between Lana's shoulder blades. "There's my girl. So how's it going?"

"I don't know where to start."

"At the beginning. What happened when you got there?"

"No, I mean I don't know where to start with the whole hotel thing. It's horrible. The entire place is falling apart. There's only one habitable room, and I'm in it. So it's not a hotel at all right now."

"Eh, you'll do fine." Jilly's voice trailed off as if she were looking at something else. "You ran that place on Sixth for how long?"

"I didn't run it." Lana had worked front desk at a hotel with three hundred rooms. She'd checked people in, giving them upgrades when they slipped her a twenty. It hadn't been hard work. "They paid crap, anyway."

"Oh, yeah." Jilly's voice trailed away once more.

Lana said, "What's wrong?"

"Why?"

"You have that sound in your voice."

Jilly sighed. "Got fired again."

"What?" Jilly was a music producer, but in Nashville that was like being an actress in Hollywood. There were too many of them. The ones willing to do the work the cheapest way possible were the ones who got hired. If you weren't willing to sell your soul for the price of a latte, you weren't going to get anywhere. "Who fired you?" Lana would find them and chop them down at the knees.

"It doesn't matter. I'm just not sure what to do next. I kind of ... I kind of want to get away. Go far and do something else."

Lana clutched her cell. "Come here."

"I can't do that."

"Why not?"

"What's the business like out there?"

Lana laughed. "In this town? We're it. This is not a music town."

"There you go."

"But you produce. You can work remotely, can't you? You already do almost everything on your computer. Fly out for sessions, and that's it."

There was a pause on the line. "You've said there's no place for anyone to stay there."

"We've shared a bed before. Or I can buy an air mattress." Hell, she could blow off the entire idea of the hotel and buy a cheap house near the beach. She'd sit on the porch and watch sunsets while writing incredibly cheesy songs that Jilly would produce and put on iTunes where they'd make whole pennies a day. "Just come. You can help me hammer things. You good with pliers?"

"No."

"Plumbing?"

"Hell, no."

"What about electricity?"

"Strangely enough, still no."

"I'll find something for you to do. Just come," Lana urged.

"I'm pretty sure you have to rent your hotel rooms to tourists, not out-of-contract producers. Aren't you on a beach there? Isn't that expensive? I'm pretty sure that even though you hit it big with Taft Hill's song, you still remember what it's like to be a starving artist."

Lana's song. It was *her* song, not his. "Taft's in town," she blurted.

A silence followed her words. Lana checked the screen of her phone to make sure she was still connected. Wireless service was spotty at best in Darling Bay. "Are you still there? Jilly?"

"Yeah, yeah. I'm still here. I'm just trying to figure out if those words you just said actually go together. Taft Hill? He followed you?"

"You wouldn't believe vacation, then, huh? A beach getaway?"

"A guy like him goes to Cancún or Malibu or Miami. Not Darling Bay in the back of beyond."

"Hey!"

"You called it the sticks with sand."

"True. But I was here every summer growing up. It *was* the sticks to me."

"What is going on, then?"

"I don't know."

"It's because 'Blame Me' blew up. I knew he'd need more songs from you, I *told* you he would."

Lana rolled to her back and closed her eyes. It was good to have Jilly's voice in her ear. "He's a songwriter. And he didn't say anything about that."

"Then he's just in love with you."

"Um." Over the line came clicking sounds. "Are you on your computer while you're talking to me?"

"No, never." The clicking stopped. "Didn't you say he was the worst sex you've ever had?"

"Did I?"

"You said, and I quote, 'I left before he could get his rocks off, that's how weird it was.'"

"I said 'weird.'"

"But you meant *bad*."

"I meant *weird*. It was the weirdest sex I've ever had."

Jilly laughed, and Lana could almost see her dark-brown eyes dancing. She'd have an empty coffee mug next to her, like she always did. She'd pick it up, be disappointed by its emptiness and set it back down, forgetting to refill it. "Nothing wrong with kinky, lady."

"I agree. There's not. But that's not what it was."

An exhaled breath. "You have to *tell* me what happened. What could possibly be so weird that you ran away across the country? And apparently made him chase you?"

That wasn't why Lana had run. In truth, without the money she'd gotten from "Blame Me," she wouldn't have been able to go very far, and she sure as hell wouldn't have come back to Darling Bay. She had sworn she'd never return until she could stand on her own two legs.

Now she could. It felt both good – victory! – and terrible – it was money she hadn't really made. *He'd* made the money, with his fame, and she just got a good percentage of it. "I'll tell you someday. It's not a big deal." Lana held the phone so tightly against her ear she knew her cheek would be red. "I tried pulling out some drywall this morning. It did *not* go well."

"I don't actually know exactly what that is, but it has wall in the word, so I'm assuming it's important."

"Apparently not. That's what the internet said, anyway. Do you feel safe where you are? Like, do you look around the room and feel secure?"

Jilly said, "Sure. Besides the fact that the faucet is leaking and the landlord won't return my phone calls."

Lana twisted and kicked her legs up so that her sock-clad feet rested on the wall behind the bed. They landed with a hollow thump. "It's just a lie. Those walls around you? You could take them down in an hour. I always thought they were hard and strong, you know? They're *walls*. We trust them. Believe in them. Turns out a hammer and a little pressure pulls them right down to the studs. Which is a phrase I never understood until early this morning. The only things behind the drywall are studs and wires and spiders and, in this case, mold."

"How terrifying. Thank you."

"Come out. I'll show you."

"Seriously. You're not going to do this all by yourself, are you?"

Lana bristled. "You don't think I can?"

"I know you. I know you can do anything you want, but you sometimes take on stupid challenges when there's no reason to."

It was true, so true, but she couldn't admit it. "Like what?"

"Like when you unpack your car after errands and you insist on carrying eleven heavy bags inside by yourself even though your friend is standing right there with empty hands, trying to help."

"That happened once."

"It was *my* beer that you dropped. I could keep going. What about the time you walked to the ER after breaking your foot? Or the time you –"

A knot tightened at the base of Lana's neck. "Please don't. Look, I know you're right. I just called a construction company. Left them a message. More hands, you know?"

"You asked someone for help? You're *kidding*."

"Stop."

"I'm so proud of you!"

"Seriously. Cut it out." She flexed her feet, pressing her toes into the wall. She was tempted to kick, to see how much force the wall would take from her body before it gave, but damn it, this was the only usable room. She was *not* going to shack up with either of her blissful sisters. "I figure it can't hurt to ask them what they think. Even though they'll probably lie to me and tell me I can't do anything."

"Okay, I'll think about it. Hey, how is it going with your sisters?"

Lana's cell vibrated. "Hang on."

It was a text. *Can you meet at the saloon to talk about the hotel project this afternoon? Around five? Jake Ballard.*

"Oh, good. The guy just confirmed."

Jilly squealed. "Taft?"

"No, construction guy."

"Tool belts are hot."

"I thought you were in a girl phase."

"Well, yeah, that's your gender-normative brain, isn't it? Only men get to wear tool belts? I went on a date with a carpenter last week, and she showed me *her* tool belt."

"Now you're talking."

"Only it wasn't a belt."

Lana laughed. "I get it."

"But there were tools involved."

"I bet there were. Is there a joke in here about screwing something in?"

"*Oh*, yeah."

Lana snorted. "Gotta go. Come out here and stay in my run-down hotel. Bring the carpenter. I could use the help."

"Don't tease me."

"Love you."

"You, too."

Lana let the phone fall to the pillow next to her. She turned to her side and looked out the partially open curtains.

A Heart Song rose bloomed outside – it was one that their mother had planted. She'd loved flowers almost as much as she'd loved her children, Lana had sometimes thought. Lana had faked an interest in gardening (much preferring the dirt and the worms to anything that bloomed green and boring above ground) just to be near her mother sometimes. *They're my babies, too.* Her mother would rub at the dirt at her hands. *Just like you.*

Time for that to change. She'd always be the youngest. But she wasn't a baby. Not anymore.

CHAPTER FIFTEEN

Taft completed another lap around town. It took seventeen minutes to walk from the rural route turn-off to the post office, to the Golden Spike, to the beach and back. He'd done it four times already. The last time he'd passed the post office, a woman had come out and very carefully taken his picture. It hadn't been a fan. The scowl on her face had told him that. She obviously thought he was some kind of criminal casing the joint.

A few minutes later, a patrol car had cruised past him, very slowly. When it had stopped, Taft had peered inside. The female deputy had stammered. "Oh! Oh, holy crap. Oh, wow. Can I have your autograph?" She'd gotten out of her car, and he'd signed the top page of her ticket book. She'd left with pink cheeks and almost tripped getting into her car.

There was just no way he could go back to the Cat's Claw. Not before it was dark, not before he could throw himself through the bed-and-breakfast's lobby, pole-vaulting himself up the stairs and into his room, which was done up with so much flower-and-lace shit it looked like a joke. Somewhere, in LA maybe, it would be ironic. Here, it wasn't. The woman believed in the scent of strawberry and the images of fluffy lambs. It was – to his chagrin – the only place to stay in town. The proprietress, Pearl Hawthorne, didn't know country music (thank God), but she had buttonholed him anyway when he'd checked in, giving him a blow-by-blow account of her recent nasal surgery. When she'd asked him to feel the tip of her nose, he'd faked an allergy attack and gone up to his terrible room, dry sneezing all the way.

The diner, maybe? He wasn't hungry yet, even though it was almost dinnertime.

That left the saloon. Okay, then.

Would Lana be there? It was her family bar, right? Attached to the hotel that had no rooms for rent, the saloon looked for all the world as if a posse would ride up and hitch their horses outside any minute. The facade must have gone up in the nineteenth century, and the thick glass in the windows was wavy. The door stood open to the raised wooden porch. An old Darling Songbird tune floated out into the warm afternoon.

Inside, it was dim. It smelled just right: pine and peanuts and stale beer. A bleach tang hung in the air.

Taft's spine began to relax. He hadn't come up singing in bars like this – no, he'd been on stage at the Ryman Auditorium and Billy Bob's. His first televised appearance was on Grand Ole Opry when he was twelve.

But he loved bars like this. There were only a few people inside as it was still fairly early. Three men played cards in the corner and shuffled their feet on the sanded floor. A man and two women played dice at one end of the bar. Two obvious tourists, both sunburnt, peered at a guidebook at a small round table.

"Taft Hill!" a woman roared from the far end of the bar. "Finally!"

It was the older woman from the diner, the one with buzzed grey hair. She wore a dress like a tent, which made it seem like she'd move slowly, but Lord have mercy, it was like the woman flew off her bar stool on wings of fire. She tackle-hugged him around the waist, knocking the breath right out of his body.

"Hello," he said to the top of her head.

The hug continued.

Taft had practice with this. Some fans were huggers, others were criers. Nowadays most people were selfie-takers, which actually made it easier. Gave them something to do.

This woman was a hugger. He gave her a few more seconds, then he gently patted the crown of her hair. "What's your name?"

She un-limpeted and stepped backward, her hands now on her hips. Her grin was ear to ear. "I didn't tell you that, did I? I'm Norma. I did *not* know you were coming. I mean, into the bar. I knew you were coming here. Things keep surprising me, I tell you what." She grabbed a handful of beaded necklaces. "Maybe I need a new tarot deck, or maybe this is just what the universe wants for me. Perpetual surprises."

"Well, that's what the rest of us get, after all. Just surprises."

Norma's eyes went wide. "You're *right*. That *is* all people usually get. I've been gifted, for sure, and you've just reminded me to be thankful. You know, I think my father sent you to me."

"Hmmm." That was one he hadn't heard for a while. Taft looked over her head (not hard to do) to see if anyone was working behind the bar. Was that Adele Darling? A slim honey-blonde woman pulled a beer for someone, and when she smiled, he was sure of it. When he was younger, she'd been his favorite Songbird.

He'd been stupid when he was young. Lana was the electric one.

"I need new tarot cards. I think I'll make them this time. Decoupage. That's it. Decoupage." Norma trucked back to her seat, apparently done with him for now.

"Well, sweet Dolly Parton. I heard you were in town, but I didn't quite believe it," said Adele Darling with a smile.

"Your sister told you?"

"You saw my sister? Which one?"

Taft didn't answer. If she didn't know, then maybe she didn't need to. Not yet. "How'd you know, then?"

"Barbara Dow was over at administration at the high school, and they had the police scanner on. Dot Rillo called in a suspicious male casing the post office."

"I knew it."

"I heard Deputy Dinario came up screaming on the radio that she saw you and you gave her an autograph."

"She seemed excited."

"She sounded so insane on the police radio that they all thought someone had been shot for a second."

"Shot in the heart. You know how it goes."

Adele smiled. "I do. I'm Adele Darling, by the way."

"I know." Of course he knew. "Didn't we play a set together, back in the day?"

"Before us Songbirds broke up? I don't think so. There was one on the books that summer, but Dad died and we cancelled the tour."

"Right." That was it. This was getting awkward. "I really did love that song I almost bought from you ..."

Adele laughed. "Don't worry about it. LeAnn Rimes did it justice."

"She did."

"Now I'm a Songbird-turned-barmaid, which suits me just fine. What *are* you doing in town?"

He smiled in a way he hoped was inscrutable. "Business."

She squinted at him, as if determining how hard she should try to get it out of him. "Business having to do with my sister?"

"Secret business."

She paused. "All right, then. I won't bug you about it. *Yet.* What can I get you?"

"Bourbon, neat."

"Best or worst?"

"Only two choices?"

"Yep. Small town, small bar."

"Give me the worst, then. When in Rome."

She slid the drink across the bar. Her mouth opened to say something, but a tour bus wheezed to a stop out front. Through the open door, they watched as a herd of senior citizens tottered off the coach steps and inside. "Oh, no. There's gotta be about thirty of them. I'd better put the decaf on. Half will want free coffee, and the other half will order something complicated. You watch."

Taft spun on his stool and surveyed the room.

When he and his father had been on the road, his pa had liked nothing more than finding the darkest little bar in town and making an appearance. A regular working bar, filled with the clack of pool balls and the familiar laughter of friends who gathered every day. As his father walked in, there were always a few confused seconds. Indrawn breaths, whispered questions: *Is it? Is it really?* Then the place would explode. Someone would press a whisky (or three) into his dad's hand. Someone else would ask (always tentatively, as if supplicating a god) if they could get him to sing a song or two. *What you want to hear is this boy of mine. This kid can sing. He's the best thing that ever happened to me.* Palmer would act humble and push Taft forward.

No, that wasn't fair. Taft's father really *had* been unassuming. Palmer was the one who'd come up from nothing, who'd built a life and a legacy to be proud of. He'd never forgotten his roots, and he would fit into little road-worn saloons because they were where he'd come from.

Taft, on the other hand, had grown up in the back of a tour bus. People (okay, mostly his mother, Davina) bitched about the buses. *Too small. Too smelly.* Taft, though, thought they were nothing but luxury. Someone else drove them where they needed to be while they slept. The fridge was always well stocked, and good, hot food was always a truck stop away. When Taft's mom had put her foot down, saying she wouldn't be touring anymore, Taft had been thrilled. He'd been less so when she'd made him stay home with her to finish high school in Nashville. Never close, they'd grown so far apart after Palmer's death that he hadn't visited her newest house.

Maybe he never would. That would probably be okay by him.

The jukebox shuffled with a whir, and an old Tanya Tucker song came on.

Crap. The jukebox. Usually he thought of it as soon as he walked in a place, but he'd almost forgotten.

He got to it in time. The Tanya Tucker was the last one queued up, so he spent ten dollars on almost every song on the jukebox except his own. Out of respect for Adele, he skipped the Darling Songbirds tunes. He knew for certain she was as sick of hearing her own songs as he was of hearing his. Nothing in the world would drive him out of a bar as fast as almost any cut from his first album, and he had to spend some time in here since he really didn't want to go back to the bed and breakfast anytime soon. If he was really lucky, Lana would come in at some point.

Maybe he should ask the tarot lady, Norma, if Lana was in his future.

Taft picked the last song, turning to go back to his barstool.

As if he'd conjured her, Lana stood near the front door, talking animatedly to a man. There were approximately four thousand senior citizens between them, though, and the noise level in the bar had risen so loud Taft couldn't hear what she was saying to the man.

She was laughing, though. The sound cut through the air, pouring right into his ears. Suddenly, he was back in his own apartment, listening to her laugh after she'd bitten his wrist while they were still revising her song.

As he watched, Lana waved at Adele. She and the man sat at a tiny table near the low stage.

It was a table for two.

The man said something to her, his head lowered to listen to her response. Then he went to the bar to order.

Taft would be a dick if he went to talk to her while the guy bought her a drink, and he tried *really* hard not to be a dick. He was mostly proud of his not-a-dick status, in fact.

But this burned.

The man was good-looking enough, Taft supposed. If a girl liked that kind of chiseled face and dark hair and rugged strength.

Whatever.

Did the Darling girls have a non-musical brother? His spirits lifted. He pulled out his cell and typed in "Darling Songbird Brother." But the reception was lousy, and the little wheel just spun. No connection.

Besides, he was pretty damn sure there were just the three girls. When their father died, it had left them orphans. He remembered the headlines.

Oh, shit.

A memory slammed into him, one he'd completely forgotten until this very moment.

Taft had *gone* to their father's funeral.

CHAPTER SIXTEEN

Tommy Darling had died in New York putting his girls on the first leg of their tour, but the funeral had been held in Nashville, of course. Tommy had been a sound guy in country music since the old days, and he'd gone on doing that job when his girls got famous. He'd managed them *and* their sound. Everyone knew him. More than that, everyone loved him.

The funeral had been in St Mary's church. The rafters had soared high above, and a choir had sung "Fly Home" so sweetly that the sobs in the audience became audible. The girls stood at the front. Taft, in his standing-room-only spot, had just been able to see the sides of their faces. Adele had stood stock-still, tears running down her cheeks. Molly had swayed a little and kept her eyes mostly closed.

Lana, though.

Lana had been so furious it had come off her in waves. The sheer anger she'd pushed out of her body, the rage that had shot from her eyes every time she'd turned around to look back at the crowd, had been so palpable Taft had felt shoved backward when her gaze had met his once.

He hadn't understood it then. Taft remembered wondering how someone could be angry at a funeral, how someone could be anything but sad.

Then Palmer died of pneumonia. Taft had understood the anger.

Taft looked at Lana and the guy, sitting together.

So, yeah. That wasn't her brother. He had to be a date. Now the man was back at the table, and they were leaning over something – gazing at some piece of paper. Lana laughed. Even through the crowd, her voice carried. It was such a pure sound, clear and sweet. She should laugh more often.

She was the kind of woman to tell him to go to hell if he said that to her.

And he liked that about her. A lot.

Taft picked up his drink and stood. Casually. He would just check out the place. Give it a once-over. He was visiting, after all, a tourist in a tourist town. The other visitors were poking around the saloon like they were treasure hunting – nothing said he couldn't do the same thing. He walked to the front, past Norma, who grinned at him. He poked his head out the front door.

"Whatcha looking for?" Norma called.

"Horses and buggies. I keep thinking they might be out there. This place is great."

"Oh. They *are* out there. In another dimension, sure, but I think that's a possibility. Don't you?"

Taft needed to keep moving. That was key. "Oh, sure."

Lana was listening to the guy, nodding as he spoke. She looked downright chipper. Taft could only see the dark-haired man from the back, but he didn't like him. Untrustworthy spine, for sure. Or something.

Adele caught his eye. "Bathroom's around the corner." She pointed.

"I'm just looking around."

"Oh, then, go outside. It's prettiest out there."

He looked out the back door. Adele was wrong. Sure, it was pretty in the back arbor, all twined vines and twinkle lights shining in the dropping twilight, but the prettiest thing was still in the bar. He was wasting his time trying to pretend she wasn't.

What was the worst that could happen if he went to talk to them? The guy could try to fight him. This did feel like the Old West, after all. Taft wound his way through clumps of elderly people who were chatting and drinking like teens on Spring Break. He didn't see many mugs of decaf – it looked like highballs all around.

His heart pounded as he approached the table, and his feet felt too far from his body. "Don't mean to be rude, but mind if I say hello?"

Lana's gaze rose to his and her eyes widened. "Oh."

Taft had no idea whether it was a good *oh* or a bad one. The man talking to her turned to face him, so Taft stuck out his hand. "Howdy. I'm –"

"Holy shit, you're Taft Hill!" The man sprang to standing. "Wow! I'm Jake Ballard, so great to meet you. You really *are* here! I told my brother he must have heard it wrong. You know, everyone likes your last album a lot, and I do, too, don't get me wrong, but I think that *Under the Hill* was one of the best things ever to come out of country music."

Taft liked this guy. "You and me both."

"Rumors were – hey, wait a minute." Jake looked from Lana to Taft and back again. "Are you two here together?"

"*No!*" They both said it fast and loud, although Taft didn't know why he said it. He *was* here for her, and if he were actually here with her, he'd be mighty proud of that fact.

"But you know each other, right?"

Lana smiled tightly. "Nashville's a small town."

Jake put up his hands. "Okay. No problemo. Just seems like a big coincidence, two big stars coming to town in a couple of days."

Lana crossed her arms. "One big star. And me."

Taft and Jake both started to speak, but she cut them off. "Jake and I were just talking about the hotel. I'm going to fix it up."

Taft nodded and felt his knees go loose, like he'd had one too many bottles of beer. The way she was looking at him – Lord, he couldn't figure this woman out. Her gaze was heated, practically steamy, but her body language was angry. Even though she was slouched in her chair, her hands were folded so tightly in her lap that her knuckles were white. The skin was tight at the sides of her mouth. Taft took a breath. "That explains why I couldn't get a room at the inn."

Jake dragged a chair over from the next table. "Sit, why don't you? Lana, you don't mind, right? Tell us where you're staying."

Taft sat, even though Lana's expression didn't make him confident that she didn't mind. "I'll only stay a second. Don't want to spoil your date." The word tasted sour in his mouth.

Jake laughed. "A date? No, dude, this is business. I'm with Ballard Brothers Building. Trying to talk this smart woman into hiring us."

Taft was rocked back by the wave of relief that smacked him. Not a date. It wasn't a date. He shook his head to clear it. "Sorry, I was going to answer a question, but I don't remember what it was."

"Where're you staying?"

That was it. "I'm at a place a few blocks from the water. Cat something."

Jake grimaced. "The Cat's Claw. Sorry, buddy. I'd offer you space, but I live on a boat in the marina myself."

"Any boats for sale? I would seriously consider buying one to get out of that place. There was a bowl of potato chips on the dining-room table and I took a whole mouthful before I realized they were potpourri made to *look* like chips. Who would do that?"

Jake laughed. "That's just plain rude."

"And my bed has a canopy."

"Whoa."

"Pink."

The right side of Lana's mouth quirked upward. Taft relaxed incrementally.

She was here.

So was he.

And she wasn't on a date. Not that it should matter as much as it did – he was here on business, too, after all. Three songs were all he needed.

Three songs and another kiss. Or more.

Rein it in, Hill.

Okay, three songs would do. He would just think of her like the wild rabbits he and his pa used to see in the hills behind their huge house. A creature with a lot of quiet twitches could move fast and unexpectedly, in any direction. If you sat still long enough, though, they'd quiet down. Once he'd seen a jackrabbit fall sideways in his sleep, stretching out his legs and exposing his belly like a dog did in front of a fireplace.

Maybe he could be still enough not to spook Lana.

Jake leaned forward. "What are you here for, then? Just a vacation?"

"I saw Taft not long ago in Nashville. I told him how great Darling Bay is." Lana's face was serious again. "I just didn't think he was listening."

"I always listen to you."

"Always? We've only spoken on one occasion, right?"

One night's long conversation, then a lot of back and forth about song rights, communicated through Sully. "But when you speak, I listen." It was true. In his mind, Taft could play back almost everything she'd said that evening, and had, many times. "Yeah. A little vacation, a little work. I'm going to try to talk this woman into writing some more songs with me."

Another woman would have sat up straighter. This was Lana, though, and there was nothing normal about her. She slouched farther down in her chair. "*Oh, no.*"

Jake slapped the table top. "Best idea I've heard in a long time!" He caught Lana's look. "Besides the idea of helping you fix up the hotel, which is, of course, an even better idea. That's okay, though, because I'm a big fan of both of yours." He gave a wide, nervous grin.

Taft continued. "She'll say no, but I'm pretty determined to get her help. I think she's the best songwriter in Nashville. When a man says that, he means the nation, because they don't get better than the writers in Nashville."

"I thought you sang, too," said Jake to Lana.

Lana snapped, "I do. I *did*."

Oh, she was fiery. Taft didn't want to get in the way of her blaze. He needed those songs, though.

He had time. "So," he said, addressing Lana. "What needs doing in this hotel of yours?"

She sat straighter and sighed. "What doesn't need doing? The more I learn, the more I freak out." Interesting. She was more comfortable talking about the hotel than writing songs. That was fine. He could do that. Now he knew she slouched, going to ground like a frightened cat when she was threatened, and straightened when she was more relaxed. He filed away the information.

"She's not over her head," said Jake. "She might have been had she decided to go ahead with her plan of doing everything herself."

Taft couldn't help it – he laughed.

Lana shot him the scowl he was starting to get used to, but there was something behind it. She might be on the verge of laughing at herself, too. "I don't like asking for help."

Jake shook his head. "Hiring help and asking for it are two different things. Smart people hire the right people. Less smart people get their friends to help. They end up with sagging roofs and bad interior paint jobs."

Taft had an idea. "Well, if you're hiring him, Lana, can I be a friend and help out? I promise not to make the roof sag. I'm actually good with a paintbrush."

Lana stared at him.

It did sound kind of ridiculous when Taft said it out loud. But how many projects had he done with his dad? Between albums, his pa loved nothing more than hammering and sawing. Taft had gotten that from him. His mother hadn't liked it much, and complained about the sawdust they tracked into her nice house at the end of the day. That hadn't stopped them. They'd built the cabin in the Smokies themselves, just the two of them. They'd gotten help with the wiring because they weren't stupid, and the plumbing because they'd been clueless. They'd done the rest themselves.

"No," she said. "No way in hell."

CHAPTER SEVENTEEN

Taft Hill was offering charity now? Was that what this was? Worst case, it was pity, and that would be just unbearable.

"No, no, no. Also, no," she said again, in case he hadn't heard her over the guffaws of the four guys playing darts in the corner.

Jilly had been *right*. He *did* want more songs.

More of her heart. More of her pain.

It was pretty ballsy of him to ask. Of course, she hadn't exactly told him that it had broken her heart that she'd let him rewrite her most agonizing song and buy it from her. That was entirely, one hundred per cent on her. It had been up to her to tell him no, to take the song off the table the second she'd realized it was the wrong thing to do. Nothing had required her to sign the paperwork when it had finally come through official channels. No one had forced her to do it.

Lana had *known* she shouldn't sell it. Not that song. Any other song, maybe. She knew she'd been overreacting, but it had honestly felt like handing him her newborn and walking away when she had dotted the "i" in Darling on the papers. She could hope that he would take care of it, but the song had been heard by less than a couple of hundred people by the time she had sold it to him. It was new, still green. Then he'd added his slick sound engineering and his well-known Taft Hill swaggering voice to it. Now it was played *all the time* on country stations. She'd heard it at least three times a day as she'd driven cross-country. She hadn't even been actually searching out country stations – they were just so popular in the Midwest that it was hard to flip the dial and not land on one. And in doing so, land on her song. No, *his* song.

It had ceased being hers the minute he'd changed the words, even a little bit.

She gave Taft her sweetest smile, the one she used onstage and when asking for more barbecue sauce at Peg Leg Porker BBQ. "Thanks, but we've got it. It was hard enough for me to ask Jake and his brothers for help."

"But –"

Jake nodded. "She's only getting part of the brotherly act, since Aidan's busy on a job out of town, and Liam's on a backpacking trip in South America with his new bride."

Lana turned her attention brightly to Jake. "It's usually the three of you on a project?"

"Nah, Liam's useless with anything that isn't a computer, but usually Aidan is project lead. I mean –" He looked down and then up again. "I, uh, he told me not to tell you that. Whoops. I'm good at my job, I swear! I'm just the youngest, so they don't ride me too hard."

Lana tilted her head. "Huh. The opposite is true in my family."

Taft set his beer on the table with a clunk. "So you're a man short is what you're saying."

The wine in Lana's mouth turned sour. "No charity. I flat out refuse."

"No charity." He winked at her. Winked! The nerve.

Taft turned to face Jake. "I happen to be available. Hire me."

Jake boggled. "Come again?"

"I can do it all. I might need some guidance sometimes, but my father and I worked for years together on all sorts of building projects. I can pour concrete and tear down walls. I know how to install both tile and wood flooring. I'm great at roofs, from top to gutter. I haven't worked too much with plumbing, but I can learn. There you go. That's my résumé. My best reference is my pa and he's dead, but I can get others if you need 'em."

Lana sat in stunned silence. Her mouth opened to say something – anything – to discourage this crazy idea.

Nothing came to her, so she closed it again and just stared.

Jake held his hands open in front of him, like he was holding an invisible beach ball. "You're a country star."

"I am. And I'm a builder."

"You must have to be ... doing country-star things."

"Thing about country singers, and Lana, back me up here –"

She would do no such thing. Her mouth flapped open then closed again.

"– we have a lot of down time between albums. At most, I bring out an album once a year. I tour for seven months at a time. The rest of the year I've got nothing to do but write songs."

Lana finally found her voice. "Are you straight out of your goddamned mind?"

Jake said, "I love it."

Taft took a satisfied sip of his beer. "Great."

"No!"

Jake ignored her. "But ... payment."

"How about fifteen bucks an hour?" Taft offered.

"Oh, *come* on." Lana set down her wineglass before she snapped the stem.

"I pay the new guys on my crew twenty an hour. I can't pay you that little."

"Twenty's fine."

Lana turned to Jake. "You can't be serious. What about your liability? Your insurance can't cover him on a site.

What if something happens to his picking hand? You can't afford that."

Taft smoothly said, "I've got my own. Covered wherever I am."

Damn it. "Think about what a field day the press will have with it. You know someone will find out and they'll run to the tabloids." She held up her fingers in air quotes. "Taft Hill Goes Broke, Stoops to Manual Labor."

Taft held up his finger punctuation. "Taft Hill Works with Darling Songbird to Bring Historic Golden Spike Hotel Back to Life."

Double triple damn. She focused on Jake again. He was tapping on his phone. "But the press. For your business. Won't that make you look desperate? Or something?"

"You kidding? It'll be the best press we've gotten since we started doing *On the Market*." He pointed at his screen. "Oh, it's a reality show we've been doing, me and my brothers. We sell houses, fix 'em up and go on dates with the buyers. We'd do more episodes except both my brothers got caught on the love hook a little quick. We have an actual agent now. I'm texting him. The top of his head is going to pop right *off*. Liam is going to think I finally did something right." With a *ping*, the text was sent. Jake stuck his phone back in his pocket. "Lana. Come on. This is the first project Aidan's ever let me manage and it's only because he's too busy to do it. It's not like he *chose* to let me run this. If I screw up, I'll never hear the end of it. You're the youngest, too. You feel me, right?" His eyes were sweet. Pleading.

Taft pressed his hands together at his heart. "Come on, Birdie. What do you say?"

What was the point in continuing to argue? She'd lost. It was obvious. "It's none of my business who you hire, Jake."

Jake gave a short whoop, pointing a finger gun at Taft. "You're hired! I just need your social security card and two forms of ID." He appeared to think about his words for a moment. "Okay, I'm pretty sure I know who you are. Just your card."

Taft reached across the table. He shook Jake's hand.

Lana crossed her arms over her chest. Men. She made sure she kept her face in solid disapproval, but secretly, deep in her body somewhere between her heart and her brain, a tiny flower of happiness bloomed.

Taft lit something inside her.

He obviously wanted to be around her, too.

Of course, that was about the songs he wanted her to write with him, which weren't going to happen, obviously. Lana pushed her hands through her short hair. Suddenly, desperately, she wondered how she looked.

Oh, no.

She was *not* going to play this game.

"So!" She clapped once. "It's settled. Anything else, Jake?"

"Nope. I've got to finish a job with my crew tomorrow. Then it's the weekend, but we can be here on Monday." He turned to glance at the clock over the bar. "Now, if you'll excuse me, I have a date waiting for me."

"Nice," said Taft approvingly. "Someone special?"

"Nah. I'm not my brothers." With a grin, Jake was gone.

It was good to remember. Siblings weren't all the same. Lana wasn't her sisters. While Adele and Molly might have been capable of falling for anyone who crossed their paths, Lana wasn't like that.

She wasn't like *them*.

Lana stood. "Okay, then. I guess that's that."

Taft held out a hand. "Wait. About those songs I mentioned."

"Nope."

"Can we talk about it?"

"Hell, no." Something sharp lodged itself at the top of her lungs. "I mean, no, thank you."

His hand dropped to the table. "I have to say I'm disappointed."

"Do you always get your way?"

He looked surprised. "No."

"Really?"

"I get my way as often as anyone else."

"You're *Taft Hill*." She almost winced as the words left her mouth. Did she really have to point that out to him?

"And you're Lana Darling. I know you."

"You know nothing about me."

"Fair enough. But I know "Blame Me.""

It smacked her right in the chest. "I've got to go. I guess I'll see you on Monday if not before. Small town, right?"

Adele passed their table carrying a tray of empty bottles and glasses. "Wait, Taft, you're *staying*?"

"I am. Working with Jake Ballard to help your sister here fix up the hotel."

Adele's eyes widened as she looked between the two of them and then back again. "You're kidding."

This Lana couldn't take. No way. "I'll let you fill her in. I'm going to bed."

"It's not even seven o'clock, Lana. What about dinner?"

"I'm still on East Coast time," she lied. Without saying an extra goodbye to Taft, she ducked through the bar and out the back door into the arbor.

There she stopped, spent.

She felt as if she'd been running for days. Years, maybe. She'd made it all the way home, and she couldn't take the last few steps to bed.

The arbor was unoccupied. Lana sank onto a picnic bench. The fog had rolled in hard and fast, and it hung now, draped through the garden, as gauzy as a veil. The white lights twinkled overhead, twined in the still-bare grapes. The night-blooming jasmine had just gasped out its thick, sweet fragrance.

It was heaven, or as close to it as she expected to find on this earth.

Lana blinked, hard.

She was soon going to be armpit-deep in a new project, one that had nothing to do with music. This was what she'd wanted. This was what she'd *chosen*. Her old life – her dream life – had abandoned her, and she'd thought she would pick herself up consciously, if not totally gracefully.

She'd figure out a way to make peace with Adele because she had to.

That, she'd thought, would be the hardest part – Molly and she were fine. Totally okay. But Adele – she'd never managed to forgive Adele. The real problem was that Adele didn't know what she was in trouble for.

Lana had never actually told her.

That was supposed to be her challenge, *that* was supposed to be the most difficult step of being back in Darling Bay.

Then Taft Hill had arrived.

Lana groaned and covered her face. She took a moment to think what Taft Hill meant.

He meant Nashville. He meant stories of people she'd worked with for years. Just by being near her, he'd symbolize everything she'd thought she'd be able to put behind her.

He meant failure.

"Taft fucking *Hill*," she muttered, her fingers heavy on her eyelids.

A boot scraped the gravel in front of her.

"You called?"

CHAPTER EIGHTEEN

It was kind of best-case scenario, actually.

Taft had gone out the bar's back door hoping he'd be able to take a quick peek at the work site. Maybe Lana would be looking at the roof or walls or something.

But there she was, under the romantic lights, her face in her hands.

Moaning his name.

Couldn't be better, that was a damn fact.

Except Lana had leaped to standing as soon as he'd spoken. "What are you *doing* sneaking up on me like that?"

He jerked a thumb over his shoulder. "I came right on out the door. The one you can see from where you're sitting. I don't call that sneaking. It is hard to see what's going on around you, though, when your face is covered and you're saying men's names."

She thumped back to sitting again. "I wasn't – I was just –"

"My name, in particular." He sat next to her, leaning his elbows on the table behind them. "There could be worse things for a man to hear than a beautiful woman groaning his name."

Lana glared at him. "I'm not doing this. Not right now."

"Look, Lana. I'm honestly not trying to be a pain in your ass."

"You're failing, then."

"The honest-to-God truth is that I need three more songs for my next album, and I can't write a single damn word."

She bit her bottom lip briefly. "You took that song and made it yours. Good for you. I'm glad for you that it's been such a hit. But I can't help you with the writing."

"I bet you're glad for your bank account, too." He injected as much cheer into his voice as he could, but it wasn't enough, clearly. She got a look in her face like someone had just lit a firecracker under her seat.

"Is that what this is? You think now I've got money from a song you sang that I'll feel *beholden* to you?"

Oh, God. It was the exact opposite of what he'd meant. "Lana, I owe *you*. My career was flatlining. My last three albums were so alike I can't even tell them apart.

You were my lucky charm. You brought me back. That's why these next songs are so important."

Lana shot a look at the bar's door. "Look. Don't tell anyone I wrote "Blame Me.'"

Taft dug his boot heel into the dirt. "Why not?"

"Because I say so."

And that just about confirmed it for him. It *was* her. It was autobiographical, he'd *known* it.

But he also knew enough not to push her on it. Lana, who appeared so tough she could chew up nails and spit out tacks, was actually deeply wounded. It was all an act.

Just like everybody else. Just like him. "I won't tell a soul." And he meant it.

Sharp tension lines left the corners of her eyes. "Thank you."

"But –" he started.

"Still no."

"Just consider it."

"Taft ..." Lana sighed. "Oh you are incorrigible." There was no heat in her voice.

He laughed. "That's what my pa always said. I like hearing it. Say it again."

The side of her mouth screwed sideways, and she shook her head. Just like that, he could see she was trying not to smile.

"Thanks," Taft said.

"For what?"

"For letting me stay. No matter what I say, no matter how I talked Jake into it, it really is up to you. If you said that you honestly wanted me to get on a plane tomorrow, I'd leave."

"Really? You would?"

"Yes." Of course he would. He'd hate it, but he wouldn't *make* the woman see him if she actually hated the very sight of him. "You were so angry that night."

She sighed. "I know. It wasn't about you. It was about a lot of other stuff."

It was a relief. A big one. "Okay."

"You're welcome to stay and help. I'm sure I'll appreciate it once I get used to the idea."

With difficulty, he stopped himself from pumping his fist. "Maybe you'll change your mind on the songs once you get used to *that* idea."

Lana poked his thigh, hard. "I'm stubborn. You might have heard."

"Me, too."

"Hmmph." She tilted her neck so she could look up at the stars.

Taft followed suit.

For a long moment, there was no noise but the faint bass beat from the jukebox and a man's laughter coming from the street. In the distance, the fog horn sounded. The night smelled of pine needles and wet salt.

For the same long moment, Taft was happy.

Perfectly happy right through to his booted feet.

Damn, it felt good.

Lana gave a long sigh. "I really am going to bed."

He had an image of her in it. She was probably one of those women who slept right on her face. Enthusiastically. She probably woke up with a pink, flattened nose, her hair sticking straight up. Without thinking what he was doing, he raised his hand to touch the black end of a jaw-length strand. "What made you dye your hair?"

Lana stilled but didn't draw away. She kept her eyes on his, as if making sure she knew exactly where he was. "Just wanted a change. The new, non-country me."

"Country girls have long, blonde hair, that's true."

"I'm not one anymore."

"You can take the girl out of the country ..."

In a move he didn't expect, she raised her hand to catch his, to press it against her cheek. Her skin was cool, soft. He caught his breath and ran his thumb along her jawline. His heart rate juddered, accelerated.

She gazed softly into his eyes.

His heart literally skipped a beat.

Lana said, "That really was the worst sex of my life."

He wanted to roar with laughter, but only allowed the corner of his mouth to twitch. "If by worst you mean strangest, sure. We just didn't find our rhythm."

"You think?" She pushed her chin against his thumb, like a cat would.

Lord, she was dangerous. He was a pile of kindling. She was both gasoline *and* the match. "Yeah," Taft said. "You ever get a song that comes to you, just the words?"

"Mmm-hmm." Her voice was a purr.

"Sometimes it takes a while to figure out the music it needs, that's all."

"Mmm."

If she kept making that sound ...

As if she'd heard his almost-thought, she drew back. "Sorry. I'm sorry." She rubbed her cheeks. "I'm just tired."

"Yeah."

"Yeah." Her eyes caught his again.

Taft's throat thickened. "I want to kiss you."

"I'm ... not sure that's a good idea."

He would take the high road. It was the right thing to do. "Probably not."

Was that disappointment on her face? "Yeah."

Taft gave up his effort. He leaned forward and took the kiss he wanted, the one she almost seemed to sway forward to give.

It was innocent at first. A closed-mouth kiss, something sweet. A goodnight kiss. That's what Taft told himself it was.

It turned into an all-night kind of kiss fast. Yeah, *this* was the kiss he'd remembered. He hadn't gotten that wrong. In fact, if anything, it was hotter. Her lips seared his, and when she opened her mouth, she tasted of red wine and flame.

All he wanted in the whole damn wide world was to pick her up and carry her through the garden behind the arbor, up to the hotel. He'd set her on her bed, he'd take off her clothing, and they'd start over, from scratch. From the beginning. She wouldn't be scared.

He pulled away. "Whew. Damn, woman." That was him, moving too fast, expecting too much. Expecting more than he was worthy of. As usual.

Lana's lips were wet, her cheeks were pink, and there was no one he'd ever wanted more in his life.

But Taft had three months before the studio needed the song drafts. He'd spend that time here. In Darling Bay. With this incredible woman. He had time.

No, scratch that. That made it sound like it was his decision. He hated it when men put it that way. *I'll bag her. She'll be mine, easy.* It sounded like women were prey, the men their hunters. Taft had never liked taking down a kill. His father had liked to hunt rabbits and squirrels in the hills. Taft thought it had been his one weakness.

They had time. He and Lana both. They could see if there really was something between them. This was about way more than just the songs, he'd known that from the start. This was about what had happened between them that night, the feeling of *connection*, like she and he were both running on the same electricity feeding into something even bigger.

"What? Why are you staring at me?" She wiped the back of her hand across her mouth, rubbing away his kiss. "I'm sorry. I know I started that."

Taft touched her cheek again. "We both did. Can I walk you to your room?"

She jumped, as if remembering she *had* a room to go to. Standing, she tugged the hem of her black shirt. There was a hole at her side, and in the low light he saw a flash of her skin beneath it. The woman was sex walking. Taft wondered when he'd be able to take a full breath again.

"No." Lana turned. "I'll see you Monday."

Then she literally sprinted away from him, up the low rise through the flower garden to the path that must lead to the hotel rooms set back on the hill.

She moved so quickly that it was almost as if she'd flown away.

"See you Monday, Birdie," Taft said into the darkness.

Three days. A damn eternity.

CHAPTER NINETEEN

L ana spent Friday night up in Uncle Hugh's old quarters where Adele and Nate were now living, the big apartment above the bar.

Knocking on their door was difficult, especially with her heart jammed into her throat. If Adele said *one* wrong word, criticized even one small thing about her – she'd what? Have the fight they'd been spoiling for, for the last twelve years?

Adele, though, opened the door with a smile so big it warmed Lana right through to the bottom of her pitch-black, ice-cold heart.

Adele always *had* been the one who could do that.

"Come in. Look what I've done with the place. Oh, Lana. I'm *so* happy you're here."

Hugh had been a hoarder, by nature and then by habit, but Adele had done an amazing job cleaning out the old place. The parlor really looked as if nineteenth-century women in leg o'mutton sleeves could walk in at any moment. The bathroom, always pink to please Hugh's three nieces, was clean and bright (still very, very pink). The kitchen had been totally redone. The stove was new, industrial and *huge*, and the fridge didn't whir or thump like Uncle Hugh's had. The windows he'd painted shut had been pried open, and the ocean breeze came in. Lana sat in a chair at the small yellow kitchen table, watching as Nate and Adele made dinner for her – fresh lingcod cooked in homemade teriyaki sauce.

Adele and Nate were the real kind of happy. It was obvious. They squabbled cheerfully about how much salt to add, and she caught them kissing when she came back from the bathroom. All three of them ate dinner on the back porch, the one that faced the hotel rooms. It had a great view of both the garden and the bright-blue tarps that flapped over most of the hotel rooms.

"It's a hell of a job you've got ahead of you," Nate said.

"Yep."

Adele cut the apricot pie (homemade – when had Adele started to bake?).

What if Lana had stayed in touch with her older sister? What if she'd reached out and stayed linked, instead of being so stupidly caught in an angry cycle of longing for connection and being sure she didn't deserve it?

Mama, standing in the kitchen, smiling as Adele and Molly ran in from outside, cheerful and clean and chirping. Her smile falling as Lana rolled in, covered in mud after tussling with a recalcitrant frog at the creek.

Lana's mother had loved her. Lana knew that. But she's always been disappointed in Lana.

Adele took after their mother.

Not tonight, though—Lana didn't want to hash anything out tonight. She was in town now. Plenty of time to feel jealousy of her perfect sisters, to build up a resistance to the looks on their faces (especially Adele's) as she inevitably let them down by being the last, smallest, weakest Songbird yet again.

As if her sister could hear her thoughts, Adele said, "Lana has never been scared of a challenge."

Lana almost laughed out loud. It was Adele who'd never been scared, who kept songwriting in Nashville, competing with the big dogs. Or Molly, who'd said screw all of it, who had gotten a real degree in nutrition and had put it to use.

Lana had just run. She'd kept running for almost twelve years. Singing, songwriting, moving from town to town, from busted futon to sagging mattress in town after town where she knew one or two people, well enough to crash with them but never well enough to really connect other than physically. She'd had strings of one-night stands that had turned into every-other-yearly stands. When she rolled into San Francisco, she stayed with Jesus, who had amazing legs from his day job of bike messengering. He'd never once pronounced her name right. "It's Lah-nah. Not LAY-nah," she'd corrected him a million times and had then started pronouncing his name like the biblical figure. He'd only laughed, saying he'd heard it so much growing up in church that now he took it as a compliment. In Tucson, there was Jonathan, who wrote computer code during the day and put together the local open mics at night. In Miami, there was Douglas, who drove a different beat-up car every time she saw him. All of them she met through the music scene, none of them close enough to her to know her middle name.

Adele and Molly.

They were probably the only two in the whole wide world who knew her middle name was Mirabelle.

After dinner, both Nate and Adele went downstairs to work the Friday-night rush with their other bartender, Dixie. They invited her down, of course.

And of course, she said no. What if Taft took it in his head to get a drink in the local watering hole? She wasn't ready to face him.

Monday, when they started work: that would be soon enough to see the man who scrambled all the circuits of her brain.

So she stayed out of the bar.

Saturday night, she had dinner at Molly's sheriff's place. Colin seemed great for a cop. He was down-to-earth and funny. He seemed like he'd actually be a good leader. He listened carefully and asked excellent questions. He seemed genuinely interested in not only what Lana said, but in every single thing Molly said or did. He probably didn't know – which made it nice – that his eyes followed Molly wherever she moved in the room. When she spoke, he listened. Molly did the same for him.

Freaking love.

What the hell?

Colin even pointed it out to her. "You'd better watch out, Lana. There's a shacking-up epidemic around here when it comes to the Darling girls. Careful, or you'll be next."

Lana saw Taft Hill's knuckles in her mind. She'd stared at them so hard in the bar while they'd been talking, and she hadn't been able to get them out of her mind. They were broad and bony at the same time. Thick cords of muscles had sprung up every time he'd flexed his fingers (picking up his beer, pushing his floppy blond hair back off his brow) and one large blue vein had popped on the back of his hand.

She'd wanted to bite those knuckles. Taste them.

"Oh, my God, look at you." Molly laughed. "Where did you just go? Are you thinking about Taft Hill, maybe?"

Lana managed to change the subject, though she wasn't smooth at all. Colin had driven her back to the hotel. She'd put herself to bed mildly tipsy. In her dreams, she'd seen Taft's left hand with a broad matte gold band on the third finger. She'd woken up so embarrassed she'd buried her head in the pillow until she'd run out of oxygen and had to come up for air.

Stuck without a plan for the rest of the weekend except reading through the home-repair book she'd gone back to Floyd's to buy, she ended up painting room one's interior. The walls had been dingy white for long enough – she cleaned and primed the walls, then painted them a dusky gold color with a bright yellow feature wall.

Even that didn't take up her full weekend.

It was strange. In the past, time had always flown in Darling Bay. She remembered the summers and Christmas holidays they'd spent in town when they were children as weeks that had flown by in a matter of hours. They'd arrive in June and she'd wake up, a minute later, suddenly smack in the middle of early September. Her skin would be dark brown from spending almost all day outside.

Back then, Adele (the Good Daughter) would follow their father and Uncle Hugh around the bar, offering to help in whatever way she could. Molly had naturally gravitated to the café. Arnie, the cook back then, had aided in Molly's first foodie forays. She'd spent hours in the kitchen with him, thrilling the customers when they peeked over the pass-through to see a little girl making their pancakes. Child Protective Services had been called out once by a nosy woman from Santa Barbara who'd been driving through town. "This can't be legal," she'd sniffed, before going home to make some calls. The complaint was waved aside when it was established that no one was paying Molly to work, nor were they forcing her – she desperately *wanted* to be in that hot, small space, laughing with the teenage busboys, getting hair tips from the waitresses on college break.

Lana had been alone.

For a majority of the time, she'd had no one to hang out with, which was exactly as she'd liked it. She spent time on the pier with the kids who smoked a lot of weed and performed jump tricks on their skateboards that defied the laws of gravity. She was friends with the woman who owned the riding stables, and would sometimes be allowed to trundle the ancient Darby down the beach to the river's end and back. Darby was twenty-seven. Lana spent a lot of time just trying to get her to do a pace faster than a plod. At the water's edge, Lana would close her eyes, pretending to be on a silver-white Andalusian, imagining they'd just finished a breathless, breakneck gallop instead of the trundling sway they'd actually done.

Always alone.

Even when she was with others.

Well, it sure seemed like she hadn't grown out of that.

It turned out Sunday was the worst day of all.

She finished the painting. The faucet assembly in the bathroom could stand to be replaced – it was dull and old, wiggling a little when she pushed at it, but when she honestly assessed it, it could go another year or two. She spent the day in a corner of the café reading her home-improvement book, learning about dry rot and smoke damage. From time to time Molly would plop next to her, telling her stories about the clientele, and Nikki kept her coffee cup so full that Lana's hands started shaking by two o'clock.

"Come to the saloon tonight," Molly said when Lana had finally decided to go back to her room. "It's open mic, which is *so* fun. You can't imagine the range of talent and non-talent we've got in town."

Lana? *Lana* couldn't imagine? Lana had spent the last twelve years listening to hopeful people croon into twenty-year-old mics that squealed with feedback and outrage. "No, thanks. Been there."

But at nine-thirty, so caffeinated she was sure she wouldn't sleep until dawn, she went onto the hotel porch. She sat in the swing in front of her room (the only swing safe to sit in, according to Adele, who'd been sure to let her know that she'd fixed it by herself).

From the saloon below, she heard a telltale shriek of a mic set too close to an amp. It was silenced immediately. A woman's voice floated up the hill from the open back door. Even at a distance of a hundred yards or more, she could tell the woman didn't have experience in front of an audience. Her voice shook, fading in and out. This far away, Lana couldn't quite understand the words, but she knew the singer would never climb out of the open-mic world. That was fine. That was where most people wanted to be, honestly. They wanted to write and sing for friends and family. That was great.

Lana had always wanted more than that.

Sitting on the swing, staring into the low, foot-level lights on the path that ran through the roses, she realized for the first time that she'd failed.

"Oh, God," she whispered, putting her hand across her mouth.

She'd *failed*.

She'd given up. Sure, she'd written a hit so huge it would probably keep paying her big for the rest of her life. Someone on a radio station had compared it to "Friends in Low Places" in terms of instantly working its way into country-music culture.

Lots of people – maybe most – would call that a success.

But she'd wanted one thing: to sing her songs in front of people who appreciated them enough to pay her enough to make her way in the world.

She'd never quite made it.

She'd really, really thought she would. Deep in her bones, she'd always *known* she would. Now she'd quit.

With her toe, Lana pushed the swing. It gave a creak as loud as the one coming from her soul.

She was never going to make it.

That was just a fact.

She was just going to have to get used to it.

The female singer stopped, and a smattering of applause rose through the night.

A man started singing.

From the first notes, she knew.

"Blame Me."

Her best song, the one she'd never claim as her own in this town.

Moving as quietly as she could, she ran down the path to the side of the building. The path continued down to the street, but from here she could see in through the window placed high above the rear of the bar. How many hours had she and her sisters sat outside, peering in at the cowboys dancing below?

There he was on stage. Her song came from Taft Hill's throat.

His perfect, long, corded, sexy-as-hell throat.

The crowd in the room that she'd heard chattering at low volume all through the last singer's song was completely silent. Totally still. They stood at attention, all faces turned toward Taft. He was below Lana's gaze, and she could only see the side of him – from his cowboy hat to that gorgeous stubbled jaw, down the planes of his body and over his red guitar, to his good-looking jeans-clad ass all the way down to his right cowboy boot. Even though she couldn't see his face, she could see the expression of each audience member.

Some people wiped at tears. It wasn't limited to the women. An old man wearing a blue handkerchief around his throat unknotted it and dabbed at his eyes. Others moved their lips to the chorus. They actually swayed a little, back and forth, in that unconscious way crowds sometimes did.

For a moment, Lana willed him with all the force of her mind to turn his head, to look at her over his shoulder. *Over here. See me.*

He didn't. She remained alone.

It wasn't so much that it hurt.

It was just kind of ... empty. Her chest was hollow, and her feet were cold. She pressed her thumb against her tattoo.

Two teenagers whooped as they ran past the saloon, and a patrol car idled in front of the café while the officer inside gossiped with one of the Homeless Petes. Darling Bay was just as it had always been.

And so was Lana.

CHAPTER TWENTY

M onday morning, Taft appeared where he'd been told to, at the base of the rose garden. Standing slightly uphill was the U-shaped hotel. Rooms stood to the left, to the right, and in front of him – twelve in total. Every square foot represented a reason for him to stay in town. It felt good, reporting for duty.

He hadn't seen Lana all weekend. The disappointment had been sharp.

Jake Ballard greeted Taft with a hug, a California thing that never failed to surprise him. Not that men didn't hug in Tennessee, they did. But that was brother to brother or good friend to another. Other men did the friendly guy handshake, the lean-in-tap-the-shoulder thing. An almost-hug.

Jake came at him like a running back, as if they were the oldest and best of friends.

"What's up, bro? Sounded great last night, just great." He grinned. "I brought a girl with me and told her you were on my work crew."

Taft raised his eyebrows in appreciation. "Good move."

"It was, it turns out." Jake rubbed his eyes. "How about you? Have you met any of our fair Darling Bay girls yet?"

Before he could say that yes he had – only he'd met her in Nashville – footsteps came up the path.

"Good morning!" Lana led a small parade along the side of the hotel, followed by two men and a woman. She could have been surrounded by a thousand people, though, and Taft wouldn't have been able to see anyone but her. A woman had never looked so sexy in overalls in the history of the western world. She wore another of her ubiquitous black shirts, nice and tight. Even the shapeless jeans material of the overalls couldn't hide the curve of her hip, and the T-shirt left her small biceps on display. As she spoke to the woman, she pointed up the hill. Taft could see her breast's curve where the overalls opened. *He* was probably the one who should be paying Jake for the honor of being on this crew.

Lana finally looked at him. "Hey." Her voice was soft, her eyes guarded. Good Lord, had he been so wrong about the kiss in the arbor? He'd really thought she'd been there with him. Until she'd bolted, that was.

Then she smiled, and at the exact same time, the fog burned through behind her, dropping a shaft of sunlight onto the top of her head. Taft realized that no, she didn't appear to be mad, and yes, he probably *could* rebuild the whole hotel by himself. By midnight. If she wanted him to.

"Taft, this is Sturgeon and Bass." She pointed to two young guys who looked alike enough to be twins, both wearing Giants baseball caps.

"Those aren't our real names," said Sturgeon.

"We fish," said Bass.

"Are you brothers?"

"Nah," they both said at the same time. "We get that a lot."

"And this is Socal," Lana continued, gesturing to a woman with short brown hair.

"They call you that because you're from southern California?"

The woman – as tall and angular as a slide rule – said, "Where I was conceived, actually. They call me that because it's my real name."

Hippie Californians.

Socal went on, "Nice to meet you. I admire you as a musician very much. I'm sorry, though, I'm not going to trust you on a job site with me until you prove your worth as a builder."

"Annndd," Jake broke in. "We should tell you that Socal came without a filter. She'll always tell you exactly what she thinks."

"I appreciate that."

Socal said, "I also think that as a performer, you're probably well trained in pleasing people by appearing, chameleon-like, to be able to charm anyone. I will also distrust *that* until I get to know you more." She gave a bright smile.

"All right, then!" Taft had no idea what else to say.

Lana, at least, looked as awkward as he felt. "Okay. Jake and I talked on Sunday afternoon. We're going to start with the roof and work our way down. Since all the rooms are connected, it should be pretty smooth sailing."

Jake snorted, and his crew outright laughed. Taft kept his mouth still, but he knew that nothing – ever – went smoothly in construction.

"What?"

Jake said, "What I meant was that was the easiest way to do it. I don't think any of this is going be as easy as we want it to be."

"It never is," said Sturgeon. Or maybe it was Bass.

Lana nodded. "Well, fingers crossed. Jake, can you put the crew to work? Then you and I can walk through the next steps?" She looked at Taft as she said it, and there was just something so damn sexy about the way she said the word *crew*.

He was on her crew.

How many crews had Taft had working for him over the years? Every tour, every album ... Crews worked for him, which got pretty boring after a while, if he was honest with himself. Taft was handled and managed every step of the way. He didn't even have to spend three hours in hair and make-up like the women of country did. He put on the clothes, he played his songs, he went to either the hotel or the bus to sleep afterwards.

Now he was on the crew.

And he wanted to sleep with the boss.

◦◦◦

Taft and Socal were assigned to roof removal, while the Indistinguishable Fish Men were tasked with hauling everything out of the hotel rooms that could be moved. He supposed it would be a dick move to ask to be reassigned to grunt labor at sea level, since the only reason he wanted to be down and not up was so he'd have more of a chance to interact with Lana.

Hell, though, it was a beautiful day. He was working outside. Just like a normal man. As he waited for Socal to climb the ladder so he could follow, he said, "This is great. Can't wait to do this. I haven't ripped off a roof in ..." he paused to make it sound like he had to count through years even though he knew exactly how long it had been. "Six years." Two years before Palmer had died. They'd redone the old barn together.

"You better not fall off. If you do, better not blame me." Her feet disappeared. Taft hurried to catch up.

Once on the roof, he said, "What if you push me? Then can I blame you?"

She gave that bright smile again. "Maybe you'll find out!"

"Your tone is ominous."

"Let's call it cautious."

They worked for three hours and took a lunch break. Molly Darling – whom he'd spoken to briefly at the café over the weekend – brought up bagged lunches. They ate on the shallow steps leading to room five.

"How's he doing?" Jake asked Socal.

Socal narrowed her eyes at him. "Hasn't screwed up too bad yet."

"Hey, thanks," said Taft, meaning it. It was a better compliment than the last *Rolling Stone* article, and that interviewer had loved him.

Lana didn't seem to hear it, though. Her head was turned, and he could see the back of her ear, curled like a perfect seashell. She was talking to one of the fish guys about what he'd done over the weekend.

He didn't spend each moment wishing you were walking into sight.

Lunch was over quickly. As the afternoon wore on, the task got boring. His eyes actually drifted shut at one point, which didn't make a hell of a lot of sense since every muscle in his body burned with overuse. He hadn't done this much crouching and bending since his last CrossFit challenge. Yeah, he worked out, but this wasn't a workout as much as it was endurance training. He stripped off his shirt by two and accepted the sunscreen Socal pulled out of her tool belt. His borrowed tool belt was an obviously old one, probably discarded because of an upgrade by Jake, and it didn't fit him right. His own belt – still resting in the master closet at home – fit his waist, bent at the right places. Like leather shoes, a man grew into his tool belt. Taft stopped working to send an email to Sully to have someone FedEx it out. He should have thought of that earlier, over the weekend.

"Don't text while you're up here!" Socal's voice was a shriek.

"You worry too much." It was the sixth time she'd corrected him since lunch. First, she thought he was being too careless prying up the shingles at the edge. She'd said he wasn't being careful enough to remove the roof jacks. True, he had lifted too big a course of shingles all the way up, and the piece had slid off whole. It could have been really dangerous. He'd felt as stupid as hell.

Her yelling at him constantly wasn't making him work any safer, though. "I'm fine. I can handle standing and looking at my phone at the same time."

Then, with an ominous creak followed by a *thunk* that travelled up his body, he dropped down, both his legs going through the roof. He was stuck. Right up to his waist. Hanging like a baby in one of those snuggly things.

From somewhere below him, Lana's voice floated up. "You've got to be fucking kidding me."

CHAPTER TWENTY-ONE

I t wasn't funny. There was *nothing* funny about it. Everyone else was howling, including Taft himself, but Lana wasn't laughing. No way.

Taft was fine. It had taken the firefighters from Truck One less than five minutes to free him. The only damaged parts of him were a bloody hand from where he'd scraped it on a roof jack and a scratch that ran right down his side.

Because he hadn't been wearing a shirt up there.

No, he'd just been up there sweating in the sun, wiping his forehead with the back of his wrist. Once he'd lifted a water bottle high up and squirted a long stream of water into his mouth from a foot away or more.

It had been so intensely sexy – his body was taking so much *pleasure* in the primal urge to drink – that Lana had had to look away. Not that she would have ever admitted she was watching in the first place.

Now that he was safely on the ground, she pretended she'd barely known he was up there. She certainly didn't act as if her whole body had turned to jelly as soon as she'd heard him fall. "What happened?"

He mopped at the back of his neck with his T-shirt. "I'm sorry. That won't happen again."

"He was looking at his phone," said Socal.

"Seriously?" Jake looked pissed, his eyebrows drawn together.

"That's not why I fell through."

This was Lana's site. These people were her responsibility. "Why the hell were you looking at your phone?"

"I needed my tool belt. I was asking my manager to send it out, overnight."

There was a pause.

Jake nodded. "Well, that's okay, then. Don't do it again."

"I won't. I'm sorry." Taft said this to Lana, but she turned away. Her hands were still shaking – they had been since she'd heard him fall through.

For the rest of the afternoon, Lana helped the fish boys load the last of the movable storage units with the salvageable pieces of furniture, of which there had been dishearteningly few. The entire dumpster was full, and they'd taken to storing next week's trash behind room twelve. She was going to be able to fill maybe two completed rooms with original stuff. The rest she'd have to buy. Today had been the first day, and she already knew her money wasn't going to last nearly as long as she'd hoped it would. Luckily, "Blame Me" was still playing out of the open windows of every car that drove down Main, so hopefully her bank account would get another good cash infusion soon.

"That's everything?" She waited to close the door of room two until everyone had nodded. Yes, it was Darling Bay, but Jake had asked for a room that had a working, lockable door in which to store their tools every night.

"That's it!" Jake raised his arms above his head. "Time for a beer. First day on the job, so I'm buying. Who's coming?"

"Me! Me!" The fish boys jiggled up and down like antsy six-year-olds instead of the just-twenty-one they actually were. They'd proved to be hard workers who didn't seem to have a single problem with being told what to do all day.

"Yep." Socal attached her hard hat to her belt with a carabiner. "Hell, yep."

Taft was last to answer. "Sounds good." He looked at her.

Oh, *Lana* was last to answer. "Um ..."

"Come have a drink with us." Taft tugged on his now filthy T-shirt and jammed his wide hands through his hair.

If she went to drink with that man, she'd end up back in bed with him.

While it sounded like an incredible idea, one any sane single woman would run with, she wouldn't. She couldn't.

Everyone was already trooping down the hill to the saloon. No one but Taft was left to hear her decline. "No, thank you. Not tonight." She didn't offer an excuse. Let that be enough.

"You want to write a song later? I'd shower first." He tucked a thumb in a belt loop. Lana's knees went warm and wobbly.

"No, thank you. Not tonight."

He smiled that 400-watt grin at her. "You have a good night, then, okay?" He touched the brim of his ball cap like it was a cowboy hat.

She watched him walk away, the back of his T-shirt broad and somehow as dirty as the front.

What if he'd gone all the way through instead of landing on the attic floor? What if he'd broken a leg? Or worse, his *neck*.

Or worst of all, what if he'd died?

Lana sat on the same step he'd been on while the firefighters had been checking him out.

She'd give herself a month.

One month of working with him. She wouldn't do *anything* else with him. Not one thing. Nothing in town, nothing at the bar. She wouldn't let her sisters talk her into doing a small concert with them (it would be just like Adele to set up something like that). If she saw him at the café, she'd head to the bagel shop.

She knew herself too well. She'd already had (strange, weird, odd) sex with the man once. Just seeing him did something to her. It made her feel like she was riding on top of a speeding freight train, trying to slow it down by pulling on useless reins.

One month.

Then she'd reassess.

Thank God she had a vibrator. Her Hitachi Magic Wand with its plug-in power would be her saving grace.

CHAPTER TWENTY-TWO

Taft unlocked the front door and ushered Jake inside. "It's unassuming from the front, right?"

Jake looked at him suspiciously. "Yeah, I know what view this row of houses has – holy *crap*. You lucky bastard." Jake stopped dead in the middle of the living room. Taft grinned.

"Packs a punch, doesn't it?"

"You lucky son of a bitch."

"I know." It *was* luck, Taft knew that. A pure dumb streak of it, from being born to the right family.

Jake walked to the glass window that ran from ceiling to floor. "Dude, I live *on a boat*, and my view isn't this good."

The sun was just dropping into the ocean, the fog still a thin grey strip on the horizon. With no clouds in the sky, the blue was going directly to orange, and soon the light would be gone. To the south was a view of the far end of town and the dunes that led to the water. Directly in front, twenty yards from the edge of the house, the cliff dropped to the water. "There's a staircase there." Taft pointed. "Goes right down."

"I know." Jake nodded. "Great make-out spot down there. I might have convinced a girl or two that it's our local nude beach."

"And it's not?"

"Well, sometimes it is."

To the north, ice plant and low scrub covered the sand like a nubby green carpet. The bluffs stretched around the curve of the coast. The water was dark blue and getting darker as the sky moved into a deep orange.

"I promised you beer." Taft grabbed a couple from the fridge. "Let's go outside."

Jake sank into a heavy wooden chair the house had come with, and gave a happy-sounding sigh. He opened the white plastic bag and dug out the plates of tacos from Dario's. "This is insane. If I were you, I'd never be inside. I've *always* wanted to get in here and see what it looked like on the other side. Man, you bought a hell of a house."

Taft nodded. He'd bought a house.

A *house*.

In Darling Bay.

Taft wondered again how long it took to stop being the newcomer here. "Did you know the people who lived here before?"

"The Adelaides. Yeah. The old guy was a music teacher, and his wife was disabled. Had a stroke in her thirties, lost most of her sight and some speech. He took care of her until they both died, in their eighties."

"Damn."

"Right? Think about that. Getting married young to someone healthy and strong, then you taking care of them for the rest of your life. The worst." Jake bit into a taco.

Yeah. The worst.

But what if they'd really loved each other? What if Mr. Adelaide's whole life was made better by his wife; what if she meant everything to him? Lana's mop of dark hair flashed into his mind.

Surely that was what true love was. Taking care of the one you loved.

What if that person didn't want to be helped?

Taft dug out a chicken taco on a soft corn tortilla. Piled with cheese and salsa, it dripped onto his work pants before it made it halfway to his mouth. "What do you think of –" he broke off, embarrassed. "Never mind."

"What do I think of the state of politics? Religion?"

"Nah, don't worry about it."

"Or are you wondering what I think about the way Lana Darling has looked at you every night for the last month when you ask her those two questions?"

The top of Taft's head went hot. "It's that obvious?"

"Dude."

Every night, when the hotel crew knocked off work, they went downstairs for a beer at the bar. Every night, Taft asked Lana to come down with them.

She said no, every time.

Then, without fail, he said, "You want to write a song later? I'd shower first."

Every night, she said no to that, too.

Each time, he wasn't surprised. Being in show business his whole life, he knew that no one got anywhere without asking, without pushing, without *trying*.

But he also knew who he was: a washed-up writer with a pretty good singing career that he hadn't earned honestly. How was that supposed to impress someone like Lana Darling, who was gifted and gorgeous and amazing and – "I think I'm in falling in love with her."

"Dude," Jake said again. He clinked his beer against Taft's. "I'm sorry."

"It's awful."

"I've gotta say, it does look painful."

Taft kicked his boots onto the deck railing. A seagull swooped by at eye level and flew away screaming with injustice. The air smelled of brine and seaweed and Tapatío hot sauce.

"So I look like as much of a loser as I am."

Jake nodded. "Yeah. You're such a fucking loser. International superstar, enough money to buy a house on a whim –"

"A cottage, your brother called it." A million had been a steal, to be honest. Three hours down the coast, and these kinds of houses started at two.

"– the kind of life where you can pitch in on a construction crew just for fun."

"Well. It's not just for fun."

"We know."

"You think I have any chance with her?" Taft tried not to sound too pathetic.

Still chewing, Jake scrutinized Taft. "Sure."

"Is that your honest opinion?"

Jake squinted. "No."

"Come on, man."

Jake lowered his bottle. "She's closed off. If any guy can get her attention, it seems like you'd be the one."

"But."

"She's the lone wolf of the group. She's always been like that."

Taft leaned forward eagerly, dropping half a taco on the deck as he did. "You knew her back then?"

"Sure. She always seemed like the one who wasn't part of anything else. They used to come here every summer, but I only remember Adele and Molly with us for the beach bonfires or drinking behind the library, not Lana. The rest of us all got stoned and stupid every summer, but Lana was always off with her notebook or her guitar. She'd come by sometimes and watch us skate. Then she'd take off again."

"So she's naturally solitary." Taft could barely imagine what that would feel like. He actively liked to collect people. No one stayed a stranger long. He'd gotten that from Palmer.

He thought he had, at least.

Jake went on, "Lone wolf, you know?"

"What if she's just shy? Or nervous about being in a crowd?"

"Would she be a musician, then?"

Heck, yeah. Taft knew plenty of musicians who preferred their own company to that of a group. It wasn't that Lana didn't like people. It was something else.

Jake kicked out his legs. "There goes the sun."

Taft barely glanced at it. "So you think I'm doomed to fail."

"Yep. Unless you need me to say you're on the right track, in which case I will, because I want backstage tickets to your next show in San Francisco."

"Maybe it's just me she doesn't like."

"Could be. Seems like she gets along okay with everyone else."

"You are *not* helping me out."

"But I'm truthful. I did buy the tacos, so I call that helpful as shit."

"No ideas?"

Jake shrugged. "Just keep asking. It's not like she's mad you're doing it. She doesn't snap at you or anything when you ask. I swear, every night she's thinking about it, but every night she says no. You know the rest of us have a pool on it, right?"

"That doesn't surprise me. Who has 'never?'"

"Um."

"You do!"

"Sorry, pal. I could use the cash."

Taft watched the last sliver of sun slip behind the back of the world. He liked having Jake on the porch with him. It was good to have friends, and he was lucky that he made them quickly. Jake was a good guy.

Damn, though, he couldn't help wishing the person next to him was a black-haired country-singing grumpy-pants-wearing country girl named Lana Darling.

He'd just keep asking, then.

CHAPTER TWENTY-THREE

L ana said yes.

It had been a crappy day, during which she'd had no intention of saying yes. None at all. She'd spent the day going back and forth to the hardware store, trying to find the right goddamn adaptor for the sink in room seven. The new faucet's supply line used three-eighths-inch female compression, and she needed to hook it to an old half-inch main-water valve. It seemed like every one she brought back was almost but not quite right. Jake kept offering to look at it for her. Sure, he'd probably have the answer. She didn't want the answer given to her, though.

She wanted to fix it *herself*. The more her crew offered assistance, the grumpier she got. Even Taft, who generally didn't follow her around the site, asked if he could help. She snapped at him and felt instantly guilty about it.

But she fixed the damn thing, and the feeling of accomplishment when the water ran fresh and clear through the brand-new taps made her so giddy that when he said, as usual, "Come have a drink with us," she answered with yes.

Jake coughed.

Socal pumped a fist.

The fish boys just nodded.

Taft broke out into a grin so big it warmed her to the center of her chest, and she started rethinking her answer almost immediately.

"Great. I'm buying," said Taft.

"That's for everyone, right?" Socal didn't wait for an answer, heading toward the saloon.

"Hang on. I don't know." Lana was disgusting, covered in old-sink sludge and sweat. "I need a shower."

"Grab one, then. We'll wait." Taft's face was happy, his eyes clear. What would that be like, to be so obviously cheerful all the time?

She looked down at her clothes. When she'd turned on the water to the room, she'd washed her hands and arms all the way up to her armpits. She'd washed her face and neck at the same time. "The rest of you are just going as is."

"Darlin', nothing tastes better than a cold drink when you're as dirty as you are."

Was that an entendre in his deep voice? She couldn't honestly tell.

Lana just smiled tightly and followed him. Maybe she'd sit outside in the arbor and have her drink quickly. Then she'd escape back to her room and the mystery novel she was reading to try to keep her mind off Taft.

Alone. A drink alone *would* be nice.

Taft held the door open for her. As she ducked under his arm, she could smell him: woodchips, grease and his own sweat. She wanted to inhale forever, to memorize the way he smelled so she could conjure it up at will, when she was lonely in the future.

She wanted to memorize the way he was looking at her, too, with those warm eyes.

Like she was someone special. "Thanks."

God help her, this yes-to-a-drink was not going to lead to anything else. She didn't need it, didn't want it. This was just to show she didn't mind going out with the team. It was the right thing to do, as head of the project. She probably should have done it before.

"Anytime." His voice held more.

The noise and bustle of the bar slapped her right in the face. This was the part that had always been hard for her. The coming in. Once she was in, once she'd gotten on stage, she'd always been all right. As soon as the spotlight hit her and the crowd was invisible, she was alone again.

Honestly, she thought as she pushed past a clump of women wearing high heels and short skirts, if she could live the rest of her life in a sound booth with nothing but writing material, a guitar and a microphone, she'd be happy. For sure. Probably.

At least the bartender knew her at this place.

"Hey." She slid into a barstool.

"Oh, my God. *You're* here." Adele looked at the whole group of them. "With the crew."

Please don't make a big deal out of this. "Yep."

"You always have an excuse not to come with them! This is great!"

"An excuse?" Lana shot daggers at the group, who had suddenly found the drinks menu incredibly interesting. "I just like to rest after we work. I go to the café and eat with Molly. Then I go to sleep." Which Adele would have known if *she* ever came down to the café for dinner instead of eating whatever perfect thing it was Nate and she ate behind the bar, the two of them sharing a fork and kisses.

"I'm just so glad you're here. What can I get for my favorite baby sister?"

Lana barely resisted rolling her eyes. "A Salty Dog."

"Are you sure? Salt will dehydrate you, and I bet you were sweating all day."

This was a bad idea. "He's buying, so make it a double." She pointed at Taft, who nodded back amiably.

Why couldn't Taft be an asshole? Why was he not only the hottest person she'd ever met but also a seemingly good, kind person? She'd given a ten to the young homeless guy who'd been hanging out on Main and First with a small cardboard sign, and she'd felt pretty good about it. Later, when she'd been getting coffee from the caboose, she'd seen Taft sitting on the curb, chatting with the man. She'd watched as the guy started rubbing his face, and she'd realized he was crying. Taft had slung his arm around him. He'd just sat there next to him, looking across the street. Just being with him.

He was a good man.

And her...what if she was just too broken?

Lana waited until the work crew were all talking about the kinds of beer that were okay to drink warm (her opinion: none), before she sneaked away through the back into the arbor. It still counted, after all. She was *at* the bar, having a drink Taft had bought her.

She was just alone while doing it, that was all. Her traitorous heart wished for a second that Taft would follow her out. Sit next to her. Lean into her ...

No. Alone was best. Alone was the way Lana operated. It was safe. If you put your trust in anyone else, they always let you down. She was a solo artist for a reason.

Lana tasted salt at the back of her throat. She wasn't sure if it was from the drink or not.

The back door opened with a creak, and she busied herself looking at her phone. A pair of feet stopped in front of her, bright-green cowboy boots stitched with gold thread. The person inside the boots was a purple-haired girl who couldn't be much older than the fish boys, maybe twenty-two or three. She flapped her hands. "Are you ...?"

Lana waited for a moment, but the girl didn't seem capable of more. "A Darling? I'm Lana." *The baby.*

"No, I meant ... do you know him?"

"Oh." Of course a woman this age wouldn't know her music. "Who?"

"I saw you talking to Taft Hill. Inside." The woman looked over her shoulder. "Do you actually know him?"

"Yeah."

"Oh, my God," she breathed. "Can I sit down? I'm Amber. You said your name is Darling? Like the town?"

Friendly, personable people. They were *everywhere.* "Long story."

Amber sat. "We're just in town for a couple of days. My friends and I. We're celebrating, staying in a condo up the road. Oh, my God," she said again. "I can't believe he's *in* there. How do you *know* him?"

"Nashville."

"You're a singer? Like backup?"

It was something Lana used to protest. Now she merely nodded. "Yeah."

"He changed my life."

"Mmmm." Lana took a deeper sip of her drink. Had she ever been so young? She didn't think she had. Life had gotten hard so early.

"That song. Do you know his latest single?"

Oh please, no. "I don't actually know much by him," she lied. "Nothing new."

"'Blame Me.' You *have* to hear it. Like, seriously, when you get home tonight, pull it up on YouTube. The video is the best thing I've ever seen, and I've never once managed to listen to it without crying."

"Sure thing." Luckily, she usually had no service at all in room one.

"No." Amber pulled out her cell. "I'll play it for you."

Lana shook her head. "Even if you have reception here, it won't be fast enough to stream a song."

"I have it downloaded to my phone. It's my *theme* song." Amber put one hand on her chest as if she were about to pledge allegiance to the flag. "Just watch."

"I don't want to –" Oh, it was too late. The phone was hovering twelve inches in front of her face, and there was Taft Hill, sitting on a bed in a country farm house.

CHAPTER TWENTY-FOUR

As the camera panned, the view turned to the exterior of the house, brand new with bright-yellow paint, as if it had just been built. In time-lapse photography, the whole place aged around Taft as he sat on the bed, singing. Only he remained unchanged. Just one pillow rested on the bed behind him, and just one side of the covers was pulled back. He sang "Blame Me" as the sun rose and set a thousand times out the window behind him. Dust grew up on the nightstands. The glass shattered silently in the mirror on the wall. The video was as haunting as the look in his eyes.

As he sang, "*Blame me, for looking away,*" Amber sniffled. Even Lana, who didn't think it was possible for her to be moved by the song anymore, felt something scratchy tingle the tip of her nose.

At the end, Amber set down her phone and looked at Lana expectantly. "You're not sobbing. Are you made of *stone* or something?"

"Granite. To the core."

Amber clasped her hands in front of her. "But you love it. You have to love it."

"I love it." Lana did. He'd done more with it than she ever could have. The words – his voice – told the story, all of it. The look on his face in the video was added emotion. No wonder it was a hit.

The saloon door creaked open again.

"Oh, holy sweet everything," whispered Amber.

"Ladies," said Taft. "Am I interrupting?" He'd left his tool belt upstairs, but he walked like he still had it on. His stubble looked three days old, even though he'd been clean-shaven that morning.

He was all man, solid as stone, broad as a tree.

"*We do not mind.*" Amber stood. Then she sat again. She looked desperately at Lana.

"Taft, this is Amber. She was just showing me your new video. Amber, Taft Hill."

Amber lost it then. She burst into wild tears, and when Taft shook her hand, she didn't let go of it. She took it with both of hers and held on as if she were drowning. She said words but apart from "you" and "mean it," Lana couldn't understand a single one.

Taft was perfect with her. Some stars pulled away quickly and had a genuine-sounding but very scripted, "That means so much. I can't thank you enough for saying so." Others went in for the hug and proposed a quick selfie, thereby giving the fan a chance to do something, to get out of the panic zone.

Taft, though, was different. He appeared perfectly happy to keep holding Amber's hand, forever if need be. His smile didn't falter. He nodded as she tried to get her words out. "Take your time. It's okay. It's really okay."

Lana pulled up her knees and wrapped her arms around them. If a man like Taft had ever looked at her and said those words, she might have believed them.

Amber took a shuddering breath. She was understandable now. "I'm so sorry. I just – that *song*. It's my anthem. My theme song."

"Yeah?" Taft's gaze never flickered, even for a second. "How so?"

"It's like you were singing to *me*. I know you weren't, I'm not naive, but it's like you wrote those words so I could hear them. And –" she gasped "– I didn't know. I thought *I* was the one to blame."

"You weren't."

"But I was drunk, and I was young, and I was stupid –" She broke off with another strangled sob.

Taft shook his head. "Look at me. I want you to listen to me. Okay?"

Amber nodded.

"*You're not to blame for what went wrong.*" It was the best line of the song.

"I should have –"

"You did nothing wrong. What happened to you was not okay."

"I was *really* drunk, and I'd smoked some weed, too." Amber's hands shook.

Taft repeated, "You did nothing wrong. Whoever hurt you is the one to blame. You did nothing wrong. Nothing. You get me?"

Amber nodded. "I can't believe *you're* saying this to *me*."

"Darlin', I'll say it to you every time you hear the song from here on out, okay? I am singing to you."

"*Oh*."

"Singing right to you, just to remind you again and again that you did nothing wrong. Everything you did in your life got you to this place – right here – safely. You should be so proud of yourself. You didn't deserve that. But you made it to today anyway. Good for you, darlin'."

Then Amber sobbed, and Taft reached forward to wrap her in his arms. Lana watched as he stroked her hair. He kept his flow of words going, so his soft *You did nothing wrong* was on a repeated loop, pouring over Amber as she cried into his work shirt.

Minutes later, she pulled away with a horrified look. "Oh, my God, I just cried all over Taft Hill." She stage-whispered at Lana, "His shirt is all wet."

Lana's throat tightened. "He's been sweating all day in that shirt, so you got the short end of the stick. He can't smell good."

It was a joke, but Amber took it seriously. "No, he smells *amazing*."

Taft pointed at his damp chest. "I'm right here, ladies. I can hear you."

"Thank you," said Amber.

He smiled at her. "Thank you for telling me."

"I have to go inside and die now."

"Please don't do that. I mean, go inside, but don't die."

The look Amber gave him was made of sparkling glitter and rainbow dust. "Okay. Okay!" She ran away, the saloon door banging behind her.

Lana's arms were still wrapped around her knees. A nightjar sang above her head. Her heart beat fast in her chest, flapping around like it was trying to get out.

She took a quick breath. "I'll write with you."

Taft's smile went from Nashville-big to Texas-ginormous. "Really?"

"Yeah."

"When?"

She looked at her phone. "In an hour? At seven? I really need a shower."

Taft looked down at the soggy spot on his T-shirt. "Me, too. Tears ain't enough to clean me up right now, though she made a good start. Meet you where?"

"Somewhere that's not here." She needed to get away, if only for an hour or two.

"My place. I bought a house, did I tell you?"

Shock lit her fingertips with electricity. "You *bought* one? I heard you talking about the old Adelaide place."

"Yeah, on the water. You know it?"

"Of course. But – I thought you'd just rented it or something." *A rental was temporary.*

"Nope! It's all mine."

Her breath felt tight in her lungs. "That was fast."

"Just took three weeks. Came furnished, major selling point."

Who closed a house so fast? Money talked, apparently. "So you're staying."

"Forever."

"*What?*"

For a moment, she thought she imagined a hurt look in the back of his gaze.

But he laughed. "I'm kidding. It's no big deal. Vacation house. That's all."

"Oh. Okay. I'll be there at seven."

"I'll get us something to eat. What do you like?"

She decided to tell him the truth. "I would *kill* for a big, homemade sandwich."

Taft nodded. "My specialty. Tomatoes and cheese and avocado and ham sound all right?"

"Sure."

"I'll make you the best one you ever had."

His eagerness was endearing.

His smile was contagious.

Lana should take it back, all of it. She'd go to bed early and read, after eating a plate of nachos from the Golden Spike Café. She'd see him in the morning, and tomorrow after work he'd ask if she wanted to get a drink with the crew. She'd say no. He'd ask if she wanted to write with him later. She'd say no again.

But Lana didn't take it back. She stood. "Meet you there."

"Great." He put his hands in his pockets and rocked a little. "That's great."

Maybe it was.

CHAPTER TWENTY-FIVE

L ana showered.

She picked up the pink razor and considered it, the cool water raining down on her.

No. Leg shaving was out of the question.

Lana was not going to have sex with him.

Then again, why not? It wasn't like they hadn't *already* had sex – well, kind of, anyway. She was a grown-ass adult, and so was he. He was kind. He was a hard worker.

No. Lana just wouldn't. She'd ignore the spark that jumped between them every time she glanced up to the roof to find his eyes on her. She'd deny the pull she felt toward whatever room he was hammering inside. She'd veto her own need to keep her fingers near his after he'd handed her whatever tool it was she was looking for.

It was simpler that way.

Simple was best, after all. That's what she was here for. Simplification. Like now, she wasn't going to drive the five minutes to the Adelaide place – she was going to take fifteen minutes to walk. She'd give herself that time to calm down her sudden nerves.

Lana nodded at the Homeless Petes as she passed them.

"Looking good, Darling!"

They cackled in joy. Lana resisted saying that the pun was so weak it almost wasn't one.

Lana hit the two-lane highway and headed north.

She didn't bargain on the dog.

Small and dirty grey, with a curled tail and floppy ears, it took up with her a quarter of a mile out of town.

"Hello."

The dog looked at her as if she'd been waiting for her.

"What's up?"

Lana looked around, but there was no one else out on the highway. It wasn't like it was a bad road to walk on – the shoulder was wide and the ocean views were phenomenal – but it wasn't a dog-walking area for townies. Cars went too fast and paid too little attention.

Cheerfully, the dog walked next to Lana, sticking at her ankle as if she'd been trained to heel.

She bent to look at it more closely. Burrs tangled in the dog's fur, and it had a long muddy streak on one side, as if it had fallen asleep in a puddle at one point. There was a cut on its back. "You going to let me touch you, dog?"

The dog stood still. It sniffed Lana's hand. Then it licked her, gently.

"Do you bite? Don't bite, okay?" Moving as slowly as she could, Lana lifted the dog, ready to drop it if it attacked. How did a person tell if an animal had rabies? It wasn't foaming at the mouth, so that was good.

The dog went limp in her arms, as if resting for the first time in years. It was a girl. A muddy, burr-filled, cut-up, mangy little dog. She couldn't weigh more than ten pounds, if that.

"You're a wreck, aren't you?"

A small dog like this wasn't going to last long out here on her own. Lana pulled out her cell and, one-handed, tried looking up the number for animal services.

No reception.

"Well, hell." Lana readjusted the dog in her arms, putting her carefully over her shoulder like a baby. The dog seemed to like it. She panted softly in Lana's ear. "I guess Taft is hosting two for dinner."

CHAPTER TWENTY-SIX

Taft finished the sandwiches just as the doorbell rang. He took a split second to admire his handiwork, then went to open the door.

"You have *got* to see how big and awesome I just made these sandwiches. Did you walk? I didn't hear a car. Holy crap, is that a *dog?*"

Lana marched past him, smelling like shampoo and something sweeter. "She needs water."

"Of course."

"And chicken. Do you have any chicken?"

Taft felt as if he'd spun in a circle although he'd been standing still. "I do, as a matter of fact, leftovers from dinner the other night. Will she mind peanut sauce?"

"No clue. Let's try."

Lana kneeled on the floor next to the bundle of skin and fur that was supposedly a dog as it drank from one of Taft's cereal bowls. "Do you think she looks sick?"

"Nah, she just looks lost."

She looked up at him. "How old do you think she is?"

Had she never had a dog? "You can get a good idea from the teeth, but I don't know her well enough to take those kinds of advantages."

"I do." Gently, Lana lifted the dog's wet lip. "They're white. But big."

"Maybe a year, then. Or two."

Lana had fire in her eyes. "Who would *do* that? Abandon a little thing like this?"

Taft kneeled next to her. The dog growled and her hackles went up. "Easy there, little one." He held out his hand. "Don't worry, dogs love me."

Well, it was usually true. Not this dog, though. It snapped at him, a vicious click of sharp white teeth closing so close to his fingers that he could feel the air they stirred. "*Damn.*"

"Careful!" Lana patted the dog's head.

"I was trying to pet her!"

"She's traumatized. She needs to eat and drink."

Taft stood. "Okay, then. So do we. By that I mean I'm starving. You want one of these?" He held up a plate. The sandwiches rose six inches high.

Lana nodded. She washed her hands at the kitchen faucet. "That looks amazing."

No, Lana was the one who looked amazing. Taft cleared his throat. "Come onto the porch. Let the dog work on the food. We'll leave the door open so she can see us. She can come out when she feels like it."

To his surprise, Lana followed his instructions. Her head kept turning to look at the little beast, but she sat next to him at the outside table.

He watched as Lana took a huge bite.

"Oh," she groaned around a mouthful. "Thish ish perfectch."

"Nothing like a good sandwich." The woman in front of him was the thing that was "perfectch," not her food. Her dark hair was as messy as the dog's, though with fewer burrs. It was still a little damp, as if she'd just towel-dried it before she left the hotel. She had no make-up on, and her cheeks were ruddy from the walk. Her black shirt was ripped at the shoulder, and her jeans (these were a tighter and darker blue than her work jeans) were a little too long for her, so all he could see of her cowboy boots were the toes. She looked like a street musician, someone who'd be busking for money outside Grand Central in New York, or on Powell Street in San Francisco.

His heart ached just looking at her.

Jesus, he had it bad.

Get it together, Hill.

She reached in her back pocket and pulled out a small red notebook. "Never leave home without it."

He took his father's mechanical pencil out of his pocket. "Okay. What are we writing?"

"It's your song, buddy. What do you want it to be?"

He sure as hell knew one thing – he didn't want it to be a song about a woman who called him "buddy." He clicked his pencil. "Love."

She sighed. "Boring."

"Love hasn't been boring in the history of humankind, and we're not going to be the ones who finally hit the end of its interestingness."

Lana craned her head to look in the house again. "I can't see her. You think she's okay?"

"She's fine." Damn, the food was good. "This really is a masterpiece. The secret is toasting the bread lightly first."

Lana wasn't listening. "I'm just going to check on her. I'll be right back."

Taft watched the water crash on the rocks below while she was inside. It was the most romantic spot in the world.

He took another bite of his lonely sandwich.

Lana was taking forever in there.

"Where are your towels?" she yelled at one point.

"Closet in the hall! You need help?"

"No! Enjoy the view!"

There was only one view he'd really enjoy right now, and she was inside, doing something with a mangy mutt who hated him.

Ten minutes later, she poked her head out. "We're almost done. Do you happen to have a hair dryer?"

"What? No. I don't think so." In Nashville he did, of course. If a woman stayed over, she expected to be able to dry her hair in the morning. Here, it was just him.

Lana's hair didn't look like she spent a lot of time on it.

"Never mind. That's a really good sandwich. I *swear* I'll be out to finish it in a minute." She disappeared again.

Long minutes later, the sun had almost set. Taft was considering the second half of her sandwich when Lana came back outside.

"Look!" Lana held up a different dog.

This one was fluffy and golden-white. The burrs had been clipped out. Her feet, which had been black, were now blonde. Taft could swear the dog was smiling in her arms, and who could blame the critter? "What did you do with the horrifying animal you came in with?"

Lana stroked the dog's head. "I used the purple bottle of shampoo in your master bath. And your beard trimmer. Sorry about that. There's some clean-up in there I still need to do, but I wanted to show you first." She reached for her sandwich. "I'm dying to finish this."

"Are you keeping her?"

"No!"

But Lana's fingers stroked the dog's ears, which looked silky soft now. Not that Taft was going to try to find out. Just meeting the dog's eyes had earned him a low growl. "Mmm-hmmm."

"No way. I don't have a place for a dog."

"Why not? Hotel rules?"

"Nah, I'm always on the ..." She broke off.

Taft finished the sentence for her. "On the road. Didn't you say you'd retired from that?"

"Still."

"Seems like a perfect time to get a dog. Even if said dog hates men."

Lana gave him a dazzling smile. "She doesn't hate men. At least, we don't know that for sure yet. We only know she hates you."

"Wouldn't be the first girl."

"Oh, I doubt that."

"You shouldn't."

She looked honestly perplexed. "Who could hate you? That's like hating ice cream or ponies."

"Oof. That's how you think of me?"

"Of course." But she bit her bottom lip and didn't meet his eyes.

"I'm mean and cold and bitter."

Lana pointed the dog's foot at him. "And this is a Great Dane."

"I'm just worried you have a guard dog now. Her job seems to be keeping me away from you."

Lana seemed delighted by the idea. "Really?"

He could prove it. Taft touched Lana's elbow. The dog made a rumble in the back of her throat.

"That? That's practically a purr." Lana offered the dog a small piece of ham, which it took, of course.

"She's looking at me like she wants to eat my face."

"Only if you're made of ham." Lana wasn't pulling away from his touch. In fact, she'd leaned against him a little.

Carefully, Taft slid his hand up her arm to her shoulder. Her skin was warm through the thin fabric, and his heartbeat sped up.

The dog's rumble became a growl. Taft jerked back his hand. "I want to keep all my fingers, thanks."

Lana laughed. "I wonder what she'd do if you tried to kiss me."

CHAPTER TWENTY-SEVEN

The words tumbled out of Lana's mouth before she could stop them. She pulled in a breath and held it.

Taft's eyes darkened in a way that made Lana's insides feel like Louisiana swampland, all heat and steam. "I've been wondering that, too."

Maybe you should try. She didn't say it. She wouldn't.

He heard her anyway. He shrugged. "Her teeth look sharp, but they're small. Probably won't need stitches." He reached forward to put his hand behind her head.

Lana registered the dog's growl and felt the rumble on her lap. But when Taft kissed her, she forgot to worry.

Heat rose between them. A solid wall of flame rushed over them, and every nerve in her body lit with electricity. His mouth was firm, his lips demanding. He smelled like soap and when she put her fingers into his hair, she found it still damp.

He drew her closer, and she didn't mind giving him what he wanted – her mouth was his to plunder, completely. The bottom of her stomach plunged and she felt herself getting wet.

The dog was pressed between them. Her growls became louder.

It didn't matter. All Lana wanted to do was to keep kissing Taft, to keep her mouth on his, to keep feeling him take her mouth in the same way she wanted him to take her body, and –

"Jesus!" Taft pulled back sharply.

"Did she bite you?" Lana looked at the dog on her lap. "Did you *bite* him?"

"She started to. I pulled my arm away in time, but I felt her teeth brush my skin."

"She wouldn't really bite you." Lana's breath was short, and she felt as flushed as Taft looked. The man was made of sex, wasn't he? He was just a tall piece of sex walking around, all broad chest and rugged jaw and eyes that a girl could lose herself in. It was amazing that he didn't have women trailing behind him, grabbing at his ankles as he moved through the world. How did he function in life, being that devastatingly hot?

"You have no idea whether she'd bite me or not."

Lana grinned. The inside of her mouth tasted like him. Delicious. "I have no clue."

Taft folded his arms across his chest. She could see that chest in her mind's eye, shirtless, the way it had been when he'd been working on the roof of room six earlier in the day. Her palms grew damp.

"*Both* you girls are biters. You have a guard dog."

Lana snorted. "I totally do."

"Congratulations. You must be so happy."

Happy? Her emotions were in a tangle. More than anything, she was turned on – more than anything, she wanted to kiss him again, deeper and harder and longer.

But yeah. She was a little happy. This tiny animal wanted to protect her.

That was kind of nice.

"Bad girl," she said to the dog. Her heart wasn't in it.

"You're sunk."

"I might be."

"You're in love."

It was a bolt of light, sent into her midsection. It was three parts fear and one part joy. "*What?*"

He pointed at her lap. "That mongrel seems to feel the same way."

Obviously, that's what he'd meant. "Maybe so."

"Sometimes love strikes fast. At first sight, right?"

Was he still talking about the dog? "Sometimes. It happened to my mom and dad."

Taft ate a piece of bread crust. "Was it real?"

"Yeah." Lana stroked the dog's head and remembered the look her mother had sometimes sent her father over the dining-room table. It had been a private look, one that Lana had never understood, not until she'd grown up. By then it had been too late to ask either of her parents what it had felt like. "It was. What about your parents?"

Taft looked at her. "I can't think about them. I was just kissing you."

He had been. Kissing the hell out of her, to be precise. Lana's stomach flipped. "Yeah."

"Gotta get my bearings back." He rubbed his face. "My parents. No. They weren't like that."

"They looked so happy in photos."

"My dad loved the hell out of her. He was happy."

"Not your mom?"

"Davina doesn't really do happy, I don't think."

Lana shook her head. "The day you were born?"

"Her two epidurals failed and labor lasted forty hours. I've never heard the end of it."

"I'm sorry. She's still alive?"

"Yep. She can be charming as hell—that's how she gets people to fall for her. Afterward, she goes back to being miserable. She's that way now, miserable with her second husband. Maybe even more miserable than she was with my dad."

Sometimes Lana had felt cut off from her mother, like they didn't really understand each other, but she'd always felt loved. "That sucks."

"Yeah." Taft ran his hands through his hair. "Honestly, Birdie, I'm too overheated to talk about my mother anymore."

Lana understood. She was having a hard time remembering to breathe, herself. "We should write."

"God. Writing. Yeah."

She pointed at her notebook on the table. "What are we writing about?"

"Not mothers."

"Not family in general," said Lana.

"Home towns?"

"No." Maybe someday she'd write about Darling Bay, but that day wasn't this one.

"The dog." Taft reached out a finger, and the dog snarled. "You can't keep that thing."

Lana pulled the dog's ear. "Oh, *now* I can't keep her."

"Yeah, I thought she was cute. But she's a terror." Taft's eyes softened again.

It shouldn't be legal for a man to have eyes that were so expressive.

Lana's insides melted.

He said, "Now you're in her thrall."

"And she's in mine."

"What are you going to name her?"

"I don't know." Lana looked into the dog's teddy-bear-like face. Her nose looked like a button, and her dark eyes shone bright. "She was a loner out there. She should have a loner's name."

"Ranger."

Lana shook her head. "Cliché. Plus, not very girly."

"Emily."

"Why?"

Taft nodded. "Emily Dickinson. She hid in her house and growled at anyone who came by."

"She did hide in her house, but ..."

"I'm pretty sure she was known for biting other poets."

Joy bubbled up in her chest. "I think I heard that. She was a vampire, right?"

Taft nodded. "Not many people knew."

"It explains so much. How does a guy like you know about poetry?"

"Not as dumb as I look, huh? English. High school. I loved the poetry sections. I thought she would have made a good songwriter, actually." Taft put out his hand again, much slower this time. Incrementally, he got closer to the dog without looking at her.

He kept his eyes on Lana's. Her heart rate galloped. "Be careful," she said.

"I know how to treat a girl who's scared."

Boom.

The *thunk* of his words juddered in her chest.

She was a wounded, growling dog to Taft? Who exactly was he hoping to touch with that slow hand?

She stood, Emily Dickinson held tightly to her chest. "I should go."

"Lana —"

"We can write another night. I just realized how tired I am."

"I'm sorry. I didn't mean anything by it."

Yes, he had. He was good at it, at getting damaged women to give up their secrets, to tell him their pain. His newest hit song (her song!) was making him even better at it.

Lana didn't want to be just another girl.

She wasn't going to fall for it. She wasn't going to fall for *him*.

"I'll see you in the morning." She turned and walked through the house, ignoring the fact that Taft stayed at her heels.

"Let me drive you."

"No, thanks."

"It's dark now. Being on the highway has to be dangerous."

She paused. It was true. Pedestrians had been hit out there. Years ago, one had died. "Fine."

The short ride to town was quiet. Lana was furious at herself, but she didn't quite know why. She couldn't be mad at him – he hadn't done anything wrong.

She *wanted* to be angry with him, though. It would make everything so much easier.

When they pulled up, Lana jumped out, the dog still in her arms. "Thanks." She shut the door before he could speak. She hurried up the walkway through the garden. Emily Dickinson peed under a trellis. Then they both went into the hotel room.

Taft hadn't followed her.

Good. She and Emily Dickinson just needed to be alone for a bit. A good night's sleep. "We're fine just the way we are, aren't we?" Emily Dickinson pushed her small head into Lana's hand and gave her a deep look Lana couldn't quite decipher. Then the dog jumped up onto the small sofa under the window and curled up, as if she'd slept there a million times before. The dog skipped light sleep and went right into snoring, almost immediately. The poor thing must have been exhausted.

It was hard to run all the time.

Twenty minutes later, after she'd washed her face and brushed her teeth (getting rid of the perfect taste of him), there was a soft knock at the door. Emily Dickinson didn't stir.

Please let it be Molly with a late milkshake. Or Adele with a criticism about the way Lana was fixing something.

Anyone but Taft.

Please let it be Taft, said her traitorous heart.

She opened the door.

Taft held up her notebook. "You forgot this."

She stepped onto the porch and pulled the door shut behind her, before Emily Dickinson woke up and went after him. "Thanks."

"And," Taft's gaze was smoky, "you forgot this."

He cupped her face and kissed her.

The kiss was mutual, damn it, and it was *searing*. It went from hot to molten lava in less than ten seconds. Lana lost the ability to breathe, but it didn't matter – his mouth would keep her alive. His tongue found hers, and he tasted like peppermint and sin.

He pulled her against the length of his body, and she felt how hard he was. He made a sound in her ear that was pitched low, full of need and lust. Just like she was.

Lana wanted him.

Goddamn it, there was nothing wrong with that.

"Hey," she said against his mouth. "Move."

He kissed her harder in response but kept up with her as she walked backward. Luckily, she knew every broken board and warped piece of wood between them and room five. Since they'd patched the roof, it was the room closest to being habitable now. In a freak rainstorm the week before, the crew had eaten lunch together inside, seated on blankets Lana had found in the laundry room.

The blankets were still on the floor.

They'd make a fine place to get naked.

CHAPTER TWENTY-EIGHT

"Wait." Taft wanted to make goddamn sure he got this right. This was too important to screw up. This was *Lana*. Everything in his body wanted her, but his mind screamed at him (a lonely sound, coming from miles away) not to scare her. Again.

"No." Lana bit Taft's lower lip. "Don't want to wait."

"I want this to be right."

"Oh, it's right." She nuzzled under his neck, her lips nibbling until he thought he might die from the electricity of it.

He grabbed her by her belt buckle, pulling her farther into the room. He turned with her in his arms and kicked the door closed. Her mouth was greedy and her hands were more so. She'd unbuckled his jeans without his noticing, but he sure as hell was noticing the way her palm slipped into the front of his briefs. She wrapped her fingers around him, and he groaned low in his throat.

"You're trying to kill me."

"Yes."

Though it hurt every cell of Taft's body to slow her down, he tugged her forearm so that she let go of his cock. "You first. Take off your clothes."

Lana grinned and ripped her shirt over her head. Low light filtered past the ancient curtains from the garden lights. She stood in front of him in her black bra. No lace, not for Lana. She wore a good old plain cotton bra, and she looked like a goddess in it, her breasts high and firm. Taft had spent a lot of time remembering what she'd looked like with fewer clothes on, but he'd gotten it wrong. She looked even better.

She undid her belt buckle and then her fly. A heartbeat later, she'd stripped off her boots and jeans and stood there in her matching black bra and cotton panties.

Taft decided he didn't need to breathe. It was overrated anyway. "You're incredible."

"Come on." She pulled at his shirt. "Hurry up."

No. Damn it, he'd scared her last time. They'd gone too fast and it had gone bad. That had been his fault. He wasn't going to let it happen again. He stripped off his shirt, with her help. "Tell me what you need."

She frowned. "Too much talking already. Less talk. More naked."

Taft lifted her hands away from his fly and held them still. "Your guard dog's asleep in the other room. I'm the only protection you have right now, and I want to make sure I get it right."

Lana narrowed her eyes in what looked like honest anger. "Seriously, Hill. Snap out of it. I want you to fuck me."

The words were an explosion in his head, in his body, a blast that would normally set off a chain reaction leading to sex – hard, fast, fulfilling every need.

But Lana was important. So very much so.

"Tell me what not to do."

She crossed her arms over her breasts. "Talk."

"I blew it somehow last time, and I'm not doing it again. You were hurt in the past. I know that."

"You know nothing." She changed it up on him, pressing herself against his body. "I'm fine. I'm strong. And I'm really, really wet." She took his hand and dipped it into her panties. Yeah, well, fuck. She *was* wet.

He was at his absolute limit. *"You're not to blame for what went wrong."*

Tears filled her eyes, and he almost regretted quoting their song.

Almost but not quite.

She stepped back, leaving coldness where there had been heat.

"Not fair."

Trusting his gut, he said it again. "You're not to blame for what went wrong."

"I *know* that," she said. She wrapped her arms around her stomach and sat on the blanket. He followed her down, keeping one hand on her bare knee.

"I'm here."

"Whatever." She bit her lip and looked away from him. "I'm fine."

But she was shivering – he could feel the small tremors rocking her, and it was more than just lust. "I don't think you are."

"This is bullshit."

"You're angry."

"Damn straight I am." She glared at him.

"Not with me."

"Like hell."

CHAPTER TWENTY-NINE

This was a nightmare. Taft Hill, shirtless, jeans open, sitting on the floor, being kind to her.

Feeling *sorry* for her. Quoting her own song to her!

She needed to pull her clothes on. Or screw it. As soon as she got the strength back in her legs, she'd just streak to her room in her underwear. The chances that anyone saw her were next to none, and she didn't give a crap anyway.

"Want to tell me about it?" He paused. "You don't have to. It's totally your choice."

She did *not* want to tell him.

Lana took a breath. She would just ignore the fact that his eyes were soft, that his body language was open, that he looked like he was listening with every fiber of his being.

She still wouldn't tell him.

Lana met his gaze, hoping to scowl him out of the room.

Instead, he just looked at her. As if she was someone important.

As if he had all the time in the world.

As if he was content to just be here with her.

"I was sexually assaulted." The words were acid in her mouth, sour and painful.

Taft nodded, as if it didn't surprise him. He kept his gaze on her, as if she didn't disgust him.

"I was drunk."

His voice was soft. "It wasn't your fault."

"Yeah." Lana gave a laugh she didn't feel. "That's what the song's about, obviously. But it didn't work."

"What do you mean?"

"I wrote it because I was trying to talk myself into believing it, that it wasn't my fault, that it was his."

"Why do you think it didn't work?"

Frustration filled her like too much air in a balloon. Soon she'd pop and it would be like she was never here at all. "I get it. I'm not stupid. I've read about victim psychology. I know what my brain is doing. I'm trying to reframe the situation in a way that makes me less culpable, but it's just not the truth."

"So what is true?"

Her hands shook so much she tucked them under her armpits. "I'd had a shitty day. Maybe the worst day ever."

"How so?"

"My dad died. We were in New York, getting ready to go on tour, and he went down during sound check. You might have heard about it. It was big news back then."

He nodded.

"Adele made us go on stage anyway. The show must go on and all that crap. I took something, I don't even remember what, but I blacked out on stage. That night, after they bandaged me up, we had a huge fight. All three of us. I said some awful things and so did Adele. I left the hotel and found a dive just off Times Square. I got drunk as hell and when I woke up, I was having sex in an alley. The guy said I'd asked for it, that I'd begged him for it." Lana's voice broke and she hated herself for it, for showing weakness in front of him.

Taft just nodded. He was so goddamn good at listening. It wasn't fair.

"I just kind of believed him. I tried to say no, but it was pretty much too late. If he said I wanted it, I probably had. It messed me up pretty badly. I didn't recover for years."

The implicit lie – that she'd recovered – hung in the air between them.

Taft's voice was steady. "It shouldn't have happened to you. I'm so sorry it did. You didn't deserve that."

That was the whole point, though. Lana knew she hadn't deserved it on a global level. All human beings deserved to be treated well, with compassion and care. But she *had* gone into the bar with an attitude and the intention to get fucked up. She'd told a man she'd wanted it (she was sure she'd done that). If anyone deserved to be sexually assaulted, it was her. "Yeah, I know."

Taft moved slowly. He took her hand in his. He didn't try to touch any other part of her. He just held her hand and looked at her. His dark-blue eyes were the color of wet beach glass. "Do you? Really?"

"Of course." Lana felt sick. She didn't know a damn thing.

"You didn't deserve that. It wasn't fair."

"Can we just –"

"Did you report the rape?"

It was like he'd dumped her into a bucket of ice-water. "Not *rape*. I just told you. Assault. I put myself there. He was rough." She choked. "I'm sure it was true I'd asked him for it. I just don't remember doing it."

"Were you drunk?"

"So drunk." And high. And in the worst grief spiral she'd ever been in. She'd lost her father *and* her sisters.

"It was rape."

Lana laughed. The sound rattled – brittle – in her throat. "That would mean lots of women are raped."

"True. Seriously, Lana. Listen to me. If you can't give consent, it's rape. People who are mentally altered by substances can't give consent. They are literally considered unable to do so, even if they think they can."

The muscles in her neck went rigid. "Really?"

"Think about college girls. You think when they drink so much they can't remember what happened the next morning that they gave consent? They might have had their eyes open, they might have been speaking and even saying yes, but when they see themselves later on tape having sex with guys they don't remember meeting, that's rape. They *teach* that now. I've been part of the frat awareness meetings in Nashville. We're training guys to know that if a girl says she wants to have sex with them but she's blasted out of her mind, it's legally considered rape if they go ahead with it."

The inside of Lana's head felt hollow, as if everything she'd ever known had been lifted right out, leaving her with only a few words.

Those words filled her mouth, sitting like rocks on her tongue. "I was raped."

Taft squeezed her fingers. "I'm so sorry that happened to you. You didn't deserve it."

"I really thought I ..."

"Deserved it. You didn't."

Something light filled the top of her head, something light and warm. It flowed through her, honey sweet and thick. "Oh, God."

"Take your time with it."

Lana touched her lips. "This shouldn't make me happy. Why is this making me happy?"

"Maybe because you finally have the right name for it. When you call it an assault that could have been avoided, you blame yourself. When you call it rape, it makes it more black and white. You know *he* was to blame. Not you. Never you." Taft held her hand loosely but his skin was so warm. "Maybe that's why you wrote the song."

"Because I already knew it?"

Taft shrugged. "Don't know about you, but half the time I write a song, it's because I don't understand what I'm talking about until I do."

"Taft."

"I'm right here."

He was. He really, really was. Lana had never felt so seen. It wasn't because she was still stripped down to her underwear. It was because he'd named the demon she'd been carting around with her for so long.

She had a name for it.

By naming it, maybe she'd *finally* get to the point of letting it go. Someday.

"Taft," she said again. Would that be weird? If she just kept saying his name from now until forever? No other words seemed necessary.

He just smiled at her. Softly.

Okay, she could think of a few more words. "Kiss me."

The muscle at the side of his jaw jumped. "Are you sure?"

"Kiss me."

"This is pretty heavy. I want to make certain –"

Lana slid forward on the blanket and crawled into his lap. She wrapped her arms around his neck and her legs around his waist. "I'm not sure about anything right now except that I would really, really love for you to kiss me.

I'm not drunk. I'm not high. I'm perfectly sober, and I'm pretty freaked out. I want you to –"

Taft waited. She could feel his muscles straining. He wanted her, too, but he was restraining himself, pulling himself back like he was reining in a horse that just wanted to gallop.

She found the words, the right ones. She didn't want him to fuck her. She didn't want to have sex with him, or to sleep with him. She wanted something else, she wanted different words, more words she'd never said out loud. "I want you to make love to me."

Taft dropped the invisible reins.

His mouth was on hers, his arms all the way around her, pulling her hard against him. Lana braided her fingers into his hair. He growled – a low, sexy sound that made her need him even more – and lay back, taking her with him so she was on top. God, he was hard. For some terrible reason, he was still in his jeans.

Lana wriggled and pulled at his fly. "Off. Off, please take these off."

Taft smoothly deposited her to the side. He shucked his jeans and pointed at her bra. "What about this?"

"Gone," she pronounced. She sent it winging across the room, slingshot-style. It landed on her own toolbox. She raised both arms. "Three points!"

Taft laughed, and the sound went to her head, making her dizzy. She shimmied out of her panties, kicking them to the side. She slipped her fingers into the top of his boxers, and he grinned at her as she drew them down.

"Fun," she said in honest surprise. "This is *fun*."

"It's supposed to be, Birdie."

"What if – what if I get scared again?"

"Then we slow down. Or we stop entirely. You make the call, at any point." He rolled her with him so she was underneath his body. "You understand me? There's no too-late-to-stop. At any point."

"Please," she said. "Don't stop."

Then somehow he had a condom in his hands, and she helped him roll it onto his shaft. He laughed as it made a funny *snap*, and she laughed, too.

It didn't make the moment less hot.

In fact, the laughter made it better.

His mouth moved from her mouth to her neck. He kissed his way up to her ear. He held himself over her, and she could feel his back muscles tremble.

"I need you," said Taft. His eyes were so dark they looked black. "That doesn't mean you have to keep saying yes."

"Yes," she said. "Yes, yes, yes, *yes*." For the first time in her entire goddamn adult life, Lana felt perfectly safe. She tilted her hips. His cock pressed against her. With one long thrust of his hips, he was all the way inside her.

"You," Taft said.

"You," she agreed.

Then they didn't talk. He moved in her, with her. When his eyes weren't locked on hers, it was because he was using his mouth to kiss her neck, to bite her shoulder. She cupped her hands around his buttocks to draw him deeper inside. He hit the very back of her, so deep inside her it almost hurt, but it was a good pain, an ache that only more of him would soothe.

Lana matched his rhythm, moving her hands to his waist. Sweat slicked their bodies together. He kissed her again, and she tasted salt and need and something deeper, something she hadn't even dared hope for.

How had she lived without this for so long?

As if he'd heard her – had she spoken out loud? – he whispered into her ear, "How did I live without you?"

I don't know. I don't know.

Their pace increased, their breathing quickened. Lana lost track of where her body ended and his began – all she knew was that this was perfect, this was what she'd been waiting for, possibly for her whole life. She curled her tailbone, grinding herself against him, her clit perfectly aligned with his pelvis. Short strokes now, so fast and so hard, and then she was coming so powerfully she saw bright white against the dark of her closed lids. He shouted in her ear, just a noise that had no words, no beginning and no ending, they were just together in their fall, and it took forever and it was over in a second and she didn't want to do anything else, ever.

Holy. Hell.

They panted.

Taft shifted so his full weight wasn't on her – a tragedy, really – and put his bicep under her neck.

He was the perfect pillow.

They panted some more.

He smiled at her. Lana grinned back. She laughed, but she didn't know why. It didn't matter. Time was gone, nonexistent. They could stay like this always, and they should.

For a very long time, for what felt like years, Lana considered her sex life up to this moment.

It had been fine, she thought. She was always in charge, and she'd liked it that way.

She hadn't been in charge of a single damn thing for those last few minutes, and she didn't think he had been, either.

"We flew together," Taft said against her brow.

"That's it. Exactly."

"Lana."

She wriggled to her side so she was pressed face to face, chest to chest, against his body.

"Are you cold?"

"No," she said. She could never be cold again.

"Are you okay?"

"I'm perfect."

"True," he said.

They slept a little, or at least Lana did. She drifted in and out, startled each time she awoke to find the warmth next to her was *him*. Each time she was relieved to find the same.

Thrilled, in fact.

She touched his stubbled jaw just because she could. "We should write a song."

Taft yawned. "I was thinking about sleeping some more."

"On the floor? Here?"

He tightened his arms around her. "Anywhere. Anywhere with you."

"I'm serious. I have a tune in my head." It had come to her as they'd drifted back down to earth.

"Hum it to me."

She did, her lips against his ear, her voice as soft as she could make it.

He kissed her and then hummed it back.

"Yes!" Delight felt bright yellow, like morning sunshine, even as the moon shone in through the old, warped glass. "That's it!"

"What's it about?" He kissed the tip of her nose.

Love, she wanted to say but couldn't.

He nodded. "Love. Of course it's about love."

Was he scared of anything at all?

She pulled in a breath. "Yeah. Maybe it could be a love song."

CHAPTER THIRTY

When her mouth shaped the word *love,* Taft fell all the way into the well of it.

He hadn't expected it to be a well. If anything, he would have thought that love was an ocean, or a lake, something a lot damn wider than a well. But he was at the bottom of it and he realized he didn't want to be anywhere else, which was lucky because there seemed to be no way out.

He sang, *"I'm at the bottom of the well, waiting for you to fall with me."*

"That doesn't seem very romantic."

"What if the lover in our story has always wanted to be in one?"

Lana ran her fingers over his chest, lightly, raising goosebumps. How did he get so lucky to be the man with her at this moment? Speaking of not deserving things.

"No. If she falls in, too, then they both die."

He kissed her shoulder. "What a way to go."

"What about a tree?"

"Do you feel like you're in a tree right now?"

"You're the branches and the trunk." Lana laughed.

It felt like winning the lottery. "Exactly."

She stretched and yawned. Then she curled herself back against him. She couldn't be comfortable – God knew he wasn't. The floor was hard beneath the scratchy blanket.

He didn't give one good goddamn. He could live here even longer than he could in a well.

"Okay," he said. "Song. We're writing. Post-coitally, might I point out."

She gave a small purr. "The best way to write."

He felt a thud of something leaden land in his stomach. "You've written this way before?"

"Never."

Brightness replaced the lead. "Okay. Let's pick our metaphor for our love song." *Our love song.* It was theirs.

"No birds. It's always birds in my family."

"No birds for Birdie. But honestly, didn't that feel like flying?"

Lana smiled at him, a bright, beaming grin. He could touch the moon if the glass in the window wasn't in the way.

"A plane," she said.

"A paper airplane." That was it. "A two-seater."

"Who's the pilot?" She propped her head on her fist.

"Copilots."

"That's dumb."

"Me, then."

"You fly the plane till you get tired."

"Then you take over."

Lana gave a soft sigh and rested her chin on the inner curve of his elbow. "That sounds nice. Planes are made for flying. People aren't, though."

Taft sang to the tune she'd given him, "*I was made for falling.*"

She responded, "*Made to fall for you.*"

They looked at each other. Taft's heart was stuck somewhere in the vicinity of his throat. Had he ever wanted to simultaneously kiss, cuddle and make love to a woman at the same time that he wanted to just look at her *and* hear all her secrets? He felt like he was running out of time, and maybe he was. Maybe she'd stand up and the spell would be broken. He had to cement this moment. Nail it down so there was proof.

"We have to write it down. Before we forget."

She pointed. "My notebook's over there."

"Not good enough. Something more permanent." Loath as he was to move, this was important. He rolled away and reached for his jeans. He held up his silver pencil. "This was my father's."

Lana touched it gently. "It's beautiful."

"Wahl Eversharp. Nineteen twenty-four. My dad wrote all his songs with it."

"And now you write yours with the same pencil?"

"I guess. *When* I write, which isn't often."

"That's a nice legacy for him to leave you."

"You have no idea."

He meant it as a throwaway comment, but she asked, "What do you mean?"

He wouldn't mind her knowing, he supposed.

No, he *wanted* her to know. "This was all he left me."

Lana was silent for a moment. She carefully took the pencil from his hands and advanced the lead. "Just this? Out of everything he had?"

"He asked me one day how he should split up his estate. I know my mother. She would need every dime he had – she always did. And me, I had the writing chops, inherited from him. I was already making more money than I could hope to spend, I knew I wouldn't need any of his. I told him I didn't want anything. He held up this pencil, said it should go to the Smithsonian, all the songs he'd written with it. But he wanted to give it to me."

I don't need your damn pencil. I do just fine writing with a pen. Or on my phone.

Palmer had said, *The right tool is important, son.*

Taft had knocked the side of his head with his finger. *Got the right tool, up here.*

Did I ever tell you you're the best thing that ever happened to me? Palmer had always said it.

Taft had loved hearing it, every time. "So that's what he left me."

Lana stared. "Just a pencil. Your mother must have been horrified."

"Oh, God, no. She was thrilled." Taft stood and gently took the pencil out of Lana's fingers.

"We're painting this room on Monday, right?" It was well after midnight. "Got a couple of days, then, right?" He tapped the drywall. "I'm thinking right here."

He wrote in large dark letters.

I was made for falling,
Made to fall for you,

She laughed and clapped her hands. "Oh, my God."

He grinned at her. "Right?"

"Perfect."

Under the paint, the penciled words would always be there, for as long as the wall stood. Now that the roof was sound, the insulation new and the drywall fresh, it would stand a long, long time.

A lifetime.

"Let's finish this song," he said.

Lana covered her mouth. Her eyes danced. "But the guys. And Socal."

"They won't see it. We'll write it, we'll take a picture, and then we'll put on the first coat later this weekend. Just as long as we cover it by Monday."

She grinned. "Yes. Yes, yes, yes."

It took an hour to get the verses right. Another forty-five minutes to write the song in its entirety on the wall.

Lana stepped forward to take pictures of the words with her cell phone, still gloriously naked and seemingly not shy about it. She wrapped her arm around his neck and kissed him. When she pulled away, she said, "I have no idea what we're doing."

Taft knew she wasn't talking about the song or the wall. Truth was, he didn't know what they were doing, either.

All he knew was that she was the most gorgeous woman he'd ever laid eyes on and that she was who he wanted to be with for the rest of his life.

Damn it, he wasn't worthy of her.

Not the way he was now, a successful country singer standing on a bedrock made of lies.

But he'd *get* worthy.

CHAPTER THIRTY-ONE

Lana woke up in her own bed in room one, alone. By the morning light coming through the curtains, it was after seven and before nine.

Next to her, something wiggled.

The dog. With a jolt, it all came back to her – not in flashes, but all of a long piece, like a movie trailer set to fast forward. Finding Emily Dickinson, going to his place, the sandwich, how she'd fled, how he'd followed her, making love with him, writing a song.

Her realization about what had happened back then.

Emily Dickinson burrowed her cold nose into Lana's neck. "Hey, now."

Taft was gone. Where, she had no idea. Honestly, she couldn't tell if she was pleased or disappointed. She was both, in equal measure, perhaps. No wonder it felt so confusing.

I am the type of woman who makes actual love with a man.

She rubbed her eyes. They couldn't have slept more than a few hours, four at most.

Lana felt amazing. She felt *free*.

He'd listened to her talk about the worst thing she'd ever done, and he'd named it.

It wasn't her fault.

The idea was so huge that it was terrifying.

Almost as terrifying as the way she was feeling about the man himself. Were the two things linked? That she'd confided in him, that she'd *trusted* him?

There was a knock at the door, and Emily Dickinson barked so sharply Lana's ears rang.

"It's me," called Taft.

Confused as to what to reach for first – her robe or her bra – Lana turned in a small circle. The barking Emily Dickinson did the same.

"Coming!" Okay, bra *and* robe.

A few scrambled seconds later, she pulled open the door. "Hey." She felt her cheeks color and stepped backward to let him in.

"Breakfast!"

"Mmmm."

"Most important of all, coffee." He handed her a cup, and found when she tasted it that he'd made it just right – light cream with a little sugar.

Suspicious.

She poked at the Golden Café takeaway plastic bag. "What's in there?"

He smiled. "Full eggs Benedict with scrambled eggs instead of poached. Side of home fries." He obviously hadn't been to his house yet – he was wearing the same clothes as last night, and his stubble was thick. He smelled like coffee and toothpaste.

"Molly," she said.

"Good guess."

"Not too much of a stretch. There aren't many people in the world who know my favorite breakfast."

"Now there's one more." He put the bag on the bed and reached to kiss her.

"Whoa." She covered her mouth. "I need to brush my teeth." What she needed was another chance to breathe.

"I don't care."

But she did. "Go sit on the porch? Take the breakfast. I'll join you out there in a minute."

He frowned but said, "Sure."

In the bathroom, Lana leaned on the sink and gazed at her feet. She took a deep breath. Finally, she looked in the mirror.

She looked the same. Overall, that was. Her lips might be a little swollen, and she had heavy circles under her eyes, but the overall effect was the same: girl with messy hair and no clue what to do next.

She didn't look guilty.

Maybe she really wasn't the one to blame.

At her feet, Emily Dickinson whined.

"You need to go out. Okay." Lana threw on an old red dress and pulled on black cowboy boots. Once upon a time they had been her best clothes. Now both the dress and the boots were so thin she wouldn't have worn them on stage. But they felt good, like her own skin.

She needed that light coat of armor now.

Outside, Taft sat on the porch swing, his coffee in hand. "Morning, Birdie."

The way his low voice rumbled those words – Lana discovered it was possible to get turned on just by sound.

Or maybe that was the effect of his gaze, too.

Whatever it was, it felt good and completely disconcerting.

"I'm not sure how to feel about you this morning," she said, surprising herself with her own honesty.

"How do you want to feel about me?"

"Honestly?"

"Yeah." His gaze was steady.

"I want to run."

"Where?"

"Away. Out of town. Far away by nightfall." She could make it to Portland, maybe farther. (But she'd always run. That was why she'd been lonely for the past twelve years.)

"How about just sitting for a little bit?"

She sat on the porch swing next to him. It gave a happy creak but it held. Taft swung it gently and handed her back her coffee. "All right."

"What's with your tattoo?" He pointed at her inner wrist.

"Oh." Lana pressed her thumb into it. "When I was a kid, I chewed on things. Everything."

Taft touched the side of his neck, and she felt her face color again.

"Yeah, I guess I still do. This is a marker from the game *Sorry!*. Remember that game?"

"Kind of?" He touched her skin lightly, and the ink suddenly burned. "What does it mean to you?"

Sorry for all the things I've never said sorry for. Sorry for running. Sorry for staying away. Sorry for not being a better sister.

"Just a reminder."

Emily Dickinson gave a bark from the garden and raced to Lana's side. She had a tennis ball in her mouth.

"She's a ball dog?"

Relieved to have the reprieve, Lana threw it. "I don't know."

Emily Dickinson chased it, skidding off the top step and tumbling down the next three. She brought the ball back up the steps. She growled and shook it like it was a small animal so hard it flew from her mouth and back into the garden. She gave chase again.

"Now that," Taft pointed, "is a good dog. Throws and fetches her own ball."

"You didn't think that last night."

"Because she didn't want to let me near you."

It had been hilarious, to Lana at least. They'd made their way to Lana's bed just after three in the morning to find Emily Dickinson sleeping right in the middle of it, as if she'd always been there. The small dog had yipped and snapped at Taft every time he got close to Lana. All three of them had slept in the bed, with Lana in the middle. When Taft had slipped his arm around Lana's waist, Emily Dickinson had growled low in her throat.

"At least she didn't bite you," said Lana.

"She's getting used to me. Might even like me! Watch." Taft stuck out his hand for Emily Dickinson to sniff as she raced back up on the porch. Emily Dickinson dropped the ball and started barking like she might never stop.

"Damn it. She *hates* me."

Who could hate you? Lana took a sip of her coffee.

"Oh, well. Hey, let's eat," said Taft. "We burned a lot of calories last night." His grin was frank and happy.

"About that."

He turned so he was facing her. "Yeah?"

Lana realized she had no idea what she'd been meaning to say. "I – never mind."

"You can tell me anything."

"Um ..."

Taft leaned over the plate of food and kissed her. His lips were soft, but the kiss was hard. Direct. The feel of him brought back every moment of the night before.

Lana placed her hand on his cheek and marveled at the stubborn sharpness of his stubble. "That was the best sex I've ever had."

"Me, too."

"You *were* also the worst sex I'd ever had. Maybe that's why I'm so surprised."

Taft shook his head. "I'm not surprised."

"You knew that was in us?"

"I knew it was in you." He cleared his throat. "Lana, I've been head-over-heels since that night in Nash–"

"Whoa." Lana held up her hand, feeling something important in her chest slide sideways. "Seriously. I've had one sip of coffee. I. Cannot. Think. Yet." *Lone wolf Lana.*

Taft turned so they were both facing the garden again. "I like this. Getting to know you in all different lights."

"We've been working together for a month." In that time, Lana had been angry (at warped wood), sad (at finding yet more dry rot), and ecstatic (at putting up her first ceiling fan by herself). Taft had seen her at her best, at her most exhausted, and at her most frustrated worst. "You've seen it all."

"I haven't even scratched the surface." Taft took a mouthful of home fries. "Holy crap, this is good."

"It is, isn't it?" Lana wasn't talking about the food. For this moment, she decided, she was going to let herself be happy.

She wasn't going to pick it apart until it fell into pieces. She wasn't going to ask too many questions. She wasn't going to run.

At least for a little while.

Lana took her first bite of Benedict. "Holy cow. Molly outdid herself. This is the best she's ever made it."

"I made it."

Lana grinned. "You did not."

"I did. I asked her if I could, with her supervision. She said yes. She told me what to do, but I did it all." He looked abashed. "Honestly, I just toasted the muffin and scrambled the eggs and put the hollandaise on top. It wasn't hard."

Lana took another forkful. "I don't cook. That sounds impossible."

Taft patted himself on the back. "*That's* what I meant to say. It was the hardest thing I've ever done."

"Thanks," she said simply.

Emily Dickinson skittered up the porch steps and rocketed herself into the space next to Lana on the opposite side of Taft. She growled over Lana's plate in his direction.

"I really don't know what I did to her."

"Maybe you look like the person who abandoned her." It wasn't likely, though. No one but Taft looked like Taft.

"Yeah, maybe. Hey, I got a call from my manager this morning, while I was at the café."

"Uh-huh?" Lana wondered how long this kind of feeling lasted, this giddiness in the center of her chest. It felt good, like her blood, which had been still for so long, had suddenly come to life.

"Sully, that's his name – he needs those three songs."

"You'd better get to work."

"What if I told you his wife is sick?"

"I'd say I was very sorry to hear it."

He frowned. "Good answer. But for real, I need to find a wooden spoon to bring Ellen when I go visit. She collects them. Is there a place in town where they have that kind of thing? Local arts and crafts?"

"Check the shop next to the Grange Hall. They sometimes have artisan goods, wind chimes and stuff."

"Thanks. Okay, back to what I was saying. I had some thoughts."

Lana raised an eyebrow and took another bite.

"Can we record the song we wrote last night?"

Lana's fingers tightened on the plastic spoon. "In a studio?"

"No, no, nothing like that. Just here, on my phone, so he can hear how it sounds. He's got to tell the label I'm working and if he could show proof, that would give me a little more breathing room."

"You don't need me for that."

"It's a duet."

"Get one of my sisters to sing it with you. They're both still in the industry."

"So are you."

Lana shook her head. A drowsy-looking bee bumbled slowly past, and the sun poked through a hole in the fog. The cool late-spring morning would soon give way to a warm summer's-coming afternoon. "I told you, I quit."

"And you're serious?"

"Yep." *I failed.*

"So quit after you sing this with me. Help me write two more. Then we'll *both* quit."

"You'd quit breathing before you quit singing."

But he didn't smile. "What if I was serious?"

"You can't quit." Lana tried to get rid of her grin, but she couldn't. It was too ludicrous. "That would be like Kim Kardashian giving up expensive clothes."

"I know it sounds funny, but I need a change."

"So grow a beard."

"A big change."

"A moustache *and* a beard."

"Lana."

"Dye your hair purple? Get a Mohawk?"

"I'm sick of it. All of it. Everything I've ever known – I'm ready to chuck it. I guess it's been at the back of my mind for a long time, but being here, working with the crew – it's changed me."

He *was* serious? "Taft, that's crazy. Just take some more time off."

"I want a smaller life."

"Lucky you." She'd always had one of those.

Taft shook his head. "I've made up my mind."

"This very second?" Shit, had she *caused* this?

"When I decide something, I go all in. Just gotta get out of this contract."

"But your family!"

"There's only my mom. She won't care."

Lana shook her head. "Surely she will."

He frowned. "*You* don't strike me as the type to care what anyone thinks."

"Not people, no. But family?" Lana stuck her fork into the potatoes and left it standing there, for emphasis. "That's different."

"You care what your sisters think."

"I'd love to say I don't. But I do. What about your father?"

Taft cleared his throat. He opened his mouth and appeared to be weighing words. Finally, he said. "He's dead. You might have heard."

"Come on."

"He's beside the point."

Lana pulled up a leg underneath her. "I'd say he's very much the point. You're Palmer Hill's son. You can't quit country. You *are* country."

"Yeah, well, the truth is I'm not Palmer Hill's son."

CHAPTER THIRTY-TWO

T aft had said it. He wanted to smack himself in the face, and at the same time he wanted to shake his own hand in congratulations.

He'd said it out loud. Taft had sworn to himself he wouldn't ever tell anyone. Not a single person.

Honestly, though, he'd known he would tell Lana the truth at some point. Maybe not this soon, but as long as she was the first person to know he was going to quit country, she might as well be the only person to know his biggest secret, too.

His stomach hurt, and he put the plate that held his leftover home fries on the small table next to the swing.

Lana just stared at him.

Finally, she said, "Run that by me again?"

Taft shrugged. His shoulders were hundreds of pounds each. "I'm not his son."

"Is that actually true?"

Taft nodded.

"How do you know?"

"My mother told me."

"When?"

"My birthday. The day I met you at the Bluebird."

"Why?"

Confusion felt like cotton balls in his brain. "Why am I not his son? Because my mother's a liar."

"No, why did she tell you then?"

"Because she was angry at me. She'd asked me for a loan.–"

"A loan? Didn't you say she got everything?"

"She spends every dime that crosses her path and then some." Davina's new husband helped her in that goal.

Lana's voice was soft. "Okay. So she asked you for money."

"For the first time in my life, I told her I'd have to think about it." There was no reason he'd needed to tell her that. He could have just written a check, which was what he always did. It was just the *way* she'd asked him that day. As if she was owed it. He'd gotten angry.

It was all his fault, really.

Lana was waiting patiently for him to continue.

"Davina got angry. She got drunk. Nothing new there – she's always been a drinker. But she called me that night. I didn't answer, but she left a slurred message on my phone." *He's not your dad. You're a bastard, always have been. Don't even know where your real father went. Doesn't matter. I got the man I needed, and now I have a better one.*

As if the loser she'd married – Teddy, the sunburnt golfer – could be even half the man Palmer had been.

"Palmer never knew?"

Taft said, "When I confronted her about the message, she swore he didn't. But I do sometimes wonder if he guessed." Taft and Palmer had different eyes. Different hands. Palmer was short, and so was Taft's mother. But Taft had grown to six two, and he'd outweighed Palmer by at least thirty pounds. Palmer had asthma and Type 1 diabetes, Taft had neither. "When I was about sixteen, he and I were on a tour. Mom had stayed home, but we'd brought a tutor with us, and we'd been on the road for a couple of months by that point. I asked if I'd been adopted because I couldn't see a single thing that was similar between us."

"The music, though."

"That's what he said. Of course I was his son, he said. Look at the way I played, he said. It wasn't until my mother told me the truth that I realized just because I could sing and play guitar didn't mean shit. Half the men in Nashville play. Probably more'n half."

Lana petted Emily's ears. "Who was your father, then?"

"Apparently, he was a nobody guitar player who was passing through, right around the time she met Palmer Hill. Palmer was already famous, and she wanted in on that action. My actual father never returned her letter. She lost track of him."

"Would you want to find him?"

"No." It was a lie. Her expression told him she knew that. "Okay, I did look him up. I found him on Facebook. He died last year."

"Oh, God. I'm sorry."

He couldn't grieve a man he'd never known. "Not my loss. He has a daughter."

"You have a sister!"

"Nope. Just my biological dad's daughter. Anyway, no one knew but my mother, who had a bigger plan. And it worked. Palmer raised me as his own."

"Did you contact her?"

"The daughter? No way."

"Did you want to?"

Yeah, he had wanted to. But he'd been too chickenshit to do it. He didn't answer.

Lana's eyes were deep and clear. "Palmer knew."

Shock pulsed through Taft. "You can't know that."

"You're saying he met your mother, and nine months later, she has a baby? He would have wondered. He would have been watching for the same things you were looking for."

The words made him feel a little sick. "No, she swears he didn't know."

"I bet he *chose* not to know, then." Lana's voice was soft. She'd put a hand on his forearm. "I bet he just chose to love you, no matter what."

It would be nice to think that. But he'd never know for sure. And *that* was the fucking rub.

"Look." Lana wrapped her fingers lightly around his wrist. "Does it actually matter?"

"Yeah."

"How? Why?"

"Would it matter if you weren't a Darling Songbird?"

She was quiet.

Taft crushed the paper cup his coffee had been in. "Exactly."

"It's just I can't imagine *not* being one. I've always been the little sister."

"I've always been Palmer's only kid."

"So you're going to quit that, too? You're going to tell everyone?"

"No," he hurried to say. "This is between you and me. No one can ever know."

"Why not, if it's the truth? If you're leaving country music – and I honestly don't see you doing that, I have to tell you – then why would it matter? He's gone."

"But his legacy. His fans. They matter."

Lana folded her arms and nodded. "*That's* why I think you're going to stay in music. It matters to you."

Suddenly irritated with her sensible and highly annoying logic, he jabbed his forefinger toward her. "What about you? How are you supposed to quit? You gonna divorce your sisters?"

"If I was going to do that, I would have done it a long time ago." Her voice was quiet, and she didn't look at him as she spoke. One hand rested on the dog's head. She took back the hand that had been on his wrist. "But I guess I got as close to that as a sister could. I'm here to ... I don't know. Make it right, try to fix all the crap we have between us. It's finally time. I didn't make it in music, so it's a good time for me to work on something else. *You* made it, though."

How could he make this any clearer to her? "I would have made it if I'd had no musical ability at all. They would have auto-tuned me. They would have made me into a guitar player if I couldn't sing. Drums if I couldn't play guitar. I was born into Nashville royalty, and that whole king's robe they've been trying to make me wear for years has never fit."

"You wear it just fine." Lana's face was breathtaking in the way it shifted with emotion. Her expressions reminded him of the way the ocean changed color with every variation of light.

"I've been fooling the world." Telling her was exhilarating. He was making her complicit. She was his partner in this secret now.

It felt good. And terrifying.

"I'm still not buying it. I'm sorry. You have it in your blood, no matter what. I've seen you on stage. You have what it takes."

"Wait." He turned on the swing to look at her more directly and for his action, got a face full of small Emily Dickinson teeth as she leaped into Lana's lap and yapped. "You've seen me on stage?"

CHAPTER THIRTY-THREE

It didn't matter if the dog bit him. He had to know. She'd been in a sea of faces while he'd sung, and he hadn't known it? He hadn't felt her out there?

"Easy, girl," said Lana. The dog looked like she really *might* bite him.

"Tell me."

"Who hasn't seen a show by you?"

"When?"

She smoothed the dog's ears. "Oh, God. A while ago."

"Which tour?"

Without hesitation, she said, "Bolt of Lightning."

Taft nodded with satisfaction. "I had a great crew on that show. Those were my favorite fireworks ever. What did you think?"

Lana nodded. "Yeah."

"That's not an answer." He wanted to touch her, but the guard dog was on duty.

"Great fireworks."

"But the show?"

"Come on, you don't want me to answer."

"I do." Oh, how he did.

She raised her eyebrows. "Okay, but don't get your feelings hurt."

"Feelings?" He thumped his chest and got a small smile out of her. "I don't have those."

"You're a country singer. It's *all* you have."

"I told you, I'm quitting."

The corner of her mouth quirked higher. "You were overproduced. The budget was blown on the spectacle, and not enough was put into the sound. The fact that you flew in –"

"I wasn't flying, I was a bolt of *lightning*."

"Well, you could have saved, what, ten grand a show, if you'd just walked out on stage? You should have spent the same cash on the soundboard. You sounded too poppy. Not even new country."

"Ah." *There* were the feelings he didn't know he still had about a tour that ended three years before.

She was right, that *had* been the problem. The lead sound engineer had been fresh off a Katy Perry tour, and Sully had sworn the guy would impress him. He'd impressed him, all right. "Somehow I managed to tell myself I was imagining it."

"You didn't see the reviews?"

"The trade reviews? No way." He stayed as far away from those as possible. He only checked Twitter every once in a while, but even that was pretty safe, since Sully did a good job maintaining it for him and blocking the haters. "They said it, too? Seriously?"

"See." She folded her arms. "I knew I shouldn't say anything. It was a great show."

"Hell. I'm *so* out of the business."

"You are so not."

"Not yet. But I will be." It wasn't a joke. She was taking it as one – he could tell by the incredulity on her face – but he wasn't kidding, not even an inch. For the last few weeks, working with the guys and Lana and Socal, he'd felt more alive than he had in years. Maybe in his whole life. "Being with the crew here, doing good, honest work – it's made me realize that writing songs is kind of doing nothing, when you look at it."

"Building a song is nothing to sneeze at."

"Building walls is way more satisfying."

"Songs last longer."

"Not the songs I've been writing for the last few years. Can you even name one? Besides the one you wrote?"

She opened her mouth and then closed it.

"Enough said." Taft stood. He took out his cell and turned on the video camera. "Let's grab the song so I can send it to Sully."

"Now?" She pushed at her hair, which looked exactly as it had looked last night – disheveled and completely, totally sexy.

"You remember the words?"

She smiled in what looked like surprise. "You wrote them on the *wall*."

He grinned back. "Sure did. The best way to memorize something is to write it down. Mind if I grab your guitar?" They'd sung it the night before with no accompaniment, but the simple chords on strings would make it better, stronger.

She shook her head. "Go ahead."

Taft went into the room that smelled like her – like peach and honey and cotton left to dry on the line – and brought out her guitar, an old Epiphone.

Emily Dickinson growled softly as he sat back down on the swing.

He growled back. The dog blinked in surprise and then stretched herself out on Lana's lap.

Taft strummed a G. "Ready?"

Lana bit her bottom lip (the one that he'd bitten last night). She nodded.

Taft reached out to the porch rail and hit "record" on his phone.

They sang:

I was made for falling,
Made to fall for you,
You were made for loving,
Made to love me true.

Damn, the song felt good. The tune of it made his heart ache in all the right places, and the chorus was just right. Their voices were meant to sing together, and the harmony that Lana broke into on the third verse was so pretty it could make an angel cry.

We were born for loving,
For you I'll always yearn.
You were made for passion,
I was made to burn.

They sang the song to each other.

The fact was this: every word of it was true for him. He couldn't speak for her, not totally, but he knew when they'd written it that this was a love song. For them.

When he'd written it on the wall, he'd written it for Lana.

For the woman he wanted to spend the rest of his natural-born life with, in this town, on this sandy soil.

For the woman who was perpetually on the run – an admitted lone wolf, who'd just adopted a guard dog that happened to hate Taft's guts.

She was the only person who knew he wasn't the man everyone else thought he was. A fake. A liar, when it came right down to it. By not admitting he wasn't Palmer's son, didn't that just make him as big a liar as his mother?

I was made to love you true.

I was made to love you true.

The last line rumbled out of his mouth, answered by her sweet response, and Lord help him, he couldn't help it. He leaned forward and kissed her as the guitar's last chord died in the cool morning air.

Lana smiled against his mouth.

Damn it, no man in the world could be happier than he was at that exact moment.

All the hopes and dreams he'd ever had paled when set next to what he wanted from this woman.

A lifetime.

From the bottom of the garden came a voice. "That's a pretty song! I just want to make sure y'all ain't naked before I walk up this path."

Jake. "Shit. I forgot! Jake and me are supposed to go fishing!" Taft grabbed his phone and turned off the video camera.

Lana pulled the dog into her arms as if Emily Dickinson were a flotation device. "You'd better go, then."

Taft stole another kiss, braving the wrath of the dog, which grumbled a warning but didn't bite his chin.

That was fine.

It was all so very fine.

CHAPTER THIRTY-FOUR

Lana sat in her spot in the kitchen of the Golden Spike Café. It had been so long that she'd *forgotten* she even had a spot, but she had and apparently, she still did. Tucked between the walk-in freezer and the second sink was a pile of plastic crates. In the morning, they held the juice bottles. At night, they were turned upside down and stacked two by two, so they made a perfect seat. She drew her knees up like she always had and watched Molly work.

"Old times, right?" Molly grinned at her as she plated two steaks Jackson had just pulled off the grill.

"Except you were smaller then."

Molly patted her stomach. "I was."

Horrified, Lana said, "I didn't mean it like – I meant littler, younger."

"I know how you meant it. Don't worry." Molly smoothed her hands over her hips. "I'm fine."

"I'm sorry."

Molly's smile seemed genuine. "I'm really fine. I like these curves."

Lana's heart lightened a bit, rising like the grill smoke going into the hood. "The sheriff does too, I hear."

"Eh." Molly flapped a rag as one of the waitresses grabbed the plates to carry them out. "I'm glad he does. But it's more important what I think."

Lana felt her cheeks color. Of course. She knew that. She *believed* that. "I'm in the way here. I'll go out and sit at the counter. Come out when you get a break." Or she could get something to go and hide in her room again. She had always liked eating alone best. She still did. Although did it count as alone if Emily Dickinson was there? Lana had left the dozy little dog sleeping in the middle of the bed.

"No, I need you to stay in here."

"You need help?"

"Just sit right there."

"Why are you acting weird?"

Molly tilted her head. "Am I?"

Prickles ran along Lana's arms. "I know you are. You're up to something."

Molly just shrugged.

"Oh, now I *know* you are! What are you doing?" Did it have anything to do with Taft? Lana stole a look at her cell, but there was still no message or text from him. He was either still out fishing with Jake or doing something more important than texting her back.

"Nothing." Molly washed her hands and dried them carefully on the cloth she had draped over her black apron. "Just a little surprise I've cooked up."

Lana sniffed the air. "I smell pizza and bacon burgers and that insane raspberry cheesecake. But I don't smell anything else."

"Just you wait." Molly fished her cell phone out of the apron pocket. "Oh! You don't have to wait!"

"What is going on?" *Taft*, her heart sang. *Taft.*

"Stay." Molly pointed at her. "Right there. Don't move. In fact, close your eyes."

"I don't want to!"

"Just do it," Molly insisted. "You won't regret it."

So Lana closed her eyes and sat by herself on the pile of milk crates, listening as Nikki and Boris clipped orders to the order wheel, as Jackson scraped the grill and threw on more potatoes, as Chris used the paddle to slide more pizzas into the wood-fired oven. Through the perpetually flapping door, she heard laughter from the dining room. A family sang happy birthday to someone. Other patrons joined in.

She wondered if part of whatever the surprise was had to do with Adele. They still hadn't talked, not really. Not about anything that actually mattered.

Not about the past.

Would Lana ever feel grown up enough to try? To want to mend the holes that had worn through in their relationship? If she couldn't blame herself for that long-ago night anymore... And if, by the same token, she couldn't blame Adele for making her run out into Times Square... What would Lana have to be angry about anymore?

She wasn't *ready* to lay down the arms she'd borne for so long.

Dishes clattered in the sink. It turned out that sitting with her eyes closed in the kitchen was actually relaxing, even with the thoughts ricocheting around in her mind. Lana reverted right back to being five years old, invisible if she shut her eyes, sitting in the kitchen with her sisters, watching Uncle Hugh and Arnie trade friendly insults back and forth. Chris and Jackson laughed exactly the same way they had. If her sitting area was just a little wider, Lana would have been able to curl all the way up and go to sleep.

She'd forgotten she used to do that.

Taft. What had his special place been as a child? She'd have to ask him – no. Was that fair to herself? Wondering about things she'd ask a man who would probably leave soon? Even with the house he'd bought, he wouldn't stay here – no musician in his right mind would stay in Darling Bay.

Wait. She was staying.

So. No *successful* musician would stay in Darling Bay. Taft could dream his dream of leaving the music industry, but –

"Open your eyes."

Lana jumped.

Molly stood in front of her, a plate in her hands.

No Taft.

Lana swallowed her disappointment. She pushed a smile onto her face. "What do you have there?"

"What do you think? Abalone!"

"Oh, my God."

"The season is short this year – I was barely able to get this."

Lana reached for the plate and looked at the thin slices. "This was my favorite."

"Every birthday."

"But it's not my birthday."

Molly looked pink-cheeked. "We missed too many of those. This is the start of making it up to you."

"Oh, Molly. You don't have to do that." It was so *sweet* of her sister. It wasn't Molly's fault Lana had been hoping for a man, not a mollusk.

"I know, but it makes me happy."

Lana nodded. Fair enough. "Can we eat at the counter?"

"You can."

"No, you eat with me."

"Nuh-uh. I did not pay Kirk Lombard to dive for that in order for *me* to eat something I don't even like."

"Then sit with me."

"That I can do." Molly tugged off her apron and led Lana out to the counter. It was late enough to be completely dark outside now. The patrons' reflections danced in the windows, doubling the apparent size of the dining room. The front door banged and Lana couldn't help turning her head to see who'd just walked in. A small family, parents and a red-faced boy, all of them looking hungry and cranky, stood at the hostess podium.

They weren't Taft, either.

Molly poured Lana a glass of white wine without asking. "This pairing will blow your mind. It's a White Rhône blend."

Lana took her first bite. Then a sip of wine, which was indeed perfect. "You actually serve abalone often enough to have a pairing?"

"Haven't served it even once yet. You're the first. And no, it would be too expensive. I just read about this wine in the *New York Times* when they did a piece on abalone. I ordered a couple of bottles just in case."

"You're very fancy."

Molly preened. "We are, yes."

"Not we. This is all you." Lana gestured with her fork. In one corner a child screamed as if he'd been stabbed by Elmo, but otherwise the entire room seemed happy. Laughter held the conversation up high, and ribbons of joy seemed to unfurl over the diners' heads. "This is magical. You did this."

"Eh. I just cleaned it up."

"No. I know better than that. I'm so proud of you."

Molly's eyes widened. "Oh. That's so ... That's so nice to hear."

"Adele doesn't say it to you?" Lana was honestly surprised.

"She does, she does. It's just different coming from you."

Because the baby of the family couldn't be proud of her sister? She was an adult, after all. Just as Lana was gearing up to be offended, she looked at Molly's face again. The happiness was visible, almost tangible. Feeling something rough at the back of her throat, Lana said quickly, without giving herself the chance to stop herself, "I love you."

"Oh," said Molly. She blinked hard and fast. "I love you, too, and so does Adele. You know that, right?"

If Lana thought too much about it, she'd want to cry, so instead, she just took another bite. "This is heaven. Pure and perfect heaven."

"Speaking of heaven, where is that divine man of yours?"

Lana choked on her bite and coughed for a moment. "Who?"

Molly bounced her knee against Lana's. "I know he was fishing with Jake today – Jake stopped by for coffee early this morning."

"Is there any time you *don't* work?"

"Don't change the subject. How's it going?"

I'm doomed. I'm done for. I'm dying. "It's fine."

"You're falling for him."

Lana shook her head.

"Ah," said wise Molly. "It's too late. You already fell."

"Damn it."

"I knew it. You've done fallen!"

"Call me Icarus."

Molly propped her head on her fist. "Tell me more."

"Do you know the myth?"

"I'm a singer and a hash-slinger. I'm not illiterate."

Lana nodded. "Yeah, yeah. I got too close to the sun too fast, maybe."

"You haven't been burned. Your wings haven't melted. I think your metaphor is off."

Molly had no idea. Last night, Lana had soared all the way to the sun, and then she'd free-fallen the whole way back to earth. When they'd sung their song together on the porch, she'd felt too lucky already. Like she'd been at too high an altitude, like she'd be punished for it. "If I fly any higher, I might lose my wings for good."

"No, you won't."

"I know it sounds stupid. It's just a dumb fear. I swear to you, though, I don't think I can do this."

"Good." Molly nodded and crossed her arms, looking satisfied.

"What do you mean?"

"If this thing is so scary you think you can't do it, then it's just about right."

Someone in the kitchen dropped something made of glass. "Is that how you felt about the sheriff?"

Molly didn't seem to mind whatever it was that had broken on the other side of the swinging door. "Oh, yeah. Still do. Every day."

"How is that a good thing?" To be scared every minute of losing the one thing that felt better – more right – than anything else ever had?

"It's the best thing."

"How?"

"Because it has the potential to be the worst thing. That's what makes it the best. When you know that losing it would break you, you're in exactly the right spot."

"Crap."

Molly's eyes twinkled happily. "Yep. Eat some more. You're not letting a single bite go to waste."

"I told you, it's heaven." Lana took another perfect bite, and realized she meant it, completely. This was heaven. All of it. This place.

This family.

This town.

Taft.

A line from one of her older songs played in her mind.

Fear never killed no one.

The double negative had pleased her when she'd written the line, years before.

It felt true now.

CHAPTER THIRTY-FIVE

L ana wasn't in the bar, and Taft was surprised at the disappointment he felt. She hadn't been up in her room, either. Or at least, she hadn't answered when he'd knocked at her door, and she *probably* hadn't been hiding behind the closed door. The dog had barked from behind the door like Taft was Satan on fire, so she was probably out somewhere, dog-less. He texted her, just a simple, *Wanna grab a drink at the bar?* but got no reply.

Taft had *really* hoped he'd see her. A whole day of fishing and listening to Jake talk about how great the bachelor life was had made Taft realize he hated the single life. Sleeping (actually *sleeping*) next to Lana the night before had made him happier than anything he could remember: the feeling of her skin on his - the way his arm tucked around her waist - had been perfect, the softly growling dog notwithstanding.

Lana's sister Adele waved at him from across the room where she was writing names on a chalkboard. Some kind of open mic was happening before a band called Dust & Rusty was going on. If Lana didn't show up before the singers went on stage, he'd leave. There was almost nothing as painful as an open mic in a small town, and Taft had hosted too many of them for charity to want to listen to one for free.

"Hey, did you hear me?" Jake poked Taft in the shoulder.

He shook his head. "Sorry, no."

"Just call her."

"What?"

"You're obviously spun out on Lana. You have her number. Just give her a call and ask where she is."

He'd texted her. There was probably a good reason she wasn't responding. "That's not it."

Jake rubbed a bruise on his forearm. Taft knew he'd gotten it when a piece of lumber had slipped on Wednesday, when they'd been reframing the window in room eight. Taft *liked* knowing that. It made him feel like part of the town, part of this world.

Jake shook his head. "Yeah, that's exactly why you're so distracted. Don't even tell me you're not thinking about her constantly."

"Come on." His protest was weak.

"You let me talk all day on the boat, and you didn't once mention her. You think I didn't notice?"

Taft studied the label on his beer bottle. "Why would I mention her?"

"Because you can't keep your eyes off the doors of this place. If you were to fall asleep right now, you'd probably start mumbling her name."

"Whose name?" Adele leaned on the bar.

"Your sister's." Jake's voice was cheerful. "He's got it bad."

"I figured."

Taft shook his head. "No, I don't."

"Yes, you do." Adele smiled, and it suddenly felt ridiculous to deny it.

"I do. I do have it so fucking bad."

Adele looked at the level of his beer. "You all right there?"

Was she checking his level of drunkenness? "This is my first. I've only had half of it."

"Just making sure you don't need another before I drag you outside to chat."

Jake hooted. "Hoo, I'm glad I'm not dating a Darling. That's not gonna be a chat. Good luck with the interrogation, buddy!"

Adele smirked. "Chat." But her tone said Jake was right. Taft felt sudden nerves play in the pit of his stomach. It would be good to keep Adele on his side.

"Let me get myself some ginger ale and I'll be right outside. Wait for me there." Her voice was polite, even sweet. But it wasn't a request.

Taft waited for her in the arbor, hoping against hope that Lana would come through instead. She could be holding three rabid Emily Dickinsons and he would brave all their teeth.

But by the time Adele made her way out, no one had passed through the arbor except a young female couple who looked extremely disappointed they didn't have the darkness to themselves.

"Hey," Adele said. She sat across from him and clinked her drink against his. "Cheers."

"Yeah."

"You sound nervous. I'm not going to yell at you."

"I wasn't worried."

"Yes, you were."

"Yes, I was," he agreed. "Are you going to ask me about my intentions regarding your sister? Ask if I know her middle name?" He didn't, he realized. And he wanted to know.

"Do you?"

"No."

"It's Mirabelle."

God, that was pretty.

"Oh, wow, look at your face," said Adele on a laugh. "I do like directness. But no, I figure whatever you do with my sister is your business and hers. Not mine."

The relief he felt was mixed with something else – could it be disappointment? Did he actually *want* to be interrogated by Lana's sister? "Okay, then ..."

"No, the reason I wanted to talk to you was about a fundraiser we're doing in a couple of weeks. It's for Migration, the women's shelter hotline Molly started."

"Yeah, I read about it." Sully had sent him an online article about the nonprofit the week before. All Taft remembered about it was that Molly and Adele had both been in the attached photo, and he'd wished Lana had been in it, too. "Good for her. For both of you. I'd be happy to help."

"Great. I wanted to talk about you and Lana maybe performing the song you wrote together."

Taft blinked, surprised. "She told you about "Blame Me?"" Lana had said no one should know she wrote it, but he now realized her sisters were exempted. He supposed that was what siblings were for.

"What?" Adele sat straighter, and a single white twinkle light burned out over her head. Her voice was tight.

"'*Blame Me?*' No, I was talking about the new song Jake told me about while you were talking to Nate. The song he heard both of you singing this morning."

"Oh."

She frowned. "But go back to that. What about 'Blame Me?'"

Taft thought quickly.

If Lana's sister didn't know about what had happened that night so long ago, shouldn't she? Wasn't that the whole point of having a family?

It wasn't his place to say anything.

It wasn't his right.

They'd hurt her, though, by not being there for her. The fact that she'd had to go through it so alone—so totally by herself—gutted him. It wasn't fair, and it wasn't right.

The words tumbled out before he could stop them. "She wrote it. She didn't want you to know, but I think you should."

"Are you serious?"

"Yeah. I am." What the *hell* was he doing? This wasn't his secret to tell.

Goddamn it, Lana had been hurt. *Really* hurt, both physically and emotionally.

Her sisters – who'd been right *there* – hadn't been there for her. They hadn't seen what she'd needed.

It made him angry. "She could have used you guys back then, you know. When your dad died. Instead, you pushed her out of the nest."

"She wrote that song?" Adele's voice broke. "Who hurt her?"

"Ask her yourself."

"Oh, God." Adele pulled out her phone. "Where is she?"

Taft felt sick. He shouldn't have said it.

Without saying another word, Adele turned on her heel and began making her way toward room one.

Taft pulled out his cell and considered texting Lana one more time.

No.

Give her some space.

Let her breathe.

Hopefully, it had been the right thing to do. She needed the love of her sisters now, needed to be held up and comforted by them. There was so much pain in Lana's eyes, and some of that came directly from them not being there for her.

Maybe they could fix that now.

Yeah, and hopefully she'd forgive him for telling Adele she'd written the song. That's all it was, after all – it wasn't like he'd told her anything else.

If she didn't forgive him, though ...

Well, then he'd deserve the heartbreak he'd just signed himself up for.

CHAPTER THIRTY-SIX

The abalone was gone. The wine was gone, too –
she and Molly had drunk two glasses each and
Lana was happily, groggily tipsy. Most of the
restaurant was empty now, all the tourists cleared out.
Nikki dried wineglasses and swayed to the music on the
overhead speakers, an old Willie Nelson tune.

Bed would be good.

Sleep would be good. Good God, Lana was tired,
which made perfect sense when she thought about the
fact that she'd been up most of the night prior. She'd
napped, yes, but most of her day had been spent
stripping wallpaper from the two good walls in room
five. That motion had made her shoulders ache.

She twisted on the counter chair. Other parts of her
ached, too, sweetly. Still no text, though. She'd sent one

earlier that had merely said, *Hope the fishing was good.* He hadn't responded yet.

That was fine. Sure. All good. He was probably tired and had gone home. He was probably crashed out on his couch right now, still smelling of the sea.

What Lana wouldn't do to bury her nose in his neck and smell the brine of the open ocean.

"Well?" Molly had asked her something.

"Um ..."

Molly ate a cold fry. "Never mind. You're hopeless."

"No, sorry. What were you saying?"

Before Molly could repeat herself, the main dining-room door banged open.

"Adele!" Molly waved, a grin on her face. "Come sit with us!"

Adele didn't look like she wanted to sit. She had that look on her face, the one she used to get right before she shouted at both of them for being too little, too slow, too wrong. "Uh-oh." Lana felt guilty and she didn't even know what she'd done wrong yet.

As she drew closer, though, Lana could tell Adele wasn't angry, exactly.

It looked worse than that.

Adele's voice was tight as she spoke to Lana. "Can I talk to you outside?"

Molly said brightly, "What's going on?"

Adele lifted a hand as if to forestall her. "Just Lana."

"Want to go up to the hotel?" Lana was tipsy enough that the thought of arguing with Adele in public probably wasn't a good idea.

"Sure."

"Molly, you come, too."

"No," said Adele.

"Yes," said Lana, and she meant it.

"Fine."

They tromped out of the café's back door, Molly carrying a new bottle of wine and three glasses. "Fine," Molly muttered. "I'm glad it's *fine* for me to come along."

Adele made a frustrated noise but didn't rise to the bait, thank God. Fear gathered at the base of Lana's skull, fear that she didn't have a clue what to do with. If Adele needed to tell her that Taft had perished at sea (on this calm, clear day), she wouldn't look angry, would she? If she'd found out that Lana had ... had what? Adele had been plenty mad at Lana over their lifetimes, and plenty of times Lana had deserved it. At this particular moment, though, Lana couldn't think of anything she'd done wrong.

Nerves made the abalone dance in her stomach, and she felt a brief surge of seasickness.

They wound up the path that led past the side of the saloon. Lana peeked in the high side window, but there were too many people doing a line dance on the dance floor to see if Taft was inside. "Are Dixie and Nate both working?" she asked politely. Of course they were. It looked too busy for Adele to be out of the bar at this time of night if they weren't.

Adele blazed ahead without answering. As always, Adele in the lead, Molly solidly in the middle, little Lana dragging behind. Piqued by being ignored, Lana said, "You planning on talking at all?"

Adele said, "Oh, yeah. I'm going to talk." She turned right at the fork, going up the stairs that led to her and Nate's above-bar apartment. The white lights strung around the deck twinkled, and the grouping of mismatched outdoor chairs around the round table were cheerful, in stark contrast to whatever Adele was going to say. Lana was grateful for the fog rolling in, cloaking the deck in mist.

Molly plopped down in an iron chair with arms and poured wine. "I'm already two glasses in. I'm headed for three. Join me?"

Adele nodded grimly. "A tiny amount only."

Lana also nodded. "You're scaring me. What have I possibly done to piss you off this much?" She racked her brain – had she left oily rags dangerously piled somewhere? Had she tracked paint on her shoes through the saloon?

Adele seemed to realize that her features were bleak. She rubbed at her cheeks and swiped her hands over her eyes. "You didn't do anything wrong. I'm sorry. I just got thrown for such a huge loop, and I ..." She choked.

"What is going *on*?"

"Taft –"

"Is he okay?" Lana's heart shifted into overdrive, leaping against her ribs. He'd been drowned. Or attacked by a shark. Or killed in a car accident on the way back from the beach. "What *is* it?"

"He told me something."

A wave of relief washed over her. "He's not really quitting."

"Huh?" Adele frowned.

"It's just a thing he thinks now. That's he's leaving Nashville. He won't do it. You know how people get about things like that." Lana stared into the only bright light, the lamp over Adele's head, until her vision went white. "He thinks he's done with the industry, but he was born into it and he'll have to die to get out of it."

"That's not it."

"What, then?"

"Lana, who hurt you?"

Lana saw a bright flash as she screwed her eyes tight, just for a second. "No."

Adele's voice was softer. "Honey, who hurt you?"

Molly leaned forward. "What are you talking about?"

Lana shook her head.

Molly said, "Lana, what is she talking about?"

Lana's whole body felt brightly lit now, as a white-clear heat soared from her chest out of the top of her head.

Taft *couldn't* have told Adele.

"I don't know," Lana finally said. "I have no idea what she's talking about."

"You wrote "Blame Me.'"

The thud of it detonated in her chest. "What?" It was a stalling mechanism, and maybe during the brief second it would take for Adele to gather her words together, Lana could close her eyes. She'd disappear again, like she had in the café kitchen, except this time she'd truly dissipate like the smoke into the grill hood, up and out into the night sky.

"She did?" asked Molly.

"Where did you even get that idea?"

Adele just stared at her.

"So what if I did?" It shouldn't matter, anyway. Songs were fictional. So often, they were completely made up. No one thought Johnny Cash was a boy named Sue, did they?

Adele's voice was thin as she asked again, "Who hurt you?"

Lana gasped. "He shouldn't have said anything. He should never have said a *word* to you. I *told* him."

"Well, apparently he forgot, and I'm glad. Lana, tell us." Adele's whole body radiated anger, though. It was coming off her in waves.

That was not goddamn fair.

"Why?" Lana sat up as straight as she could. She set the wineglass down. She didn't need any more, and if she held the glass any longer, she'd probably snap the stem. "Why should I tell you a thing? You're already mad at me." She stuck the side of her pinky into her mouth and gnawed briefly on the skin.

Molly gasped. "What are you *talking* about?"

Adele shook her head so hard her hair, which had been up in a loose knot on top of her head, fell in messy waves. She looked about twenty, vulnerable and young. "You think I'm mad at you?"

That same thump reverberated in the middle of Lana's chest. "You're acting like you want to kill me, yeah."

Adele covered her mouth with her hand and stood so abruptly her chair fell backward with a heavy thud. She took a few steps away and then set her chair upright and sat again, as if it had been her intention all along. "I'm not mad at you, you idiot."

Lana just shook her head, her mouth empty of words.

"I'm furious at *myself*. For not realizing."

Adele was angry at herself? Lana had a hard time believing it. She knew rage when it was directed at her, and Adele seemed full of it. "Really."

"Jesus, Lana." Adele's words were so ragged Lana wondered if she was about to cry. "Can you just tell us?"

"Songs aren't always autobiographical. You both know that." It was a false protest. She could tell they both knew that.

"Little Lana."

"Stop it. I haven't been the little one in a long time."

"How long?" Adele's eyes were stark. "When did it happen?"

Lana cracked, and the truth spilled out. "The night Daddy died."

"No." Adele was crying now, silently except for the sucking sound when she inhaled. "Lana."

"You want to know? You *really* want to know?" She wanted to punish Adele. Both of her sisters. For not knowing. Not seeing. The feeling was so familiar that she realized she'd felt this way for a very long time.

"Yes," her sisters said in unison. Molly reached to take Lana's hand, but she jerked it away.

She didn't need consoling. Not anymore. "I went out that night, after we fought. I got really fucked up. I was assaulted." *It was rape.* Taft's words.

"Why didn't you tell us?"

Now she would be blamed for doing it wrong. That was just perfect. "Because I knew you wouldn't believe it wasn't my fault."

"But it wasn't. Jesus, Lana, whatever happened, it wasn't your fault."

That's not what Lana had thought for years. That's not what her sisters would have thought, had they known. Especially Adele. She would have said, *You shouldn't have been there. You shouldn't have had those tequila shots. You shouldn't have gone outside with him.*

"Yeah, well, I handled it."

"By yourself." One huge tear wound its way down Adele's cheek. "You dealt with it by yourself."

Just like everything else. But Lana didn't say it. It seemed too cruel, somehow. Lana let her head fall back, and she searched the night sky for anything she could possibly say in response. A bat, black against the white fog, flapped and gave a shrill screech. What Lana wouldn't give for arms that folded into wings, so she could fly up, fly away as fast as she could go. "Yeah. I guess."

Molly folded her arms over her chest. Tears shone in her eyes, too.

Lana was suddenly over all of it. "I don't want to *do* this with you."

Adele wrapped her fingers around the edge of the table. "I just can't get my head around the fact that the moment you needed me most was the exact moment I pushed you away the hardest."

"Yeah, I got used to the idea a long time ago." It was a jerk response, and Adele's lips got thinner and sadder, instantly.

Sisters. They always knew exactly which button to push. And Lana had always been the master at pushing Adele's.

"But it's okay. It's fine."

Adele shook her head. Molly exclaimed, "No!" and then went silent again.

"You see?" Lana took a carelessly huge swallow of wine, feeling the acidic burn match the heat in her throat. "This is why I never wanted to tell you."

Adele rubbed at her eyes. "*Why* not?"

"Because then I turn into the one who has to comfort *you*. Now I have to tell you that you did nothing wrong, but honestly? You did."

Adele's expression got more miserable. Deep down inside, buried underneath everything that was good in her, Lana felt a little spark of satisfaction. There was a small, dark place in her heart that was enjoying the way Adele and Molly looked almost ready to pass out in concern.

This was what Lana had always wanted, in her secret heart of hearts.

It was agony.

And it was the tiniest bit – unforgivably – pleasurable.

"I know." Adele's voice was a rasp. "I'm sorry. You're right. I was wrong, so wrong. I *knew* that the way you reacted was more than –"

"I was more out of control than I should have been? After suddenly becoming an orphan and being pretty sure I was going to lose my band, and my sisters, too? Huh. You're right, I was totally out of line. I should have told you about being –" her voice choked shut before she could say the word.

Adele said it for her. "Raped."

Lana coughed. "I haven't told you one thing about what happened."

"Did you say no?"

"No." That was the whole fucking problem. She'd whispered it, maybe. She'd thought it, she knew. She'd wanted to scream it. But she hadn't.

Adele shook her head. "It doesn't matter. If you were that drunk, you were beyond being able to give any kind of consent."

How did Adele even know? "Did Taft tell you *everything*?" How could he? How had he betrayed her like that?

"He didn't tell me any details. You did. In your song."

Lana covered her eyes with her hands, relishing their coolness. "Not autobiographical."

"Not all songs, no. But I've known since I heard the song that the woman behind it was telling the truth."

Something struck Lana as she dropped her hands. "What if I'd told you then?"

"I wish you had. God, Lana, I wish to hell you had."

"Seriously, what if I'd told you *then*? Dad had just died. We'd just lost the tour. We all knew the band was going under. If I'd told you I'd been assaulted –"

"Raped."

The word was a knife to Lana's throat. "Okay, if I'd told you that I got too drunk and a guy had sex with me because he said I'd wanted it. Which I probably did. You would have defended me?"

"Yes." Adele looked as if she could fight a lion barehanded.

"Really?"

"Yes." But her yes was softer.

"Think about it. I'd already passed out on stage from the pills. You were furious with me. You think you wouldn't have blamed me? Even a little bit?" Lana knew she *would* have been accused of being the one who'd asked for it.

Her anger about that had been what had kept her apart from Adele for so long.

The knowing that she was right.

"I wouldn't have ..."

"Bullshit." Molly's tone was clear, bell-like. "That's bullshit, Adele. We both would have blamed her. You know we would have."

"No –"

"The reason 'Blame Me' has blown up is because people are talking about consent *now*. They're talking about it on college campuses and on public radio stations and in magazines. We didn't even have that language back then. All we knew was that Lana got out of control and we didn't like it."

Lana had to point out, "You minded it less than she did, Molly."

Adele winced.

Molly shook her head. "Well, then, I'm the one who should have noticed. We were close. I should have figured it out. I should have asked you what was wrong."

"You did ask me, remember? Everything was wrong then. That was practically the least of it." It wasn't true. It hadn't been as bad as her father dying, but it had been worse than almost anything else.

Adele wrapped her arms around her waist, around the baby still too small to really even push out her shirts. Lana knew Adele would do anything to protect that child once it came into the world. She would have done anything to protect Lana, too.

"I know you love me," said Lana.

Adele nodded miserably. "So much."

"I know. It's not your fault. None of this is. But I wish you'd seen past the walls I put up."

Adele shook her head. "Every single piece of this is my fault. I'm the one who made us go on stage that night. I'm the one who pushed so hard you broke and ran and got high and drunk and –"

"Can you give me *some* credit, please?"

"What?"

"Jesus, Adele. The whole world doesn't revolve around you."

Adele looked wounded, and her voice was quiet. "I know that."

"Maybe you do now. But you didn't know then. I would have had to make you feel better about that, too. I've always regretted not telling you both, but I'm changing my mind. I wish you'd never found out." Lana stood. "I'm going to bed."

Molly reached out a hand. "Wait. Please talk some more with us. Don't go, don't run away."

"Why not?" Lana locked her fingers around her elbows. "It's the only thing I'm good at."

"Please just don't leave town," said Adele in a tone fiercer than fire. "*Please* stay."

Lana wasn't going anywhere. Honestly, there was no other place for her to go.

But she didn't need to reassure either of them right now.

Darling girls were shit at reassurance, it turned out.

CHAPTER THIRTY-SEVEN

Sunday morning was busy on Main Street in Darling Bay. Taft watched people stream into the double doors of the Baptist church. They waved at the Catholic churchgoers coming out of ten-o'clock mass next door. Kids ran in and out of the bagel shop, and the Golden Spike's parking lot had been converted to a rummage sale, fundraising for the high school track team.

In his car, Taft pressed "play" again.

There they were, on his phone's screen, singing together. He'd watched it a dozen times already, of course.

But this time he was watching it on YouTube.

Sully had leaked it.

Taft could tell by the account name – Sully had a burner account named ProSongs32 that he sometimes used to test the waters for up-and-coming talent.

Nothing on that account had ever blown up like this one had.

In just the last day, there were four hundred thousand views. Every time Taft hit Refresh, there were several hundred more views.

He prayed to God Lana would like it. That it wouldn't make her angrier.

Lana.

She'd finally texted him back about meeting him in the bar. *No.*

Yeah, she'd talked to her sister.

She probably wanted to kill him already – he sure as hell didn't want her finding out about the YouTube video from anyone but him.

He strode into the Golden Spike Café and flagged down Nikki. "Have you seen Lana this morning?"

Nikki pointed west. "She came in for coffee. I tried to get her to take a muffin, but she said she was going to take her new dog to the beach and do some yoga."

Just the words set his brain on fire. He imagined Lana stretching, wearing something tight and made of spandex, bending and folding on the sand as the waves pounded the shore behind her. "Thanks."

Seven minutes later, he was at the shore. Lana wasn't visible on the beach before the bay's curve, so he trucked on foot over the dunes, hoping like hell he'd have reception out here so he could show her the updated view count.

There.

By herself, at the edge of the water, Lana was doing yoga.

Sadly, no spandex, though. She was wearing a huge traffic-orange shirt that disguised her body and hung almost to her knees. Under it she wore a pair of black sweatpants so baggy he marveled that she didn't fall right out of them as she bent into downward dog, the only pose he remembered from dating Minna, the yoga fanatic. Even disguised as Lana was, she looked hot as hell. Her hair stuck straight out from her head. Her yoga moves, instead of being fluid and gentle, like the yoga he'd seen Minna do, were angry and rushed. Her back still to him, she stood and raised one foot, placing it on her opposite thigh. Stork-like, she wobbled and raised her arms. She fell sideways, catching herself with a string of curses that had probably been uttered verbatim by the captain of the last shipwreck off the coast.

He laughed. He couldn't help it.

Emily Dickinson, who'd been nose-down in a pile of kelp, looked up and barked sharply.

Lana spun around. "What? You think it's funny?"

Anger poured off her body as if she'd swum in a sea of it.

"Just admiring your ability to cuss."

"Better than that fucking *namaste* shit."

He folded his hands in prayer and gave a short bow. "I honor the pirate spirit within you."

She cocked a hip. She hadn't been using a yoga mat, and there was wet sand all over her. What *didn't* look good on this woman?

"What do you want? Other than to apologize, which I assume you're going to do, and which I'm going to reject, so we can just skip it."

"Lana, your sisters had to know."

"You didn't have the *right*."

"I know that. I knew it when I said it, and I did it anyway." He spoke as earnestly as he possibly could. He meant this. "If I had to do it over, I wouldn't. It was so stupid. I feel terrible about it."

"I can't – no one but my friend Jilly knew. And she only knew because she heard me working on the song when I was staying with her. *You* were the only one I trusted enough to tell." Lana glared, and her face was fierce in her rage, every single bit of it directed right at him.

Man, he was an idiot. It would have come out – he was sure of it. Too many people *did* know, everyone in accounting at the label, the people who sent the money into her business account.

But he'd been the one to tell her sister, and for that he was deeply regretful.

"I want to show you something." He held up his cell phone and took a few more paces forward, until Emily Dickinson blocked his way, yapping her fool head off.

Her bark was excruciating, at just the right pitch to make his ears feel like they were bleeding. "You want to call off the guard?"

She crossed her arms over her chest. "I'm not in a very chatty mood. Maybe later." Her tone said *maybe never*. She snapped her fingers for the dog. Emily Dickinson ignored her entirely and kept rolling in the kelp.

"Lana, I'm sorry. I really am."

"That doesn't change the fact that you did it." She tromped away. Some of her emphasis was lost because the sand didn't lend itself to stomping, but Taft got the message.

Shit. Taft had screwed up so far beyond big time.

She turned her head, whistling for the dog, who finally came running. Emily Dickinson shot a weak growl in Taft's direction and then ran ahead, snapping at the waves.

For racing through sand, Lana was sure accelerating. Taft's breath speeded as he tried to keep up with her. "Lana. Stop."

She turned around, and she sure as hell stopped. As soon as she did, he regretted his words. "You're giving me orders now?"

"No," he said. "Just ... just hold up a minute. Let me apologize completely." Her lips were bright red, maybe from the wind. For a second, he imagined kissing her. He could apologize *very* thoroughly if she'd let him.

Lana blew out a breath. "What are you *looking* at? You don't get it. You don't get to apologize for spilling the beans on my biggest secret. That's not something I could possibly just let *go*, just because you weren't thinking."

Taft had been thinking. He just hadn't known to keep his lips zipped. "I get it. I'm sorry. I'll say that as many times as you want me to. But I have to point out – isn't family exactly who should have helped you through that time in your life?"

"You? *You're* the one saying this to me?"

"What?" Ahead of them, Emily Dickinson chased a sandpiper that looked like it was taunting her, flying a few feet every time the dog got close, setting down again just out of reach.

"I don't think you're the one who should really lecture me on family."

He felt a jolt, like he'd just bumped another car with his own. "Hey, now."

Lana tilted her head to the side and her eyes narrowed. "Family. What a bitch, am I right? It's just the luck of the draw, I guess. You got a famous dad – who wasn't your dad. Was it mere luck, then, that you wrote such good songs back in the day?"

"I don't know." It hurt to think about it. Again.

"Just because your family helped you out in every single way imaginable doesn't mean the rest of the world wants or expects the same thing. I got where I am on my own two feet. By myself. No help."

He took a breath. "Look, Nikki said you were out here. I just had something to show you."

"So you didn't even come out here to grovel? You came to find me for a *different* reason?"

For a million reasons, number one being that he couldn't stop thinking about her, about the way she'd moved in his arms, the sound she'd made when she'd come the first time, and the second time, and the third ... His number-two reason was the video on his phone. "Just look at it." He held it toward her and prayed for a good signal. Maybe the video would buy him a slim scrap of forgiveness.

Still with the scowl on her face, Lana got nearer to him. Emily Dickinson seemed to feel that her presence was needed and came to stand at Lana's ankle. She growled softly – almost cheerfully – as if it was a little dog song she was making up as she went along.

That wasn't the song Taft wanted to hear. He pushed Play.

The music tumbled out, tinny and quiet. Taft raised the volume. The sound became fuller, even out there on the beach with the roar of the surf and wind behind them. The two of them were small on the screen, but the way they were looking at each other was visible even in low resolution. It was a love song, all right.

"You said you were sending our song to your manager. So?"

Their song. It sounded good. "Look closer."

She did, somehow managing to still stay two feet away from him. The wind blew her scent to him, light and sweet, as heady as a hundred-proof bourbon.

"It's on YouTube. Why is it there?" Lana leaned a little closer. "What is that number?"

He laughed, excitement flooding his bloodstream. "That's what I came to show you."

"Does that say almost half a million? Views? Is that *views*?"

"It's gone viral. Overnight. Sully texted me while I was walking down here that I have more than twenty press requests on it. Your agent's probably getting the –" She shot him a look, and he remembered her agent had fired her.

"We recorded it yesterday," she said.

"I know."

"It's impossible."

"Not anymore it isn't. It's kind of great, right?" She had to admit it.

"No. It isn't." She walked away without watching any more.

"Lana." He jogged to catch up and caught her elbow.

She jerked away with a hiss, rubbing at her arm like he'd burned her. "What is *wrong* with you?"

"Me? I thought you'd like this." It was amazing. Couldn't she see that?

"Why?"

Taft shook his head. "I can't keep up with you."

She slowed her speech insultingly. "I told you I. Left. The. Business. What more is there to say?"

Lana couldn't intend to walk away, not now. "Hang on, just look at the comments. They're barely interested in me."

Lana raised an eyebrow so high it almost met her scalp.

"Okay," he clarified, "they're leaving comments about me, but most of them are about you."

"Do they have any idea who I am?"

"Most of them, no. But they're learning. People are leaving comments about which of the Darling Songbird albums is their favorite, and others are linking to your solo stuff. Is your phone on?"

She frowned and dug it out of a pocket in the baggy sweatpants. She squinted at the screen. "Holy crap."

"You've been blowing up, too."

She scrolled. Then she scrolled some more. She didn't look up at him.

That was fine. He could wait.

Taft raised his gaze to the waves tumbling in to shore – the biggest ones hit with a thump that he could feel in his heels. Then the waves got sucked right into the next one, refolding themselves over and over again. If this was the surf here on a clear, fine day, it would be spectacular during a storm.

Almost as spectacular as stormy Lana was, right now. She was still sparking anger – he could feel it coming off her skin. Her tempest was glorious.

And he was responsible for it. God, he was *such* a dick for telling Adele that Lana had written "Blame Me."

Lana was still scrolling on her phone.

"Good stuff?" he finally asked.

"My agent. My ex-agent, I mean."

"Bet he's begging for you to come back."

She frowned. "Yeah."

"Media?"

"My inbox is full."

"People want more from you."

Lana looked up at him, her features tight with what looked like anguish. "But ..."

"But what?" He moved in, putting his hand against the side of her face – he couldn't stand not touching her one more damn second. Her skin was cold and damp from the ocean's spray. "How could this possibly be a bad thing?"

She gazed at him, a question he couldn't decipher in her eyes. "Taft."

"Talk to me."

"You don't get it, do you?" Her words were a push, but her body was pulling him in to her – or maybe that was her, doing the leaning. She let her head fall forward and her forehead rested on his chest.

Without thinking, he kissed the top of her head. Her sand-powdered dark hair was softer than it looked.

Just like she was.

She made her hands into fists and gripped the front of his sweatshirt.

Taft gently cupped the base of her neck. Whatever she needed, he would get for her. Whatever she wanted, he would figure it out. *I love you* swam through his mind, but it was too early. Today had held too much already. Maybe tomorrow, when they finished working for the day. Maybe she'd let him take her out on a real date, one with cloth napkins and candlelight and music. One that ended with her in his arms, one that ended with him whispering those words in her ear, the words he wanted to keep telling her forever.

Lana spoke into his sweatshirt, so quietly he couldn't quite catch the words.

"What's that, Birdie?"

She drew back and looked up into his eyes. She was so close he could drop his mouth to hers with no effort, but he didn't. Something stopped him.

"Tell him to take it down," she said.

His brain stalled, and for a second he had no idea what she meant. "The video?"

She let go of his sweatshirt, and he felt a chill run through his body that had nothing to do with the wind. "Tell him to take it down."

"Lana. He said with the rate it's being shared, it'll hit a million views by tonight. You can't *buy* that kind of exposure."

"That's the problem. I know that. I *would* have bought it if it were possible, if I ever could have afforded more than a nice poster and an email sent to my list for each of my gigs. I tried my whole career to catch the eye of the public. Over and over, I was told I was very nice, I was very talented, and to go away."

"Now they want you, though."

Lana nodded. "The irony isn't lost on me, don't worry. But now I'm telling *them* to go away."

She touched his cheek, her fingertips feathering his cheekbone, her thumb running along his jawline. A shiver went down his back. "Lana –"

"I'm telling you to go away, too."

At their feet, Emily Dickinson whined.

"Come on," Lana said to the dog. She turned, walking away without looking back.

Carefully, as if she'd been thinking about it for a while, the little dog lifted her leg – Taft didn't even know girl dogs did that – and peed on his boot. He jumped backward and swore.

Emily Dickinson trotted off quickly to catch up to Lana, leaving Taft standing alone with one soggy boot and a heart more sodden than anything in the whole ocean.

CHAPTER THIRTY-EIGHT

L ana ran away to hide.

She felt awful and stupid for doing it, but she couldn't bear it. Until the video got taken down, she had to avoid everything to do with Taft Hill and his goddamned *sharing*.

He'd shared her secret with her sisters, and she didn't think she could let it go. She *ached* to forgive him – to find one reason she could. But that kind of reason didn't exist.

Then he'd gone and shared their private song with the world (or his manager had, same thing) and that might be even worse. The world that had rejected her now wanted her back. Not because of anything she'd done. Because of him.

Lana had left the beach and walked straight toward the hotel, but luckily, she'd caught sight of the media van parked in front. Its antenna was up, springing out of the van's roof like an ugly metal mushroom, and a blonde reporter was speaking into a mic from the Golden Spike's front porch.

It wasn't too hard to guess why they were there – a video being shared that fast was news in today's market. Lana thanked the past version of herself that had attached her master-room key to her car key. She had her phone with its debit-card holder – she didn't need anything else. The reporter kept her eyes on the camera – she didn't notice Lana opening her car door as quietly as she could, not even thirty feet away.

She'd just take a drive. A long one.

Heading north out of town, she suddenly felt the urge to cry, which pissed her off so much she mashed the accelerator to the floor. She hit seventy on the highway.

Fish and chips. That's what she needed. From the old stand twenty miles up the road, she wanted to order a bag of chips, heavy with grease, and fresh petrale sole, crispy and hot and wrapped in newspaper. She'd sit on one of the benches that lined the cliff and drench everything in vinegar. She'd dip the pieces in tartar sauce, and she'd enjoy a seaside meal.

Just like the other tourists.

She wouldn't think about Taft, the tourist who did things to her heart and body that she didn't want to understand.

Or her sisters, worried about her too many years too late.

At the turn-off, though, nothing stood but a permanent wooden outhouse and a sign outlining the rules for dogs and horses on the beach.

The fish-and-chip stand was gone.

Wait, she must be remembering its location wrong. The stand *had* to be there. It had always been there, ever since she was a girl. It didn't even have a real name, not that anyone knew, anyway. It was run by the old lady with the purple hair, who'd taken it over when her husband had died.

God, the old lady would be ancient now. Maybe dead.

Lana drove to a split, where Highway One met a smaller highway that ran east, and then she knew she hadn't missed it. She hadn't misremembered its location.

The fish-and-chip place was gone.

So was her dream.

I am the kind of woman who loses her shit when she can't eat what she wants.

Lana needed to chill *out*. It wasn't like there weren't a million other places to get good fish on the coast, up to and including the Darling Bay Café.

But it was different. Everything had changed, everything had left her behind.

At the next turn-off, Lana leaned her head against her steering wheel, trying and failing to swallow the lump in her throat that threatened to choke her. Beside her, Emily Dickinson whined.

"Cooped up too long? Let's go walk. Can't get down to the beach here, but we can walk along the edge of the cliff. Would you like that? Sometimes you see hang-gliders around these parts."

As if the dog cared, as if she spoke English. All the pup cared about was that Lana fed her in the morning and at night and petted her in between. Simple creature.

Lucky.

She dug out a bottle of water from the back and poured some into a can that had once held peanuts. Emily Dickinson lapped it up. "What about food, though, huh? You ate this morning, but I didn't." She'd been planning on getting breakfast at the café when she was done with her yoga. Then she'd been going to try to figure out how angry she was at Taft.

Well, whatever she'd been thinking she might be, she was angrier now.

And sadder.

She was *so* much sadder than she'd thought she would be. Her heart ached like she'd folded it wrong, like she'd tried to stuff it into a suitcase already too full of broken glass.

Lana found another unopened can of peanuts behind the driver's seat – thank God for road food. She and Emily Dickinson walked the path that wound its way through the ice plant and bush lupines to the cliff's edge.

Far below, the water roiled on the rocks. It was good to see the waves breaking themselves against the tide pools. The way they rushed forward and then *smacked* against the continent's edge felt familiar in her very bones. If you threw yourself at something hard enough for long enough, you finally wore it down.

That's what she used to think, anyway.

She'd come to Darling Bay with one agenda: to leave music and start her new life as a hotelier. If her sisters got in the way or presented any kind of a problem, she'd imagined herself like that wave – throwing itself against the shore until she carved out enough space for herself. She had the money. She had the time. And she had no other ideas.

Lana looked down at the dog. "What kind of marine animal would you be, huh? If I'm a wave, what are you?"

Emily Dickinson grinned and gave a sharp bark.

I'm not a wave. Who was she kidding? She didn't have the entire force of an ocean behind anything she did.

No, she was more like a mollusk, alone and powerless except for sucking.

When they were kids, she and Molly had liked to pry the mussels from the tide pools. They'd read that Native Americans had used them for food and had eaten them raw, and once they'd dared each other to suck out the slimy insides. Molly had started to do it, but then she'd chickened out. Lana, never one to back away from a challenge, had. And it had been disgusting.

Emily Dickinson peed on a manzanita bush, then trotted to the edge to look down.

"Away from there, you. The last thing I need is you falling." Is this how crazy pet owners got started? Thinking their animals knew what they were saying?

"Come here." She snapped her fingers. Emily Dickinson came willingly, happy to take a peanut as reward.

Lana put her hands on her hips. She looked west over the ocean. The water looked so far down, flat from up here. The depths were more brown than blue today, and the whitecaps were few. The roar was still there – a constant that she'd missed every day she'd ever been away from the coast.

She wanted to cry.

She drove her fingernails into her palms to prevent herself from giving in.

The horizon was crisp today, with no fog visible to blur it. How many miles was she seeing right now? Dozens? Hundreds? When she was a child, she'd thought if she just got high up enough (the big oak behind the Golden Spike or the water tower on the far edge of town) she'd be able to see Japan. It was just there – on the other side of the water. She inhaled – the air smelled of ozone and dirt and sand, and if she closed her eyes and imagined hard, she could almost smell the incense that burned in the Buddhist temples far across the water.

She'd gone to Japan once, years before. Lana had loved everything about the country – the diminutiveness of some things, the cups, the plates, and the awkward tallness of others like the busses that were double-deckers but as narrow as a passenger car, and the dizzying skyscrapers.

An American promoter had heard her sing one night. He'd told her he could make her into a star in Japan. She went with him to two shows of performers he'd been working with. It was true. They were enormously popular, and both said that he was the reason for it.

Then he'd told her his terms. They involved lots of acceptable things, and one action that wasn't – sleeping with him.

She'd laughed in his face. *I don't need your help, asshole.*

She didn't need *anyone's* help.

Lana always knew she'd make it to the top on her own terms. By her own actions. With her own art.

Except she hadn't. She'd failed.

Screw this. The wind picked up, slapping at her cheeks. "Let's go!" she called to the dog.

Wait. Just a second ago, she'd been here, right here at Lana's feet.

"Emily Dickinson?"

Just the wind answered her.

Lana ran to the edge of the cliff.

There, almost at the very bottom, was Emily Dickinson.

CHAPTER THIRTY-NINE

Emily Dickinson was alive. She was running, in fact, and appeared to have gone over the edge willingly. The cliff face sloped severely downward, at what looked like an eighty-degree angle. In seconds, the dog was on the rocky shore below, barking into tide pools and scampering over the wet boulders.

No possible way existed for Lana to get down there. A mile south there was a steep staircase that led to the shore, but the tide looked high, and the way the land curved, she doubted if there was even a way to get to the rock pools. If Lana took one step over the edge, she'd tumble to her probable death. It wouldn't be a painless one.

"Emily Dickinson!" The wind carried away her puny breath.

Adrenaline surged through her limbs, prickling her fingers and toes. The dog would *have* to scramble up on her own.

As loudly as she could, Lana bellowed, "Emily Dickinson! Come back!" She gave a whistle, but she'd only had the dog for two days – how could she expect her to be trained?

Emily Dickinson looked up. She was so small down there, barely a white speck. It had to be ninety feet down the cliff, at least. The face of it looked to be made of soft shale, and plants grew out of it all the way down, but there were no handholds, nothing that Lana could hang on to if she had to go down.

Emily Dickinson started climbing toward her.

"Yes! Come on, girl!"

It took the dog long minutes – it felt like forever – to get even halfway up.

Lana cheered and cajoled from the top. She knelt at the edge, which felt steadier than standing and leaning out into the wind. "Come on, you can do it!"

The dog grinned up at her, trying her best. She slipped a little but regained her ground.

At almost three-quarters of the way up, Emily Dickinson was panting hard, her small sides heaving.

The dog got another ten feet up, scrabbling hard at the plants and vines. She was slowing. Was she wearing out?

What should I do? Lana looked behind her, but there was no one on the cliff-top walk, no one on the road to help her. Lana took out a handful of peanuts and held them over the edge. "Treat! You can do it! I'll give you so many treats! Keep climbing!"

Emily Dickinson scratched and clawed at the slope, but her back end kept sliding down. Her forelegs trembled with the effort. Another ten feet and Lana could almost reach her –

Emily Dickinson slipped. She whined.

Then she tumbled sideways and rolled – bounced and slipped – all the way down to the tide pools below.

From so high above, Lana couldn't tell if Emily Dickinson was breathing. She certainly wasn't moving.

Everything inside Lana's body screamed at her to follow.

She knew she couldn't.

She had to call for help.

There was nothing else *to* do.

She dialed 9-1-1, grateful for the signal that was weak but present. "Help!" she said breathlessly when the dispatcher answered. "She went off the edge of a cliff, and she's fallen. I can't get to her from where I am. I don't know what to do!"

The dispatcher stayed calm, asking for Lana's exact location. "Help's already on the way. Can you tell me about her condition? Is she awake?"

"I can't tell from this far away."

"Is she breathing?"

Impatiently, Lana said, "I just told you, I can't see from here."

"How old is she?"

What did that matter?

Oh, God.

Lana realized her mistake. "She's a dog. I think I forgot to say that." She heard only silence in her ear. "Hello?"

Still nothing.

The call had been disconnected. Lana hit redial, intending to clarify the situation, which the dispatcher had probably gotten wrong and with very good reason, but whatever reception she'd had was gone, completely.

She tried again. Two, three more times, but the signal didn't come back.

Lana raced to the road to try to flag someone down, but the highway was eerily silent, and she couldn't bear to be out of sight of Emily Dickinson. She ran back.

A thrumming rose in the distance, a noise that Lana knew she recognized but couldn't quite place.

She peered down. Far below, Emily Dickinson was still motionless.

Lana's breath was so tight in her chest she felt dizzy.

The noise got louder, more of a thumping now.

Jesus.

It was a helicopter.

They'd sent a *helicopter*.

CHAPTER FORTY

Two minutes later, the helicopter hovered over the water in front of her. A voice boomed down, the sound God would make if he were in the business of rescuing fallen hikers. "Where's the victim?"

Lana pointed. "Down there!" she screamed. How would they hear her?

The helicopter dipped a little lower. Lana could look right into the open door. The man crouched inside was wearing a blue helmet and dark glasses. "Ma'am, we can't see her," the voice boomed. "Did she go into the water? Nod yes or shake your head no."

She shook her head and pointed again at the small white body below. "A dog! She's a *dog*!" Still pantomiming, Lana jumped up and down, pulling her hands up like she was begging for food. She barked, as loudly as she could.

The pilot's mic opened again, and the voice boomed, "Ma'am, we don't – wait, dude, is she saying it's a dog?"

Lana nodded her head as hard as she could. In the distance, under the roar of the helicopter, she heard sirens approaching.

The distinct sound of a snort came over the microphone.

A pause. "All right, ma'am. The fire department will be on scene soon. Hold tight."

It took an hour to bring Emily Dickinson up. Lana knew the firefighters from when they were kids cruising Darling Bay during those long, boring summers. And here they were, trying to save her dog.

Who was probably dead.

Lana's heart broke into pieces at the thought. She'd let Emily Dickinson leap to her death. Because she'd walked her right to the edge of the cliff, her little dog had probably died.

Tox Ellis and Coin Keefe rigged up a rope-and-harness system. The helicopter flew away as they worked, a graceful dragonfly arcing into the distance.

Coin went over the edge. He appeared thrilled to be doing the rappelling.

The press showed up just as Coin put Emily Dickinson into Lana's arms. They managed to get a few pictures of her crying, in which she was sure she looked amazing. She had wind-chapped cheeks and red eyes from the crying she hadn't even known she'd been doing while watching Coin being hoisted up. Emily Dickinson looked stunned, but after palpating her limbs, the paramedics had said they didn't think she'd broken anything. Tox said, "Take her to the vet. The emergency clinic should be open. Looks like she got lucky, though. This here scratch on her side is the only real damage, and it's almost stopped bleeding."

Poor bloody little dog. Emily Dickinson trembled, licking the underside of Lana's chin.

Tox used his body to block the pushiest photographer. "Can't be fun to be chased by paparazzi. I'll distract 'em. You get."

"Thank you." Her voice shook.

Tox nodded and turned. In a booming voice, he shouted, "Hey! Did you see where her other dog went? You, with the camera, can you get a good zoomed-in look at the beach down there?"

Lana made it back to town safely, but her hands shook so much she could barely take the key out of the ignition when she parked in front of the vet's office. After X-rays and a few stitches to the wound on her side, Emily Dickinson got a pain pill and became exponentially friendlier. "She's going to be pretty out of it," said the vet, a short, round man with a shiny red forehead.

"Is that bad for her?" Lana asked in mild horror as the dog humped the vet's ankle.

"Her spine looked fine." He shook his leg gently, and Emily Dickinson attached herself to Lana's boot, humping the leather lightly. "This particular pain shot sometimes has that effect."

She spoke without thinking. "Like me on tequila."

The vet blinked, hard, but kept his face neutral. "She just needs a lot of rest, to heal. It'll take time, maybe about a week."

Wouldn't that be nice? If all life's anguish got better in seven days?

Lana left her car at the vet's, hoping she could sneak onto the hotel grounds without the press noticing. She carried Emily Dickinson carefully, happy that the humping stopped as soon as she picked her up. The licking of Lana's neck didn't, but she could deal with that.

"Lana!"

"There she is!"

"Over here!"

Lana forgot for a moment what the hell they could want from her. Her arms tightened around the dog. Who *cared* about Lana Darling anymore? No one, that was who.

Then she remembered. That damn song. The video with Taft.

"You're over a million views, and rising!" shouted one man wearing an orange ball cap. "Just a few sentences, Lana, how does it feel to rocket back into the public eye?"

Adele burst out the front door of the saloon, carrying a broom. If she'd been wearing a long dress, she would have looked like an old-fashioned barmaid, sweeping out the drunken clientele. As it was, she was wearing a short denim skirt and just looked pissed. "Quit it! Out! Off!" When one of the cameramen pointed a lens at her, Adele mimed where she wanted to stick the end of her broom, and he got the picture quickly, pointing the lens back at Lana.

"Go away!" yelled Adele.

Lana, though, remembered how the press got. The more they ran away from them, the hungrier and more vicious they'd get. "Adele, I'll just talk to them. It's okay. Then they can go." They would, too, after Lana told them she was out of the business. "There's really no story here. I'll explain that to them."

"Are you sure?" Adele jabbed her broom at the toes of a young woman who'd gotten too close with her microphone. The reporter squeaked and jumped backward, almost falling off the saloon porch.

Adele's fierceness was one of her best qualities. "I'm sure." Lana checked the light. "This swing is all right, isn't it, guys?" She sat, placing Emily Dickinson gently next to her.

There were only four reporters and six camera crew, but it seemed as if there were dozens as they trained their sights on her. Three of them spoke at once.

"You." Lana pointed. "In the hat. You first."

"So, are you and Taft Hill together?"

Lana should have expected it, but the question felt dropped from an airplane onto the top of her head. "No." The answer was quick and automatic.

It was true.

And horrible.

"So that was just an act?"

"What?"

The man looked at her as if she were lacking important brain cells. "The whole lovey-dovey thing on camera with Taft, while you were singing that song? You kissed!"

"Just an act."

"So you're *not* an item. Not even dating?" This came from the young woman who'd gotten her toes poked by the broom.

"Not even dating." Emily Dickinson started slowly humping Lana's forearm. A blush started at her hairline.

"But you wrote the song together."

Lana took a breath. It was always best to stay as close to the truth as possible, to save later embarrassment. "We did."

"Were you together then?"

She looked at another man, ignoring the question. "Did you have a question?"

"We hear you've written with Taft Hill before."

A chill ran through her. "What?"

"Have you?"

She smiled slightly, disengaging Emily Dickinson from her wrist. "You know, I've written with so many people over the years. The interesting part is this, though, I've decided to leave the –"

"How much of 'Blame Me' is autobiographical?"

The chill turned to ice cubes in her stomach. "Sorry?"

"You're the songwriter, right?" The man's eyes were the color of mud. He flipped a page of his notebook.

"You performed it at a venue a few months ago. Sources say he bought it and rewrote it with you, but that it's about you and an attack that happened in your life when you were younger."

Taft.

He was the only one who could have told them.

Unless one of her sisters had – but, no. She caught sight of Adele's face, and she looked as confused and upset as Lana felt.

Taft had told *reporters* she'd written "Blame Me."

He'd told them about what happened that dark night. Coldness soaked into her bones.

"I'm so sorry to push you like this –" the man wasn't sorry, Lana could tell he was almost gleeful "– but when did the rape happen? How old were you? Did you have counseling? Who else did you tell? Have you recovered?"

A standard move – ask enough different questions and hope the truth spills out. She worked as hard as she'd ever done anything to keep a mild look on her face. "Sorry, pal. You're barking up the wrong tree, I'm afraid. Just a story I was telling. Sometimes writers do that. "Ghost Riders in the Sky" isn't about real ghosts, did you ever think about that?"

The reporter looked disgruntled that his big push hadn't worked. "But –"

"Look." Lana sat forward. Emily Dickinson slid off the swing and began humping Lana's ankle in a desultory, sleepy way. Lana shook her leg, but the dog was as determined as a drunk trying to pull out a stuck cork.

"You should know. I'm leaving – no, I've *left* the music industry. Writing that song with Mr. Hill was my last action. I'm sorry to let you down, but there's just no story here."

"Are you leaving to get married? To Taft?"

"If you're not together, is it because of your previous rape?"

"Will you two have kids?"

"Is this why your sister started her women's shelter hotline?"

It wasn't fair. None of this was.

The assault had been her secret. She'd been planning on keeping it to her grave. Now the whole world would know.

Now the whole world would feel sorry for her.

Worse, they'd want to *help* her.

For the rest of her goddamned life, if she didn't fix the spin, she'd be known as the Abuse Singer. The one who was raped and wrote about it.

That's all she would be: an object of pity, a woman who deserved a soft tone, an empathetic smile.

It was Taft's fault.

"It's a fictional song, about a fictional woman. It's helped bring his career back from the brink, I've heard."

"Hey, now." Taft's laughing voice came from her right. "What are y'all talking about? Are these folks bothering you, Lana? Should I move them along?"

Oh, *good*. Her hero, to the goddamn rescue. "No –"

The reporters all changed their clamoring, like birdsong that speeded up when thunder rumbled. Their words were louder, faster.

"Are you two together?"

"Are you in love?"

"Will you write more songs together?"

"When can we expect a new recording?"

Taft – looking like a country-album cover in his blue chambray shirt and dark-brown cowboy hat – leaned on a porch post and crossed his arms. "Don't go getting overexcited, y'all." He was playing up his Nashville drawl, and Lana hated it. "There *will* be a new album. Three more songs – no, make that two now – and we'll record it and get it right out to everybody. You're gonna love it."

"Will you write the last two songs with him, Lana?"

Lana wasn't even sure which reporter had asked, but it didn't matter. She looked into the biggest camera, the one with the biggest lens with the biggest network logo on its side. "Taft Hill is known as an excellent songwriter, but the truth is a little different. He exploits the weaknesses of his fellow musicians."

All the cameras panned to pin her in their sights.

She looked right at Taft, ignoring the soft thumping of Emily Dickinson at her calf.

"Lana," he said.

"He's not the real deal, that's what you should know." Lana's stomach hurt. "He's gotten as far as he has by lying about *who* he is."

"Who's that, Lana?"

"Who is he?"

Taft said softly, "Lana, no."

"He's not Palmer Hill's son."

A muscle jumped at Taft's jaw. The sides of his mouth turned white.

"Who is he, Lana?"

"Who's his father?"

"Who knows?" Lana said. She wanted to vomit and hoped desperately she'd get out of the camera's eye before she did.

"Taft, what do you have to say to that?"

Taft didn't even look at the reporter or the camera. He looked only at her. "Why?" His voice was grief made audible.

"Because you told them about 'Blame Me.'"

He knit his brows. "You think I would do that?"

She shouldn't keep talking in front of the cameras. She should shut up. "I didn't think you would, no. That's why it hurts so much."

"Jesus, Lana." He took a deep breath and bent halfway at the waist, as if he'd been kicked in the groin. Then he straightened. "I didn't tell them anything about you. I would *never* do that." His eyes were broken glass, his gaze full of shards.

He took a step off the porch. His boots scuffed the dirt and then his heels hit the pavement.

For a moment, Lana could hear nothing but his footsteps as he stalked away. The media people were saying things, words that made no sense, sentences she didn't bother to parse.

If he hadn't told them, who had?

Her sisters wouldn't, Lana knew.

She pulled out her cell and continued to tune out the reporters' words. If she just waited long enough on this swing, they'd get tired and go away, right? Eventually they'd get hungry and leave her to dry up. She'd turn into dust, blowing away on the ocean breeze. Hopefully.

She scrolled through the texts. So many of them, from so many people she'd forgotten she'd ever known. Sam in Reno. The guitar player in Dallas. Sandy in DC, and darling Carrie from Richmond.

There it was.

Jilly's text.

CHAPTER FORTY-ONE

*T*hey tricked me. I'm so sorry. They were probably calling everyone who knew you. They got me in a weak moment. They called because of the video, but they kept pushing and wanted to know if you and Taft had ever worked together, and you know what a bad liar I am.

It was true. Jilly couldn't even tell a polite lie, the your-haircut-is-great kind of fib.

I should have just hung up, but the guy was so good about keeping me on the phone, and he kept badgering me.

Of course the guy had been good. He was probably from one of the big media sites, the tawdry online-only ones (the ones that got the truth more often than not, because they didn't fear barging into anything. They would scoop funerals when they could get away with it).

It just slipped out. He asked if there was a story behind "Blame Me" and I said no, but then I'd accidentally confirmed it.

I know he didn't believe me. He'd already jumped on it, and then he'd hung up and it was too late. I'm so sorry. I don't blame you if you never want to be friends again.

At this moment?

No, Lana didn't want to be friends with Jilly.

She stood. Emily Dickinson reluctantly detached from her ankle. "Sorry, kids, this fun is over."

Lana ignored them all. She went through the bar (they followed), into the back storage room (they stopped) and into the arbor. She started running then, and didn't slow until she was inside her room. Emily Dickinson panted ecstatically and guzzled water, doing several fast laps of the room while barking. Lana sat on the small sofa, which gave with a dusty wheeze. The dog leaped into her lap.

Lana tried very hard not to cry.

It took all her concentration, which was good. She didn't have much to spare for anything else for a minute. Maybe two.

Then the sadness crept back in.

And the guilt.

The anger, too, came back, thank *God*.

Fury was better – so much better than the regret she was starting to feel, deep red and viscous, like congealed blood.

Jilly should never have told anyone anything. It wasn't right.

Even by accident.

It wasn't *right* to share a person's deepest secret to anyone, let alone the media.

Lana would always be the rape victim, from here on out. Forever.

Then the truth sank in.

Lana groaned and covered her eyes. She drew up her legs and felt pain bloom behind her temples.

By telling the reporters about Taft not being Palmer's son, she'd done the exact same thing.

Worse.

Her assault was in the past. It changed how she looked at the world, of course, and it always would. But it was already hers, already something she knew how to live with.

Because of her, Taft would now and forever be the man who had lied about the very essence of who he was.

Of course, no matter what, Taft had never *been* Palmer. He was good – maybe even great – but his father had been bigger than Johnny Cash. If Taft had tried his entire life, he would have attained Palmer's status by the time he was sixty. Maybe seventy.

Now he never would.

Taft would never be seen as heir to the throne.

He'd be the usurper. Forever. The liar. The cheat.

It was Lana's fault.

I am the kind of woman who tells a secret and breaks a man's life.

She finally cried then, her tears so hot they burned her cheeks. She didn't cry for herself – she didn't deserve a single tear spent.

Lana cried for Taft.

For what she'd done to him.

For the way she'd blown up whatever they'd had a tiny chance of ever having together. He'd told her sister about her assault, trying to do the right thing.

She'd ruined his life, publicly, on purpose.

They were children squabbling over a swing at the playground, and instead of choosing another swing, she'd dropped a nuclear bomb that took out the whole city.

She'd blown all of it into kingdom come and she wanted to fly away into dust along with the wreckage.

CHAPTER FORTY-TWO

Bourbon on the porch.

That's what Taft had, and it was almost all he had left in the world.

He had a nice new-to-him house, on the coast, in a part of the world most of the rest of the world longed to live in. His backyard opened into the Pacific. That stretch of beach down there? Technically, he owned it.

It would be handy when he built a wall around the property. He'd brick himself in, so no one could ever talk to him or see him again. Walkers on the beach would wonder where the partition had come from, and then they'd take pictures of it to share back home. Kids would graffiti it. Eventually, years down the line, someone would come check on him and find him dead on the porch, probably of alcoholism, which he intended to acquire as soon as humanly possible. Maybe even tonight if he could figure out how to keep the whole bottle of alcohol down.

Waves crashed, and even though they were five hundred yards away at the bottom of the cliff, he could hear them as if he were *in* them, being tumbled around like a shoe in a washing machine.

His cell rang.

Davina.

Shit. When was the last time his mother had called him?

Not since she'd told him the truth on his birthday. The day he'd met Lana.

He took a long swallow of bourbon, feeling it burn down his throat and into his stomach. "You heard."

"I can't believe you told them. Why did you do it?" Her voice was a whine, and instead of making him annoyed like it usually did, he just felt sad.

"I didn't. Someone else did."

"That Darling girl. I *knew* it. I saw the video, and I've got to say, you two look as ridiculous as a pair of teenagers."

It made sense. He'd felt like one around Lana, like they'd invented kissing, like they were the first to ever fall in love.

In love.

He was such a fucking idiot. "I won't disagree with you on that."

His mother sucked in air, as if surprised. "So she *is* the one who told the media about Palmer?"

"Why is this about Palmer at all?" He was struck by something that hadn't occurred to him before this very second. "When it comes right down to it, this is about you."

"Me?"

"*You're* the one who had a baby and lied about its parentage. For thirty-six years. It's not like any of this was Palmer's fault."

"Darling." It was her charming voice. His mother *could* be endearing when she tried to be, which she did for the first six months of any relationship with a man. Problem was, Taft couldn't remember back to being in the womb.

"Nope. Not his fault, Mom."

"You're blaming *me*?"

Hell, yes, he was. "You should have been honest."

"And have him abandon me? Where would we have been?"

"We?" Rage was making his hands shake.

"Me and you."

"I'm familiar with the definition." Maybe that was the primary problem, that he and Davina had never felt like family, ever, not even since he was a child. She'd had a vested interest in keeping Palmer happy when they'd been together, and who knew? Maybe they were. She'd always lit up in a way when she'd been with Palmer that Taft hadn't seen any other time. She'd been a loving wife to him more often than not. She just hadn't been an enthusiastic mother. When he was little, Taft would run to Palmer to be soothed. It was Palmer he yelled for at night after a bad dream, never Davina. "There was never a *we*."

Another gasp. "You hurt me. Why do you hurt me like that?"

She was just a woman.

For years, Davina had been almost mythical in his mind, the guilt over his feelings toward her eating him alive. He loved her because she was his mother. But he didn't *like* her.

For the first time, he saw her clearly. She was just a broken, lonely woman who didn't know how to love a son, which was sad.

But it wasn't his problem. He could honor her – she was his mother, he was pretty damn sure of that, at least. He didn't have to admire her, though, something he'd been trying and failing to do his whole life.

"If I hadn't married Palmer, where would we be today? I'd be working in a laundromat in Tulsa. Like my mother. You would probably be a ... a carpenter or something."

"Would that be so bad? Either of those things?"

"I will *never* understand you."

"You don't have to."

"We'll deny it. I'll go on *Good Morning America* and I'll say she made it up to get attention."

"The jig's up, Mom. It's over."

His mother's wail was long and painful in his ear. "You'll end up on skid row!"

"Is that even a thing anymore?"

"Somewhere it is. You'll end up hooked on drugs and overdosing in a hotel in Vegas."

"Are you wishing or predicting?"

"Don't make fun of me!" Her voice cracked, and Taft remembered how it used to do that when Palmer would tease her, when they'd laugh in the kitchen and she'd yell at him but not mean it. Palmer would steal a kiss after her frustration about whatever it was wound down, and his mother would seem almost happy in those moments. Palmer had loved Davina. He'd loved love, period.

Taft cleared his throat. "I'll always consider him my father."

"But you'll tell the world."

"The truth, yes."

"Taft."

"I owe them that. Dad believed in honesty above all, remember?" It felt good and awful at the same time to call Palmer Dad again.

You're the best thing that ever happened to me.

"He wouldn't be proud of me for keeping a secret like this."

"You don't owe them a thing."

"I do. Because of him."

"You'll be broke."

"That's okay." Taft held out his hand and looked at his knuckles. He made a fist. "I'm strong. I'm in my thirties. I've still got a lot of work I can do with these bones. It's funny you mentioned carpentry –"

"What about *me*?"

This was the core issue. *This* was why she'd called. "You got everything of his, Ma. You're fine."

There was a long pause. "I'm running out. Again."

"Money will still come in, don't worry." The royalties in Palmer Hill's trust still brought in more money than most wealthy Americans would ever see.

"What if it's not enough?"

"Then you scale back." He watched a seagull light on the corner of the railing. It looked at him with one beady eye, as if judging how likely he was to throw stale bread.

"I was counting on you," his mother wailed again.

"That was your first problem." The seagull clucked, disappointed.

"Taft."

A sour taste that had nothing to do with the bourbon filled his mouth. "You're right. I'm sorry. You know I'll always take care of you." It was true. He didn't have to like his mother, but he'd make sure she was comfortable.

"How? You're a nobody now."

He liked the sound of it. "Royalty money will keep coming in, no matter what the press says about me. I'll be okay. And I bought a house out here. In Darling Bay."

"You're staying there? With her?"

Not with Lana. No.

No.

Heavily, he said, "I like it here. I've joined a construction crew."

"You *what*?"

"There's enough room in the yard for one of those tiny homes. I'll contract the guys to help me build it, and if you and Teddy ever split, you can live in it if you need to."

"Me? In a tiny home?"

He almost laughed. "You'd be fine. There are TV shows about it. You just get rid of everything you own, get down to four changes of clothes. Two plates, two mugs. You can eat up at my house if you need a bigger table."

"You're teasing me."

He was, but he was more than half serious at the same time. "I'm not sure about running water out to it – I think there are pretty strict laws about digging extra sewer lines this close to shore. There are composting toilets."

A sigh came through the earpiece.

He smiled – he couldn't help it. "People say they don't even smell."

"I'm glad you're finding this funny."

"I hadn't been, until you called." Honestly, it wasn't the worst idea he'd ever had. He'd always loved those tiny homes, even as he found them ridiculous and entitled. Those not able to afford much space had been living in tiny places for as long as humankind had needed shelter, and now rich people were discovering the joy of less?

It would be fun to build, and it would be hilarious to see his mother, to whom travelling light meant taking only one suitcase of shoes instead of three, try to fit herself into a space the size of her smallest closet. "You might like it. Pare down. See what's essential."

"Stop teasing me."

"Okay, okay. Look, just don't answer your phone for a month. It'll blow over in two or three weeks. No one will care. They'll move on."

"They'll want to know who your real father was."

"Screw 'em. You don't owe them anything."

There was a longer pause. "Do you hate me?"

He sighed and took another sip. The seagull took off with a clapping of wings. "No, of course I don't."

"I was only trying to do what was best for you."

The problem was that he knew it wasn't true. It would be nice if it were. If Davina had been the kind of mother who would bare her teeth and fight off the wolves at the door by doing whatever it took to take care of him.

She'd been looking out for herself.

By doing it, she'd taken pretty damn good care of Taft along the way. "You couldn't have picked a better father for me. I know that."

"Taft." A short pause. "I love you."

Maybe she meant it. He'd give her the benefit of the doubt. "You, too, Mom."

"Am I going to have to meet her?"

Lana. He had wanted them to meet. He'd wanted to introduce them, to tell Lana everything about her.

He'd wanted his mother to approve of Lana, as stupid as that sounded now.

"No, Mom. You won't have to."

"Good." Her voice was brisk. "No tiny home."

"Tour bus?"

She laughed, and for a moment Taft wiped the image of Lana betraying him out of his mind and just let the sound of his mother's laughter and the ocean's waves fill his ears.

His heart, he knew, would never be filled again.

CHAPTER FORTY-THREE

Lana lay in her bed. Alone.

Well, except for Emily Dickinson, of course. The dog made it hard to feel alone with the way she wriggled and squirmed and tried to nuzzle right underneath Lana.

But Lana was managing to feel lonely anyway.

"Come here, you." She wrestled lightly with Emily Dickinson, but the pup got carried away and nipped the side of her thigh, right through her yoga pants. "Ow!" Those little teeth were ridiculously sharp. She pushed the dog away, and then immediately felt guilty at the shocked look on Emily's face. "I'm sorry. Jeez. Sorry, little one."

Lana wanted something. Someone.

She wanted Taft.

So badly. She wanted to run to him, wherever he was, and apologize. Grovel.

But how did you apologize for ruining a person's entire life?

There was no way. It was impossible.

Her eye fell on the framed photo – Molly and Adele laughing, Lana frowning in the background.

There were twenty-two new texts on her phone, two of them from Molly: *Are you okay? Come eat. You can hide in the kitchen.* Three were from Adele: *Come upstairs. Tell me how you are. I'm worried. Don't make me use the master key on your room.*

Being in this room was unbearable.

She tucked Emily Dickinson in her crate. "Time to sleep." Emily Dickinson curled up without a single whimper, burying her nose in the blanket.

That was good. At least there was one living thing at peace.

Not Lana, though. She needed ...

I am the kind of woman who doesn't need anyone.

What a lie.

She went outside. Sitting on the porch swing in front of the room, she dialed Molly. It went to voicemail. She didn't leave a message.

Lana heard a light laugh. Adele's voice.

She crept forward in the dark, sneaking into the garden, far enough that she could look up and see Adele give Nate a kiss. Her sister said something to him to make him grin, and then he ran down the stairs and into the arbor behind the saloon.

What would it be like? To be with a man who loved you like that? Nate's eyes lit up every time her sister walked into his view.

What would it feel like to be confident in that love?

Lana couldn't even imagine.

She took a deep breath and then went up the stairs to their back apartment. She walked past the picnic table, touching a string of white lights. When Uncle Hugh had lived up here, the whole deck had been covered with car parts and spare buckets and whatever gas grill he was tinkering with.

Now the space looked like something out of *Better Homes & Gardens*.

What was best? Then, or now? Then, her parents had been alive. The girls had been young, in a band that was setting the country on fire.

Now, their parents and uncle were dead. They were – all three of the girls – washed up. Adele and Molly still sang a bit, but the reason they'd made their album earlier in the year was to raise money for Molly's charity, Migration. It wasn't to tour, or to make serious cash, or to garner critical attention.

It hadn't been the Darling Songbirds – Lana hadn't even been on the album. (Molly had asked her to sing with them, via text, of course. Of course, Lana had said no.)

Everything was different now. Maybe it wasn't for the worse, exactly, but could it possibly be for the better?

Lana was still alone.

Always little Lana the loner, off by herself.

Her hand raised to rap on Adele's door.

Then she let it fall. The last time they'd spoken, up here on this same porch, they'd argued. They'd come *so close* to finally talking about what mattered, and then Lana had run.

She turned to go.

The door opened. "Why didn't you knock?"

"What?" Lana hunched her shoulders and turned to look guiltily at her sister.

"I heard you come up the stairs. I was watching you through the window."

"Spy."

"You just stood there." Adele's voice was soft. "What was going through your head?"

Anger. Sadness. Despair. Tears burned at the back of Lana's eyes again. "I don't know. I didn't know what to do."

Adele held the door all the way open. "You just come in. That's all."

While Lana sat silently at the kitchen table, her sister made popcorn. It had been ages since Lana had seen anyone do it on the stove, heating the oil, shaking the pot back and forth. The smell made her think of afternoons at the movies and of nights at home in Nashville. "Dad always liked it without butter," Lana said.

Adele shook the pot again, holding the lid on. "And Mom would sneak it on."

"He'd always complain but he'd eat it anyway."

"We all did." Adele poured it into a bowl. "I don't know how you like it. That's terrible." She looked sad, but there was only room for one heartbroken Darling girl at a time.

"I'll tell you. Then you'll know." Lana held out the box of salt. "All salt, all the time, no butter, unless you want some, and then I'll just be the opposite of Dad and eat it without complaining."

Adele's smile was cautious. "How about the tiniest bit of butter you ever saw? So tiny you won't even notice it's there."

Her sister carried the bowl into the sitting room at the front of the building. Lana followed. A memory of lying on the hardwood floor struck her. "Remember we used to beg Uncle Hugh to drill a hole in the floor? So we could spy on the dance floor from up here?"

Adele nodded. "Maybe we'll do that someday."

"You might get sued. Lack of privacy or something." They were just words. Just noises, to give the air something to do around them. Lana felt sweat start at her temples, but she wasn't hot.

Adele sat on the old red settee. She patted the spot next to her.

Lana sat awkwardly and took a handful of popcorn.

Adele, though, didn't seem uneasy at all. She sat, crossing her legs under her. "I'm sorry about the way I acted last night. I was bossy, as usual, and I pushed too much. That's why you ran away from me in the first place, and I've been so scared I'll do it again that I don't quite know what to say."

Lana stared. Adele *knew* she was pushy? And she was apologizing for it? The world seemed suddenly upside-down.

Adele held out the bowl. "You don't have to take care of me. Tell me about you, little one."

The endearment hit her like a punch. "That's what Mama called me."

"I think she called all of us that."

It was a sentence that would have pissed Lana off a year ago. Maybe even a month ago. How dare Adele try to steal an endearment from her?

But now it crossed Lana's mind that Adele had no intention of stealing anything at all. She was just a woman, doing her best in the world.

A pregnant woman.

"You're going to have one of those. A little Darling." Lana pointed at Adele's stomach. "Unless you take Nate's name, that is."

Adele rubbed her small belly. "Never. I'm a Darling. I'll die one. If I wasn't a Darling, I wouldn't know who I was."

Lana felt a rush of unexpected relief flood her bones coolly and sweetly, like the tea their mother used to make. "Me, too."

"Good. Now. What happened? I kept getting press phone calls at the bar, and those leeches were trying to pry something out of me, so I made Nate take over."

Lana hadn't even considered the fact that obviously, the reporters would flock to Adele or Molly if they couldn't get to her. "What did they say?"

"That you said Taft was a bastard."

"They *said* that?"

"Did you?"

She guessed so. "Not in those words."

"But you said Palmer Hill's not his real father?"

Lana nodded, dumbly, struck all over again by how impossibly unforgivable her action had been.

"Is it true?"

That's what everyone would want to know. They'd pressure Taft into either confirming or denying, and then there would be a paper chase – paparazzi would dive into every bit of history they could get their hands on, to figure out who Taft's real father was. The way information was stored now, they'd find it. Taft had said the man was dead, but that he had a sister. They'd dig her up – they'd shock her with the truth that she had a half-brother. They'd probably do it on camera and film her expression, presenting it as a fait accompli. She and Taft would be front-page news for about half a day, until the next scandal broke, but Taft's career would be mostly finished.

"Yeah. It's true."

Adele shifted. "Why did you do it?"

"I was mad that he'd told you about my past. I thought he'd told the reporters about it, too."

"He didn't."

"How did you know?"

"Because Taft isn't the kind of person who'd do that."

The heat of grief seared Lana's lungs. "I am."

"No. You're not. I didn't mean it that way."

But Lana wasn't mad at Adele. All the anger in the world should be directed at her, no one else. "How do I get everything so wrong? How on earth have I made it this far? It seems like I should have been culled out of the herd by now."

"What?"

"The weak ones. You know. On all those old animal shows. The weak ones get taken down and killed by the next stronger thing on the savannah."

Adele stared at her. "You think you're the *weak* one?"

Lana rolled her eyes. "Don't pretend you don't think so."

"Lana!" Adele set the popcorn bowl on the table with a *thunk*.

"Adele!" Lana tried to mimic her sister's tone.

"I swear to God, if you roll your eyes once more at me, they'll fall out of your head."

Old irritation flamed its way up Lana's spine, and she opened her mouth to say, *Oh, yeah? Like I care! You can't tell me anything!*

Then it hit her.

They were grown-ass women now.

They weren't children.

They didn't have the same roles anymore.

Her big sister was just a person. A smart, good, kind person who was adult enough to call her on her bullshit.

Lana said, "I'm sorry I rolled my eyes."

Adele just nodded shortly, appearing to accept the apology at face value. "No problem. Back to my question. Do you really think you're the weak Darling?"

"I'm the little one. The last one. The one who fails at everything she tries."

Adele's laugh was melodic. "Lana. You're the one Molly and I look up to."

Lana kept her eyes from rolling but she did drop her head to the back of the settee. "Seriously, don't blow smoke. I don't need it, I promise I don't."

Adele grasped her hand. "Lana. We didn't make it. You're the only one who kept trying."

"You and Molly wrote an album."

"It's made the center twelve thousand dollars so far. It's not exactly going platinum."

Lana pushed further. "You're a professional songwriter."

"I took home less than fifty thousand from songwriting last year."

Holy crap. Lana had made that much in the last two months from "Blame Me." "Seriously?"

"I've never had a number-one hit, like you have. I haven't spent the last twelve years on the road, singing my own songs to people who love me."

"I don't sell out shows."

"You don't sell out arenas. I bet you sell out small shows."

It was true. Sometimes she did. The Freight and Salvage in Berkeley was standing room the last time she played. Largo in LA was the same, as was the Silent Barn in New York.

"But ..."

"I *will* tell you what you're bad at, though."

CHAPTER FORTY-FOUR

Here it was. This was when Adele would launch on her, going back to the old days and about how careless Lana had been, how she'd deserved everything bad that had ever happened to her. "Yeah?" Lana stuck out her chin.

"You're *so* bad at asking for help."

A piece of popcorn stabbed her in the cheek. "I asked for help earlier today. I got a helicopter. I almost died of embarrassment."

Adele gave a half-smile. "I heard about that, too."

Lana flopped backward again. "Is there anything you *don't* hear in the bar?"

"Not really. Look, I mean ask for help in other things, too. For everything."

"But I don't need help with *everything.*"

Adele arched an eyebrow.

Shit. Maybe she did. "How?"

"How what?"

"How do I know when to ask?"

"When you've run out of your own good ideas."

"I ran out a while ago."

"Then ask now." Adele's face was composed, but her left eye twitched. It had been her tell when they were kids – it still was now. Adele was inches from crying and the fact that this mattered – really mattered – to her big sister was everything Lana needed to know.

For the first time, Lana noticed that Adele had the same framed picture Lana carried around with her, sitting on the end table. "Look." She pointed. "Even then, I was the odd one out." Always alone. Always wishing to catch up, and being unable to. Always behind in the jokes, in the running, in the playing. She'd learned early to make her own fun, since Adele and Molly never slowed down for her.

Adele turned her head to look. She made a sound resembling a cough. "I remember that moment so well. You know what we were laughing about?"

That I was too little. That I was dumb. That I was slow. That I was in the way. "No."

"Daddy had just told us you were getting a big-girl bike for your birthday. We were giggling because we knew the secret."

"Oh." Her sisters looked so excited.

So happy.

For her.

"*Seriously?*"

Adele nodded.

"Shit." If she'd been wrong about this picture for so long...what else had she been so wrong about?

"What next, little one?"

"How do I get over a broken heart?"

Tears filled Adele's eyes. "Time. And hanging out with people who love you. Who think you're amazing and wonderful, people who want to be near you."

"Know anyone like that?"

Adele smiled through her tears. "I might know a couple."

"What if – I know it's impossible, but – how do I get him to forgive me?"

"You ask."

It couldn't be so simple. It wouldn't work. Lana shook her head.

"Just try," said Adele. "See what happens."

"I have to do more than that."

"Sometimes you just need to apologize."

"Mind if I practice?"

Adele brightened and sat up straighter. "Great idea! Okay, I'm Taft." She cleared her throat and lowered her voice. "Go."

"No, you be Adele."

"Huh?"

"Just be yourself."

Adele nodded and folded her hands in her lap. "Okay."

Lana took a deep breath. "I'm sorry."

Adele sucked in her lips, and her eyes got wet again. She started to speak.

"No. Don't say anything. You'll say something stupid like I don't owe you an apology –"

"No, I'll take one of those, if you've got one for me."

Lana drew back, unsure whether to be offended or not. But Adele had a small smile on her face, and there was love in her eyes.

There was so much gorgeous love.

Lana said, "I'm not sorry about pushing you away back then – that's just what I had to do."

Adele opened her mouth but Lana held up her hand. "Just let me get through this, okay? I'm sorry I didn't trust you. You were just trying to do the right thing by getting us back on stage. You were trying to hold us all together, and we'd always been held together by Mom and Dad. You didn't know how to do it, and you couldn't be them, no matter how hard you tried, but the fact is you tried. I love you for it. It's *not* your fault what happened to me." Lana's voice cracked. She wouldn't have admitted it until now, but she'd held Adele partially to blame for that awful night. "I'm sorry I ran away for so long."

"Stop it now." Adele's lower lip wobbled. "I get it. You're good at apologies. You're not going to need my help with Taft."

"I love him." The words were out of her mouth before she could stop them. Lana would never have predicted in a million years that the first person to whom she'd confess the outrageous, unexpected love of a man would be Adele, but there it was.

"I know."

Lana rolled her neck. "You do not."

"I do, too. You go all dizzy when he's around."

"Ditzy? No way."

"Not ditzy. Dizzy. Soft-focus. Like you're there but you're also listening to something that no one else can hear."

That's what it felt like, being around Taft. She was hyper-aware of where he was, when he breathed, how he moved. "But if we're finished – and I think we are, of course it is – how do I get over him?"

Adele shook her head. "Honey, I have no idea. I thought I'd lost Nate for a while there, and it was the lowest I'd ever been in my life."

"How did you get him back?"

"I wrote a song."

Lana snorted. "You would."

"You could, too."

"Nah. There has to be something else. Something bigger."

"Skywriter?"

"Something bigger that isn't cheesy as hell."

Adele stretched out her legs and rubbed her belly. For the first time, Lana noticed she was wearing her jeans unbuttoned under the hem of her shirt.

Lana held out her hand. "You're showing."

Adele grinned. "Yep."

"Can I touch?"

"Can you? Heck, yeah." Adele took her hand, pressing Lana's fingers to the soft skin at her bellybutton. "Get used to seeing this skin stretched out. I'm going to need you, both of you, in there with me when this kid arrives."

"In the *birthing room*?"

"That's your job. Straight up. You're not getting out of it."

It was a sister responsibility Lana had never even considered. She was terrified.

And she couldn't wait. "Okay."

Adele laughed, a round, joyful sound. "Good. Okay, now back to your man. What does he want, most of all?"

Lana folded her hands carefully in her lap. Wouldn't it be nice if the answer was her? Lana Darling? But it wasn't, she knew. "Probably that he could make it all go away."

"The truth?"

"Yeah. That I spilled."

"Want to know what I think?"

Lana tilted her head. "You know, you never usually ask. It's nice when you ask."

Adele grimaced. "I get it."

"So go ahead."

"I think that what you did was wrong. Not only that, you did it for the wrong reasons."

The dagger twisted deeper in Lana's belly. "I know."

"I can't help thinking it comes back to one thing, though, and that's truth. You spoke the truth. It was a lie he was keeping in front of the whole world, and it can't have felt good."

"The whole truth-will-set-you-free cliché?"

"Yeah, but come on. Maybe it will. Maybe he'll find the long-lost family he didn't know he's always wanted."

"He has a sister," Lana exclaimed, remembering. "A half-sister."

"Does he have contact with her?"

"No." This was hopeless. "What do we do now?"

"Now we eat all the popcorn and you tell me everything."

"What?"

"From the moment you got on the bus."

The Greyhound station in New York. Lana's heart had pounded triple-time as she'd paid for her ticket in the Port Authority. She'd been nineteen, old enough to be on her own, young enough and sad enough to be more scared than she'd ever been.

"I saw you there." The confession suddenly felt important. Just as they'd pulled away, she'd seen Adele running toward the bus.

"I know."

"From the bus. I saw you standing in the station." She hadn't yelled. She hadn't asked to get off the bus. She'd been frozen, sitting terrified in the plastic seat.

Adele nodded. "I know," she said again.

"I'm s–"

"No. No more apologies. Save those for him. Tell me your stories, and I'll tell you mine. Like we're new girlfriends, learning each other's best tales."

"Except better." Lana held a handful of popcorn carefully. "Because we're sisters."

"So much better."

And even while Lana's heart felt as shredded and heavy as lead, the popcorn tasted of salt and hope.

CHAPTER FORTY-FIVE

On the job site (because that's the way he was trying to think about it now, not as Lana's hotel, but just a site where he went to make a pay check while he decided what to do next), Taft was working in the laundry room. The old machines had been swapped out for new, shiny white models, two front loaders and one huge dryer that held four loads. He turned off the main water and started working on the plumbing. It was close to the arrangement they'd had, but different enough that every single pipe adaptor he bought at the hardware store was a little bit wrong. It took him seven trips, and his anger at the old pipes almost overtook his anger at Lana by mid-afternoon.

He swore as he banged at a washer that had probably been tightened in the stone ages. It was never going to loosen.

Taft missed hearing Lana laugh on site, listening to the way her voice rose and fell. When she laughed, it almost sounded as if she were singing.

He'd be better off forgetting it.

Lana wasn't at the site on Monday.

Or on Tuesday.

The *dog* was around. Adele appeared to be watching her, but she let her run all over the construction site. Emily Dickinson's favorite thing in the world seemed to be finding Taft and yapping up at him, painfully loudly, barely pausing for breath.

"What's her problem?"

Jake laughed. "She hates you, man."

Like dog, like owner.

When Taft finally dug up the nerve to ask where Lana was, Jake said all he knew was that she'd needed to do something in Nashville.

Yeah, right, she'd quit the industry. That obviously hadn't stuck. He couldn't blame her for it, either, though he wanted to.

He checked his phone. Ten more messages, probably all from press, about Palmer. It would blow over – it had to – but his anger wouldn't.

His disappointment.

The fact was, though, that he was equally as disappointed with himself.

Outside the laundry room, heavy footsteps sounded. A thud reverberated through the wall and someone – no, two people – sat on the porch swing in front of room five.

"Where's Taft?" It was Jake's voice.

"Saw him head for the hardware store about an hour ago," Socal said.

"Good God, he's never going to get that connection right."

Taft's spine straightened.

Socal laughed. "I know. He tries, though."

Pity? Was that *pity* he heard in their voices?

"What do you think about the rumor?" Jake asked.

"Palmer Hill's son, not actually related to him? It's crazy. I think we never have any idea what's really going on behind the scenes."

"You think he'll keep singing?"

"Dunno. Maybe that's why he's on this job. Maybe he knew it was only a matter of time and he needed a backup pay check."

Taft heard Jake sigh. "He's good enough. He knows wood, for sure. Plumbing and electricity, though? I wouldn't trust him to wire my house without me watching every move."

That wasn't fair. Taft just didn't have as much experience with wiring as he did with sawing and hammering.

"Nice guy. I like him a lot. But nah, I don't think he's going to stick around. He was here for Lana, and now that she's blown it, he'll be gone within a week or two."

Jake said, "But he bought that house."

"He's rich! God knows it's easier to find a vacant house to buy in this town than it is to rent a room."

"What would it be like, to have that kind of money?" Jake sounded more curious than envious.

"We'll never know how the other half lives. You think your show will come through on the filming soon?"

"Maybe. They're trying to get a camera crew here."

Taft frowned. Jake and his brothers were on a reality show called *On the Market*, but Jake had said they weren't filming a segment for another few weeks, until after this job.

Jake went on. "I'm just kind of worried he'll split now that Lana's broken his heart, and we won't get the press from them being together."

"Don't you think he'll figure it out? That you hired him to make the network happy?"

"Hey, that was Aidan's idea, not mine. He's the TV mastermind."

Once Taft had ridden in a small rodeo to raise money for charity. A bull had kicked him in the chest. The champion rider who'd been training him told him it was just a touch.

It had felt like the bull's foot had almost gone through his body.

This was the same feeling.

Socal said, "Let me get in the laundry room with the pipes. He can help Sturgeon out with the sheetrock. Every single time he goes back to the hardware store, it's costing you money and time, you know that. I *told* you it wasn't a good idea, didn't I?"

Taft stood from the crouch he'd been frozen in. His left knee popped so loudly he held his breath. He would step outside. He'd say, "I'm back from the store," and he'd watch their jaws drop.

They wanted him for *marketing*. To promote the Ballard Brothers company.

"Nah, I still think it's a great idea. It's nice to have him around." Jake sounded cheerful.

"He's costing you money."

"I gotta argue with you there. He came up with the ceiling fix in room seven that none of us were able to figure out."

"He's a singer."

Taft held his breath. This was where they'd say *Yeah, but he's not ever going to be Palmer Hill, huh? Especially now.*

"I know," said Jake. "Honestly, he's my favorite singer in the whole world."

Socal laughed. "Really? Even over his father-who-isn't-his-father?"

"Taft's *Under the Hill* album is genius. Every track. He produced it, too, did you know that? It got me through a hell of a rough time, I tell you what. I owe that man a lot."

Socal grunted. "Okay. I hear you."

"He's gifted. We're lucky to have him here. I don't care if the network doesn't come through. That was Aidan's idea, not mine. I'm just glad to know the man and call him a friend."

Taft's face burned. He held his breath, suddenly unwilling to risk making a single noise.

"You wanna get back up in the attic?"

Taft listened to them climb the ladder on the porch.

He finished fixing the line to the washing machine. He got it right, finally.

Jake was a fan. For the right reasons.

If Jake was out there, surely there were more people like him out there, too.

What if he just hadn't been putting on the right suit? He'd been trying for so long to be Palmer Hill's son, what if he just had to be Taft Hill?

A rush of hope filled him, one he hadn't felt for a long time. A hope that he could make the music work.

Who was he kidding? He didn't want to quit. He might want to build more things, but he wanted to keep performing.

He probably always had.

What if he could be successful just being plain old Taft Hill, son of a nobody who played guitar pretty well?

But that was a lot to hope for.

And without Lana, what did it matter?

As soon as the work on the hotel was complete, he'd pack his shit and he'd get out of this town as fast as the first flight out of SFO could take him. Maybe Thailand. He hadn't been there in years. Or New Zealand. Was that as far from California as a person could get? Antarctica, maybe.

He didn't know if it was possible to outrun a broken heart, but he'd never know till he tried.

CHAPTER FORTY-SIX

Nashville's midtown was never quiet, not where Jilly lived, anyway. Music poured out of bars and clubs, drifting like smoke down the street. The summer air smelled like the Cumberland River. Lana's backpack was as heavy as her heart as she got out of the Uber and walked down the crowded sidewalk toward Jilly's apartment building.

"Hey, Songbird!" someone yelled.

A woman squealed. "It's her!"

Lana gave as cheerful a wave as she could muster to the drunken crowd gathered in front of the Newport Inn. "It's me!" she muttered. "Large as life, twice as idiotic."

Using the key she still had to the building, she let herself in. She went up the four flights of stairs – the elevator in this old building hadn't been trustworthy since Nixon had been.

She didn't let herself in to Jilly's apartment, even though Jilly would probably forgive her if she did.

Lana knocked.

On the other side of the door, she heard scuffling. She knew that Jilly was looking out the peephole so she put her eyeball up to it, the way she used to when Lana lived here.

When they were tight.

The door flew open. "I'm so sorry! Lana! I'm sorry."

"It's okay."

Jilly looked tired. Her eyes had dark rings under them, and tears immediately swelled. "Oh, my God. I thought you'd never talk to me again."

"I thought about it."

"But you're here."

"You're not the only reason."

Jilly opened the door wider. "Come in?"

Lana planted her boots more firmly on the ground. "Look. I know you're sorry."

"Oh." Jilly's hand went out and then dropped. "I can't *tell* you how sorry I am."

"I don't need you to, that's the thing." Lana held up her wrist so Jilly could see the tattoo. "We all screw up."

"But ... why ..." Jilly looked confused.

Lana couldn't blame her. "I'm here to offer you a job."

Jilly blinked. "Huh?"

"It starts tonight, though. Want it?"

"Yes."

Lana hitched her backpack higher. "Don't you want to hear what it is first?"

"Don't need to."

"You trust me that much?"

"That's what friends are for." Jilly paled further. "I mean, if we're still friends."

"You're a terrible liar."

"I am."

"It's one of your best traits."

"Oh." Jilly looked as if she was barely breathing.

"The job comes with a place to live."

"Oh!" Jilly bobbed on the balls of her toes – long ago, before she was a producer, she'd been a dancer. Lana knew that when she was nervous, she had to move, to sway.

"That place is in California."

"Fantastic."

Lana laughed. "Don't you need to know more?"

"Girl." Jilly finally reached forward and they hugged so hard Lana could feel her ribs creak. "You know I've been trying to get out of this place for ages. What do you want me to do?"

Lana held up her cell phone. "Tonight? I have a meeting with someone. I want you to film it."

"Okay. And after that?"

"I'm starting an artist-in-residence program at the hotel. Songwriters can apply to come stay in one of my rooms. Another room will be for you to stay in, where you can produce their songs."

"I love it." Jilly nodded. "I'm in."

"You want to talk salary now or later?"

"Later. I owe you a drink first, I think."

"That you do." Lana stepped over the threshold with relief so sweet it made her heart ache.

❧

"Oh, God." Lana looked up at the stately Tudor home. "Is this a bad idea?"

"Honestly?" Jilly stood next to her on the doorstep.

"No, don't tell me."

"You still following your heart?"

It was the only thing she was doing. It was all Lana had left. "Yes. How am I supposed to trust it?"

Jilly shrugged. "You just have to. Ready?" She trained her iPhone on Lana. "Ring the doorbell."

Lana did.

A few minutes later, an older man wearing a well-cut dark-blue suit opened the door. He had crinkles around his eyes that hinted he smiled a lot.

He wasn't smiling now.

Sully Tavin introduced himself to both of them, and then led them inside. He spoke over his shoulder as they walked through an impressive marble foyer. "My wife, Ellen, wants to meet you."

"I have something for her." Lana's heart pounded so hard she wondered if the camera was picking it up.

Sully stopped in his tracks and turned. "She's sick. And while I'm sure you're normally a very nice person –" his tone said he did not believe this "– I don't appreciate what you've done to Taft. I won't have you upsetting her. Period. If you do, I'll throw you out of this house so fast you'll wind up in Knoxville."

"I hear you, sir." Lana's southern manners had come back as soon as she'd crossed the Mason–Dixon line. "Yes, sir."

"Good. She's in the solarium. This way."

The solarium, Lana mouthed at Jilly's camera.

Oooh, Jilly mouthed back.

The house itself was normal – showing off its wealth just like all the other houses in this part of Nashville. Old wood, new tile, art that was numbered on the walls.

The solarium was different. It wasn't so much a room as it was a small greenhouse. It took a minute after being ushered in even to see Ellen around all the lush greenery.

She, too, was in all different shades of green, as if in camouflage – she wore a glaucous dress and lime ballet flats and an emerald knitted wrap. She was tiny, with very short white hair that spoke of recent chemo. When she held out her hand to Lana, it shook.

"I'm sorry to bother you at home, ma'am," Lana said, lightly gripping the offered hand.

"No bother." Ellen's voice was as soft as her skin. "Let's sit, shall we? Sullivan, is the tea coming?"

"Ruth's bringing it, love." Sully looked like a different man in front of her. In the hallway, he'd been fierce. Here, his face was tender, as were his eyes.

This man loved this woman.

Both of them loved Taft.

Holy crap.

Lana settled herself in a low wicker chair. "Thank you, again, for allowing this. For letting us film here. I know it's a terrible imposition."

Ellen didn't even glance at Jilly's camera. "This is about Taft, isn't it? Anything for him. Please, tell me how your trip was."

Oh, no. This wasn't a social visit. Lana didn't want to stress out this frail woman for a second longer than she had to.

"I came to ask Sully a question about Taft Hill."

Ellen rested thin fingers against her face. "And here I am, barging in. You know women. I want to know everything. Are you in love with him?"

The question took Lana's breath away. "Yes."

Ellen shot a happy, triumphant look at Sully. "I told you so, darling."

Sully sighed. "She's always right."

"I am."

"It gets annoying." But Sully reached for his wife's hand, and the way they sat there – so very together – made Lana wistful. And angry at herself. Again.

"I screwed up. I told the media he wasn't Palmer Hill's son."

Sully shook his head. "I can't believe you did."

"I know – here's the thing –"

Ellen interrupted, "But he *was* Palmer's son, that's what I don't understand."

"I mean, I told the media he wasn't Palmer's biological son."

"Well, of course, but Palmer didn't care about that."

The air in Lana's lungs grew hot. "Wait. Palmer knew?"

Ellen waved a hand gently as if she were brushing away a butterfly. "Of course he did. He knew from the start."

Lana felt as if she'd fallen out of a tree. "Sorry?"

"Davina was pregnant when they met."

"But Taft's mother told him she wasn't sure if Palmer knew or not."

Ellen smiled with radiant sweetness. "Davina has always been prone to convincing herself there are problems when there are not. A plight many people have, I think?"

Lana swayed in her seat. "So he knew the whole time?"

"He always said Taft was the best thing to ever happen to him. Isn't that the nicest thing? Not like other men, who brag about *making* their children, as if their children are their best products. No, he was eternally grateful to Davina for giving him a son, the best gift he ever received."

"Why didn't – why didn't they ever talk about it?"

Ellen lifted a shoulder. Her shawl slipped. Sully pulled it back up gently. "I always assumed – and I still do – that he just didn't care. Taft was his pride and joy. That was all, full stop. He couldn't have been any prouder of the boy if he *had* sired him. Palmer thought – like we do – that love is where you find it. It's all that matters. It doesn't matter *how* the love arrives, or when, or where. It matters that it does, and that we honor it. You love your friend, yes?" Ellen gestured at Jilly, whose eyes widened.

"Yes. Of course."

"You love your sisters?"

Something about this woman tugged at Lana to tell the absolute truth. "Always. Even though I don't show it the right way to them. I never have."

"Oh, honey, they know. Just like Taft knows, in his heart of hearts. That's why Palmer left everything to Davina. He knew she'd need it."

"Did he love her?"

Sully answered. "So much." He looked at his wife. "We never ... well, we always thought he could do better. But she gave him Taft, and that's all Palmer cared about. Davina herself was always about the money."

"Did she ever love Palmer?"

"I think she did," said Ellen quietly. "In her own way. Now, what's your question, dear?"

"I'm sorry. I want to say that to both of you."

Ellen bowed her head as if she were receiving the apology around her neck, like a lei. "And what else?"

"How do I get Taft to forgive me?"

Ellen smiled. "Do you deserve forgiveness?"

Lana looked at her hands. Her fingers were braided in her lap so tightly the knuckles ached. "No."

"Well, that's good. It means you just have to ask for it. If you deserved it, he'd *have* to forgive you. This way, he gets to choose."

"What if he doesn't?"

"Then, my dear, your heart is broken."

"It is already."

"It won't be any different, then." Ellen touched Sully's sleeve. "I wish you the best of luck, sugar. We love Taft, and we want only his happiness. I'm so glad to meet you both."

"Ditto." God, what a dumb thing to say, but it was all Lana could think of. "Oh! I brought you something." She rummaged in her bag. "Here. It's made of walnut from a tree a storm blew down last year in Darling Bay."

She handed the carved spoon to Ellen.

"Oh, how lovely."

"A man named Mike carved it. He's a veteran, and the carving gives him focus, he says."

"Even better." Ellen looked up at Lana. "Do you know why I collect spoons?"

"No. Taft didn't say."

"A long time ago, someone told me if you hang a spoon on the wall, you'll never go hungry. I used to be hungry a lot when I was young. It sounded good to me."

A thin hope trickled down Lana's throat. "So it worked?"

She raised her shoulders. "Who knows? Now I just like spoons. Darling, will you take me to the bedroom now? I'm quite tired."

Sully nodded. In a move surprising for a man of his age, he lifted Ellen out of the chair in his arms and carried her from the room.

Lana sat next to Jilly. Both of them stayed silent.

Sully came back and walked them to the door. "Did you get what you were looking for?"

"I don't know." Lana touched the marble foot of an angel on the doorstep. "I think so."

"Palmer loved his son."

"I'm so glad."

As the heavy door closed behind them, Lana started to cry.

Jilly turned off the camera and hugged her. "Jeez."

Lana hugged her back. "What?"

"I am *never* falling in love."

"Good luck. I think it's in the water in Darling Bay." Lana sighed and wiped her cheek on Jilly's shoulder before pulling away. "You're doomed."

"I'll bring bottled water, then. When am I putting this video together?"

"I just have to play you the song. We can do that at your place, right? Will it take long to edit?"

"I can do it on the plane if you help me pack."

"Perfect."

CHAPTER FORTY-SEVEN

Taft heard her before he saw her.

He was in room two, installing the light-switch plates, the final touch that was needed. All that was missing now was furnishings, and it would be rentable.

Lana's laugh drifted up the walkway. She sounded like a song. Music in motion.

Taft was still so damned in love with her, he could barely see straight.

He was still furious, of course, too. But the fury had worn off a bit in the last few days of thinking about her. He was even considering saying yes to *People* magazine's interview request.

The fact was, now that the truth was out there, he was kind of off the hook.

He wasn't Palmer Hill's son, and that meant exactly the same.

He didn't have to be anything he wasn't. It wasn't so much a relief as it was a surprise. He was getting messages of support from unexpected places – his label had reached out and offered him another contract, even though the current one wasn't even fulfilled, for even more money. A lot more.

Maybe it was true that the only bad press was no press?

Lana's laugh got closer. She was saying something to Jake, and he suddenly wanted to know what it was that had brightened her voice so much. Taft snapped his fingers. "You hear that, dog?"

Emily Dickinson paused in chewing on the old boot she'd found behind the hotel. Her ears pricked up.

Then she gave a bark and ran out of the room as fast as her short legs could carry her. Taft wanted to do the same, but managed a more sedate pace.

Lana knelt on the ground, rubbing Emily Dickinson's ears. "Look at you. Did you grow in the last few days? You seem rounder." Lana looked up. "Oh, wow. You seem taller." Her voice was breathy.

Jake garbled something that didn't make any sense and disappeared into one of the rooms.

Taft wanted to pull Lana up, to haul her against his body and kiss the hell out of her, but he couldn't. Wouldn't. "Yeah, well."

She stood. "I have something to show you."

"Okay." He crossed his arms. Emily Dickinson moved to sit on his foot.

"Wait, she likes you now?"

"Loves me. What can I say? I'm a ladies' man."

Lana pulled in her lips and nodded. "Oh, *damn*."

"What?"

"Nothing. I mean, everything. I'm about to come apart at the seams."

Yeah? So was he. "Show me whatever you have so I can get back to work." The sooner the better.

She held out her phone. "Push Play."

He lifted an eyebrow. "Really?" Was this her on camera, being interviewed somewhere? Talking in Nashville on TV about how sorry she was she'd outed his mother's secret?

Would that help things? Or make them worse?

He honestly didn't know.

"Just ... please. Wait, come inside so you can hear it better." She hurried to unlock room one. Emily Dickinson raced ahead and leaped onto the bed.

Taft remembered the one night he'd slept in her bed. His heart hurt so much it might stop beating. It would be easier, probably.

Lana sat on the edge of the bed, too. She pointed at her phone, which he was still holding. "Watch it. So then I can pass out." Her breathing was as shallow as his was.

"Fine."

On the small screen, he hit the play button.

Lana sat in a kitchen he didn't recognize. She smiled at the camera and flashed her *Sorry!* tattoo. She held an orange guitar and strummed it slowly. E minor, always a good chord to start a sad song.

I wear sorry on my sleeve like it's a bracelet.
I hang sorry round my neck for you to see.
I put sorry on at night like it's my perfume.
In the hopes that someday you'll come back to me.

The scene faded, and went to a voiceover. Lana's voice, "I screwed up. I told the media he wasn't Palmer Hill's son."

They were – astonishingly – in Sully and Ellen's home. There was Ellen, looking pale.

He glanced at Lana, who gestured for him to keep watching. While the simple chords of the song kept playing behind the words, he heard Ellen say, "But he *was* Palmer's son."

Lana's voice: "Wait. Palmer knew?"

Ellen smiled beatifically. "Of course he did. He knew from the start."

The scene went back to Lana singing at the kitchen table.

I put sorry on at night like it's my perfume.
In the hopes that someday you'll come back to me.

Voiced over, came Ellen's words: "Taft was his pride and joy. That was all, full stop. He couldn't have been any prouder of the boy if he *had* sired him. Palmer thought – like we do – that love is where you find it."

In the hopes that someday you'll come back to me.

As the last chord died, Lana looked back into the camera. She pressed her thumb into the tattoo at her wrist and kissed it. At the camera, she mouthed, "I'm sorry, Taft."

Taft's heart landed somewhere on the floor, along with every conscious, rational thought he'd ever had. "What – you went to talk to them?"

"They're your family. I needed to apologize to them, too."

"I –"

"You don't have to say anything. Taft, I'm sorry. I've never done something as wrong-headed and stupid as what I did to you, and I sincerely apologize to you."

"Lana –"

"I put this on YouTube this morning, and linked it with a comment over at the one Sully posted. My friend Jilly helped by notifying the media. Even if you can't accept my apology, which I would understand, I want the whole world to know I mean it." She stood and reached into her jeans pocket. "And this is another small apology. I didn't even screw this one up."

It was a phone number. Not hers, it wasn't a familiar area code. Taft searched her face. "What is this?"

"Your half-sister's phone number." Lana put up her hands. "Before you get mad at me, I didn't call her or contact her or anything. I've got a private investigator friend, and she dug up the info in like ten minutes."

"My ..." Taft had no words.

"You don't ever have to contact her if you don't want to. I thought I'd just give you the option. My sisters are two of the most important people in the whole world to me."

Words came to him then, words he meant with all his heart. "I shouldn't have told Adele about your song."

"You shouldn't have," Lana agreed. "But I'm glad you did. Now they know about the worst day of my life. It was a pretty bad one for them, too."

I love you. The refrain swam in his head. Thinking the words made him feel drunk. He wanted to say them to her, but did he have the right, any right at all, to say them?

Lana looked down. "I can't believe my dog is sitting on your foot."

He hadn't even noticed Emily Dickinson had placed herself there again. "I know."

"Come on, tell me how you made that happen."

Taft felt a blush creep over his face. "I strapped a piece of bacon under my sock."

"Seriously?"

"She's been driving me crazy, and I couldn't stand it that she hated me. A man's gotta do what a man's gotta do, Lana Mirabelle Darling."

Lana's mouth dropped open. "You know my middle name," she whispered.

"I also know it means gift." He'd looked it up.

"More like surprise."

"Surprise gift, maybe." Inside Taft's chest, his heart had started thundering again, and he doubted anything would be able to slow it.

"Oh." Her voice was small and her eyes were huge.

Taft shook Emily Dickinson off his ankle. He stepped toward Lana. This – everything mattered, everything hinged on this moment.

"I love you," Taft said.

Tears filled Lana's eyes. "Oh!"

He kissed her then, and under his lips, he felt her say the words back. He couldn't hear her over his heartbeat, over the blood pounding in his ears, but he could feel them, taste them.

I love you, she said. *I love you, I love you.*

By the time he could hear the words out loud, the door was closed and locked, the curtains were drawn. By the time he heard them a second time, they were naked. By the time he heard them a third time, he and the woman of his dreams were making love, and much later, when she whispered them to him a fourth time, he realized that it was going to take a lifetime to get tired of hearing her say it.

"Hey, Birdie."

"Yeah?" Lana chewed idly on the knuckle of his thumb, while on the floor, Emily Dickinson humped his tool belt.

"Can I have that song for my album?"

"The sorry song?"

"Yeah."

"Sure. You'll have to buy it from me, though."

"How much?"

"A million kisses."

"Sounds fair." He started paying her that very moment.

EPILOGUE

I'm the kind of woman who sings with her sisters.

It felt good.

Okay, it also felt weird – but still nice – to be standing on the small stage in the Golden Spike Saloon, looking out over what seemed to be the whole town and then some. How Adele and Nate had managed to pack in so many people was anyone's guess, but the fire marshal was beaming at the door, so they hadn't gone over capacity. Yet.

In each corner were lights, and camera-people swung through the room, capturing it all.

Adele was at the mic, driving the action as usual. Thank goodness she didn't mind having that role. Lana sure as hell didn't want it.

"Okay!" Adele held up her arms, and her round belly showed clearly under her white T-shirt. "Pipe down!

We've got a real treat for you up next. Thanks for listening to us play a few oldies but goodies."

"We love you, Songbirds!" The words were shouted from the very back of the room.

Molly grinned at Lana. Lana had literally forgotten how it felt to have her voice twining with her sisters', the way they intuitively found the old harmonies and reached for new ones as they went. It had felt a little bit like flying, singing on stage with them.

Adele said, "We love you, too, Darling Bay. Thanks for coming out. Remember that every dime you spend at the bar tonight goes right into Migration, and we'll be passing around a hat in a little while, too. Please give generously. Now, Molly and I are going to leave the stage in the capable hands of our baby sister, who's back in town. You might know her as the one who's fixed up the hotel. She might have checked you in when you got to town. You may have seen her walking a small dog who barks so loudly she cracks crystal. But Lana's actually the rockstar of the family –"

"Really?" Lana said into her mic. "The rockstar?"

Adele raised an eyebrow. "Are you engaged to be married to a cop?"

Heads swiveled to look at Molly, who blushed.

"No," said Lana.

"Are you pregnant, by any chance?" Adele touched her belly.

"*Hell*, no."

"By default, you have to keep being the rockstar, then."

Lana tugged at her cowboy hat. "Well," she said smoothly into the mic. "There are worse things, I think."

Adele nodded. "So give our baby sister a big, Darling Bay welcome, won't you?"

Lana tuned her E-string. It wasn't out of tune, but it gave her something to fiddle with while she ran through the words in her mind. Nerves – she was wound so tight with them. That morning, when she'd woken in Taft's arms, she'd groaned. *Do I have to do this?*

It's going to be televised. It's an opportunity. But no, darlin', you don't have to do anything you don't want to do.

It wasn't true. Sometimes you *did* have to do exactly the last thing you'd ever wanted to.

Sometimes you just had to be brave and run off the cliff, hoping for someone to call a helicopter for you if you got hurt. Lana pressed her thumb into her tattoo and then smiled at Taft, who leaned against the bar.

His grin was huge.

His blue eyes didn't move from hers. Next to him stood a tall woman who had the same dark-blue eyes. His half-sister, Martha, had desperately wanted to meet him but was apparently as anxious as Taft had been to reach out to her. Taft and Lana had driven to meet her the week before. He and Martha had spoken for an hour, and then for four hours the next day.

They were taking it slow, but Lana had overheard him introducing her as his sister to the mayor, and her heart had just about burst with the sheer outrageous joy of it.

Now, as she stared at him, he winked.

He *loved* her.

"I'm the luckiest woman alive." Her voice shook, which ticked her off, so she hurried to continue. "For a while, though, I was the unlucky one. The loner. The one who didn't fit."

The crowd grew quieter.

"You might have seen the rumors in the country tabloids, but I'm going to confirm them for you right now. I was raped." The air left her lungs, and quite clearly, she heard a woman in the back say, *Ohhhh.*

"I didn't say those words for a long time, because I didn't have the language for it. I was assaulted, that's what I told myself. I put myself in a bad place, and I got too drunk and out of control. I'd asked for it, so I deserved what I got. I was ashamed of every part of myself. I pushed the ones I love most away because of the shame, and because of the angry lies I fed myself to try to cover it up." Lana couldn't see them, but she could *feel* her sisters behind her. Loving her.

In front of her, Taft's gaze didn't waver.

"It turns out I didn't deserve it. Period. And if I can tell just one woman watching that it wasn't her fault, it makes my story worth telling." Lana looked away from Taft and into the camera. "If you were too drunk, if you were too young, if you were in the wrong place at the wrong time, even if you made every single wrong decision possible, what happened to you when you got hurt was *not your fault*. It was never your fault." The words caught in her throat. "That's why I wrote 'Blame Me.' I was trying to heal myself. I didn't know it then, but I was trying to heal you, too."

Lana looked down at the guitar. Just a few pieces of wood and metal, but her music had saved her. It wasn't too much to hope it could help someone else, too.

"Now, I'd like to invite a man up to the stage you may have heard of." A light laugh rippled through the room. "Taft Hill, you gorgeous beast of a country boy, would you come join me on stage?"

He dipped his head in response. The crowd parted for him.

Then he was next to her. He picked up his guitar and slung the strap around his neck. "Hey, Birdie." His deep voice raised goosebumps on her arms.

"Hey there." Lana could fly – she *knew* she could. But she didn't want to. She wanted to stay right here. "Will you sing with me?"

"You sure you want some nobody bastard who never knew his father to sing on this stage next to you?"

"Nope." They hadn't planned what they'd say. Lana leaned into the not-knowing and just spoke what was in her heart. "I want the man who was raised by a wonderful father named Palmer Hill to sing with me."

"What if I don't sound like him?"

She shrugged. "Who could? If you sound like yourself, like the Taft Hill I'm in love with, that'll be more than enough for me."

Taft grinned then, and leaned down for a kiss.

A cheer from the crowd rose, and above it, they heard Norma, who was sitting with her tarot cards at the bar. "I see a platinum record in your future! I see it right here!"

Lana didn't care about a platinum anything, when it came right down to it.

She cared about her sisters.

She cared about the hotel.

And this man – this one right here, with his lips pressed against hers.

I'm the kind of woman who falls in love.

So Lana kissed Taft back.

Thoroughly.

ABOUT THE AUTHOR

Rachael Herron is the bestselling author of the novels *The Ones Who Matter Most, Splinters of Light,* and *Pack Up the Moon* (Penguin), the five-book Cypress Hollow series, and the memoir, *A Life in Stitches* (Chronicle). She received her MFA in writing from Mills College, Oakland. She teaches writing extension workshops at both UC Berkeley and Stanford and is a proud member of the NaNoWriMo Writer's Board. She's a New Zealand citizen as well as an American.

Rachael *loves* to hear from readers:
Website: rachaelherron.com
Facebook: Rachael.Herron.Author
Twitter: RachaelHerron
Email: Rachael@rachaelherron.com

CPSIA information can be obtained
at www.ICGtesting.com
Printed in the USA
LVOW01s2227190417
531466LV00006B/418/P

9 781940 785363